Dreams
of Willow
House

BOOKS BY SUSANNE O'LEARY

The Road Trip
A Holiday to Remember
Secrets of Willow House
Sisters of Willow House

Susanne O'Leary

Dreams of Willow House

Bookouture

Published by Bookouture in 2019

An imprint of Storyfire Ltd.
Carmelite House
50 Victoria Embankment
London EC4Y 0DZ

www.bookouture.com

ISBN: 978-1-78681-863-8
eBook ISBN: 978-1-78681-862-1

For Becky

Chapter One

When the flight from Miami landed at Faranforre Airport in County Kerry, Cordelia looked out through the window at the sunlit green hills with a sense of wonder. Here she was at last. In Ireland, the country of her ancestors. She had never imagined that she would ever travel here, even in her wildest dreams, but the past year had changed her life forever. All because of a woman called Philomena Duffy.

'Here we are at last,' Betsy said beside her. 'I had hoped to come to Ireland one day, but never thought it would be in such sad circumstances.'

'I know,' Cordelia replied, touching the older woman's arm, remembering that Betsy had not only been Phil's publisher but also a dear friend. 'I can't believe she won't be here to welcome us, like we planned.'

Betsy dabbed at her eyes. 'I haven't stopped crying since I heard.' She blew her nose. 'I'm such a frigging wimp. Phil would be disgusted. She was such a trouper herself.'

'She was amazing,' Cordelia agreed, her own eyes stinging. 'We only knew each other a short time, but we became so close.'

'She loved you. And you were such a support to her.'

'Oh, she would have managed without me. But I'm glad I could do something. We were a team during the last few months. I enjoyed every moment of those book tours and loved hearing her speak on the radio and on TV. That wasn't work to me, it was a huge thrill.'

'You made her look like a film star.' Betsy unbuckled her seatbelt as the plane came to a stop.

Cordelia undid her seatbelt and picked up her bag. 'Thank you so much for upgrading me. I really appreciated it. This flight would have been a lot less comfortable in economy.'

Betsy patted her arm. 'You're welcome, honey. I enjoyed your company. And I think we both managed to sleep for a couple of hours.'

'Yes. I'm glad we did.'

'Are you sure you'll be OK to drive?'

Cordelia nodded. 'Of course. If I can do New York to Miami, I can manage a couple of hours on Irish roads. Can't be too difficult. Don't worry, I won't land us in the ditch,' she added, trying to ease Betsy's concern with a joke.

'They drive on the left here,' Betsy said, still looking worried.

Cordelia smiled reassuringly. 'I know. But I don't imagine the traffic will be as bad as the freeway out of the Lincoln Tunnel or even close. All you have to do is yell "left!" if I stray across the road.'

'I will. If I don't go to sleep.' Betsy stifled a yawn as she gathered her hand luggage and they filed out of the plane. 'Bye, honey,' she said to the air hostess on the way out. 'Thanks for looking after us so well.'

'You're welcome,' the hostess replied with a smile. 'Mind yourselves now.'

'Thank you. Have a nice day.' Betsy returned her smile. 'Lovely woman,' she said to Cordelia. 'I must fly Aer Lingus whenever I can.'

Cordelia glanced down the row of passengers in economy who were still struggling out of their seats trying to find their hand luggage in the overhead bins. 'And I'll do my best to fly first class whenever I can. It was so comfortable.'

'Yeah,' Betsy agreed, 'it takes some of the pain out of long flights.'

As they walked down the steps and onto the tarmac, Cordelia breathed in the sweet air laced with the scent of flowers and newly mown grass. A soft breeze played with her hair and the warm sunshine felt wonderful after the many hours in the stuffy plane. She instantly felt at home, a feeling that grew as the Border Police wished her welcome and the personnel in the car rental office did everything to make sure she was comfortable driving a stick shift and that they would take the right road to their destination: Sandy Cove village, on the Ring of Kerry.

'It's quite crowded on the roads this time of year,' the man explained. 'July is our busiest month.'

'I can imagine,' Cordelia said. 'But I'm sure I'll manage. Can't be worse than driving in America.'

'Not at all,' he assured her. 'It'll be easy for you. Now don't forget to turn on the air-conditioning. We're expecting some really hot weather from tomorrow. Could be up to twenty-five degrees, they said.'

'We've just come from Florida,' Betsy cut in. 'Twenty-five degrees is cold to us.'

'Ah sure, in that case you're all right so,' the man said, looking impressed. 'We'll be sweating bricks ourselves. We're not used to that kind of heat. Have a nice stay in Kerry and give us a shout if you have a problem with the car.'

They thanked the man, piled in their luggage and drove off into the busy roads of Killarney, getting caught in a traffic jam only ten minutes later.

'Shit,' Betsy groaned. 'I hate being stuck. Who are all these people and where are they going?'

'Mostly tourists,' Cordelia replied, pushing her sunglasses into her short dark curls. She scanned the long queue of vehicles. 'Looks like most of the cars come from other European countries. France, Italy, Germany and over there I can see a car from Spain. It's the middle of the tourist season after all.'

'I know.' Betsy sighed and brushed her nearly white hair from her face. A tall, slim woman in her early sixties, she suddenly looked every minute of her age. Usually so well-groomed with her hair in a sharply cut bob, her red glasses and her simple way of dressing, she now looked worn out both from the flight and the grief of having lost a dear friend. She and Phil had become so close while they worked together which, Cordelia thought, had a lot to do with them being of the same generation. 'Ignore me. I'm jetlagged and upset.' Betsy leaned her head against the back of the seat and closed her eyes. 'I'll try to catch some sleep. Would you wake me up when we're there?'

'OK,' Cordelia replied. 'Looks like it's easing a bit. This round-about is like a bottleneck. Muckross,' she muttered, peering at the road signs. 'OK, that's the best road to take, then Sneem and Caherdaniel…'

She followed the stream of traffic through Killarney, out past Muckross Park, where a lot of the cars turned off and people got out to walk around the lake and to see the famous Victorian manor house she had heard Phil talk about. Her thoughts drifted to Phil and the year they had spent together. They had made plans for Cordelia to visit Phil here in the part of Ireland that she loved so much. Phil had wanted to introduce Cordelia to the people she was distantly related to, and she had promised that this would make her feel a little more Irish. But Phil had become ill before they had a chance to do all this, or even say goodbye. As she glanced out at the lovely little town and the green hills beyond, she felt a stab of loss and sadness. She would never see Phil again and hear her lovely lilting voice. Cordelia shivered as she thought of the funeral that lay ahead. How would she cope during the next few days that would be so full of sorrow?

The traffic thinned to a steady trickle and Cordelia increased the speed while she glanced out at the stunning landscape with mountains rising above green fields and glimpses of lakes and rivers through the trees. Everything was so lush and green and the houses just like the ones she had seen in tourist brochures, especially the white-washed cottages, some with thatched roofs. They were so Irish it was nearly like a cliché. She glanced at Betsy snoring softly, her mouth half-open. Good. Betsy needed a rest after all that had happened in the past few days.

An hour later, they had reached Sneem, a small village halfway to Sandy Cove. Cordelia pulled up outside a café in the main square as Betsy opened her eyes.

'What's up?'

'Pitstop,' Cordelia announced. 'I need the rest room and a cup of coffee and some kind of bun or whatever they serve here.'

Betsy sat up. 'Good idea. The breakfast they offered on the plane didn't deserve the name. More like a snack.'

After a visit to the tiny toilet, they sat down at a table by the window and looked at the menu on the blackboard over the counter. A woman in a white apron appeared and smiled at them. 'Hi there. Welcome to Sneem. What can I get you?'

'Breakfast,' Betsy replied. 'What's "the full Irish"?'

'Sausage, eggs, bacon, black pudding, mushrooms and grilled tomato. Served with toast or soda bread, tea or coffee.'

'Holy mother,' Betsy said. 'Sounds like a total health disaster. I'll have that, please. With coffee. What about you, Cordelia?'

Cordelia laughed. 'Sounds a little too much for me. I'll just have a poached egg on toast and coffee, please.'

'Coming up,' the woman said and opened the door to what appeared to be the kitchen. 'One Irish, one poached egg and two coffees,' she yelled. Then she closed the door and smiled at the two women. 'My son. Needs to be woken up at times. You're our first customers today, but there'll be busloads of tourists soon, so he needs to get his ass in gear, as you say over there in America.'

The breakfast appeared only a little while later and Betsy tucked into her huge plateful with gusto. 'This'll fix the jetlag,' she said between bites. 'How're your eggs?'

'Lovely.' Cordelia sipped her coffee, pleased to see some colour come back into Betsy's cheeks.

'It was a good idea to stop,' Betsy remarked. 'For you, I mean. Must be tiring to drive like this in a strange country.' She looked out at the sunny square lined with tiny cottages, their lovely little gardens full of roses and hydrangea bushes in full bloom. 'Gorgeous place. I love Ireland already, don't you?'

'Oh yes,' Cordelia agreed. She finished her breakfast and pushed away her plate. 'I just wish…' She stopped and looked down at her plate, blinking away her tears.

'I know.' Betsy sighed. She ate the last of her gargantuan breakfast and picked up her cup. 'Can't believe she's gone. I didn't even know she was sick. I just thought she was tired and needed vitamins or something. How stupid of me. I should have told her to go and see a doctor.'

Cordelia put her hand on Betsy's arm. 'Please. Don't beat yourself up about it. I begged her to go and see a doctor and she said she would when she got back to Ireland. But then it was too late. The cancer was too far gone. It's nobody's fault. Phil might have felt this was the end of her life and she wanted to slip away quietly without fuss.' She sighed and looked at Betsy's sad face. 'I know how hard this must be for you.'

'Yes, it is. It seemed to happen so fast. And now we'll be going to her funeral only a few days after her passing. It appears there are two services. Something called a "removal" tonight, Phil's niece Maeve told me, and then the funeral tomorrow. Weird, don't you think?'

'No,' Cordelia replied. 'That's the Irish way. The removal is this evening. That's when the… the coffin is brought from the funeral parlour to the church and then there is a service, and after that, a wake. Then the formal funeral Mass the next day. That's what I did for my mother, anyway, even though she died in America.' Cordelia blinked away tears. Her mother had passed away only three years earlier and it was still so fresh in her mind.

Betsy patted Cordelia's hand. 'I know, honey. Your mom's only gone a short time. It must be hard for you.'

'It is sometimes.'

'And when you and Phil discovered each other it was such a comfort, wasn't it? To have found someone related to your mother and who had actually known her. Incredible.'

Cordelia smiled at the memory. 'Yes. How strange it was to discover that my favourite author was none other than my mother's first cousin.'

'It seemed like a miracle. Or maybe just a happy coincidence. And if you hadn't happened to watch that show on TV and heard Phil talk about her life and her family back in Ireland, you wouldn't be here now.'

'I know.' Cordelia fiddled with her teaspoon. 'I was so nervous about contacting you. I thought Phil wouldn't want to see me.'

'Why wouldn't she?'

Cordelia shrugged. 'She had so many relatives in Ireland. Didn't think she'd be interested. I mean, she was a famous author. She must have been contacted by a lot of people.'

'Yeah, sure she was. Lots of people wanted to meet her in person, too. But you were different. She knew immediately you were genuine.'

'We clicked straight away.'

'You made her life much easier. I could see how she relaxed around you, as you helped her with her tours, and found more peace to write. You were a godsend to her.'

'That's nice to know.'

Betsy sighed and drained her cup. 'Famous author meets long-lost relative, the daughter of her cousin who ran away all those years ago. And then you became her close friend and assistant. Such a lovely story. You and Phil finding each other like that and discovering you were related.'

Cordelia smiled fondly at Betsy. She was right. It was a lovely story. If only it were true.

Chapter Two

The day Cordelia saw Phil for the first time felt like fate. At first, she was thrilled to see one of her favourite authors being interviewed on TV, but as she'd watched her, she'd been instantly reminded of her mother. And when the discussion turned to Phil's Irish family, Cordelia felt a shiver going through her.

Cordelia owed her black hair and golden skin to her father's Italian ancestors, but her bright blue eyes and the freckles smattered across her nose and cheeks were pure Irish, just like her mother's family. The sloping eyebrows and the dimple in her chin were also typical of her Irish genes: 'So like your grandmother,' her mother used to say with a sad little sigh. What her father thought about that – or anything – Cordelia didn't know. He had left when she was three and for a long time he was just a voice on the phone on birthdays and at Christmas. The calls hadn't lasted, and he'd faded away in her mind, like a ghost from her early childhood. She didn't feel sad for herself, but she did for her mother, Frances, who often seemed lonely and lost. They lived, just the two of them, in a small house in Morristown, New Jersey, her mother working as a music teacher in the local high school and giving piano lessons in her free time.

Frances had met and married Gino when she had been in America for about ten years and she had given birth to Cordelia just a year later. The marriage had been short and stormy and Cordelia had faint memories of rows and doors banging but as soon as he'd left there was peace and a sense of relief in the little house. Cordelia had grown up feeling she was her mother's only support and confidante. Together they struggled to pay the bills and Cordelia worked after school as a babysitter and in the local grocery store at weekends. They'd had no money for a college education but Frances had scraped together enough for Cordelia to train as a beautician.

When Frances' health had deteriorated and the doctor had recommended she move to somewhere warm and sunny, Cordelia didn't think twice about living nearby and moved with her mother to Miami, where she found a job in one of the hotels. And when Frances had died peacefully in hospital, with a funeral attended by a surprising number of people who had loved her, Cordelia couldn't imagine leaving Miami. Rents and food were cheaper there than in New York, too, which was a help as her mother's medical bills started to arrive.

And it was there, still grieving for her mother and exhausted by her days coping with two jobs, that Cordelia had found Phil's stories, which swept her away from reality in the most delightful way. The heroines' romantic adventures with handsome men made up for the lack of romance in Cordelia's real life and she found herself looking forward to bedtime and getting back into the world Phil had created, going to exotic places and flirting with glamorous men.

Cordelia had turned on her TV just as Phil was introduced by the talk show host under her pen name Fanny l'Amour, her heart beating faster as the tall woman walked onto the set, smiling into the camera like a pro. Cordelia had leaned forward and stared at the screen, taking in every minute detail of Phil's face. A lovely older woman with dark hair and beautiful eyes, her face lined but with a brilliant smile that instantly made Cordelia fall in love with her. What a lovely, charming, warm woman she must be.

Phil and the host chatted about her books for a while before moving on: 'I would like to talk a little bit about you and your life and who you, the woman behind these wonderful books, really are.'

Phil had laughed. 'There's nothing startling there,' she'd said in her lilting Irish accent. 'I come from County Kerry in Ireland. My darling late husband was an international lawyer and we travelled around the world all through his career. When he retired, we came back to Ireland and lived in my family home, Willow House on the Atlantic coast, where I still live, except for when I'm on a book tour. I hope to go back there in the summer and run it as a guesthouse with my other niece, Roisin, who has been managing the repairs to the house while I've been away.'

Cordelia had stared at the screen. *Philomena Duffy*, she'd thought. *What a gorgeous name. Irish, like Mom…*

'What about your family,' the host asked, 'are they all living nearby?'

'Some of them,' Philomena replied. 'My brother lives in Spain, but my two nieces live in Sandy Cove where my house is. Wonderful village. Quiet, friendly and very beautiful. The rest of my family are sadly all dead.'

'All of them?' the host asked. 'No relatives in America by any chance?'

'None,' she'd said, pausing. 'That is, apart from a cousin called Frances, now I think about it. She was ten years younger than me and went to America when she was still in her teens. I remember how sad I was when she left. Lovely young girl. But we never heard from her again. She seemed to have disappeared. I have a feeling she died, but I don't really know.'

'Maybe she's still alive?' the host had suggested.

'No idea,' Philomena had replied with a sad little shrug. 'It would be impossible to find her, I think.'

The host had turned to the camera. 'Maybe not? Why not ask the viewers out there if they know a woman called Frances—' She paused. 'What would her last name be?'

'Fitzgerald,' Philomena answered. 'Our mothers were sisters. My mother married my dad, who was a McKenna, and my aunt Clodagh married a man called Jim Fitzgerald. Jimmy Fitz, they called him. Frances was their only daughter.'

'A woman called Frances Fitzgerald,' the host continued. 'About sixty years of age?'

Philomena laughed. 'I should protest and say I'm forty-nine, but that would be stretching the truth a little bit. Yes, about that age. Sixty-four, I think. And she was from Dublin. She came to visit us in Sandy Cove one summer when she was around nine and I was a teenager. I was given the job of minding her on the beach and we read stories together. She was a lovely little girl, but later became a bit of a rebel, I heard. Then she went to America all on her own and we didn't hear from her after that.' Philomena sighed, looking suddenly sad. 'I don't think it would be possible to find her after all this time, but miracles do sometimes happen.'

'We'll hope someone gets in touch,' the talk show host had said. 'Now, about your new series…'

Cordelia had tried to concentrate on the rest of the interview while the words rang through her mind: *Frances from Dublin. Around sixty-four years of age. The same name and the same age Mom would have been…* But of course, that was the only thing in common. Cordelia's mother's maiden name had been Ó Braonáin which was O'Brien in Gaelic, Cordelia had assumed, and she had also been an only child. This was probably another Frances, but the similarities were quite amazing all the same.

Cordelia sighed. Wouldn't it have been lovely if… Then something clicked in her mind. *Maybe it would be possible*, she thought as the credits rolled on the TV screen. As if in a trance, she picked up her phone and googled the number of the TV station. Her heart beat like a hammer in her chest and her stomach churned as she dialled the number. As she waited, she began to rehearse what she was going to say. *But would it all be lies?* she asked herself. She was about to hang up, but then someone answered and she heard herself talking in a very excited but convincing manner about how she had just heard Fanny l'Amour asking about her relative and that she, Cordelia, thought she might have a few clues… She left her contact details with the TV station and hung up, thinking, assuming that nothing would happen. Maybe tons of people had rung up with similar stories, also pretending they were related to Philomena Duffy. *If it were only true*, Cordelia thought, *if only my mother were the real Frances…*

Nothing happened that day, but the following evening the phone rang and she found herself talking to Philomena.

'Hello?' the lovely Irish voice said. 'My name is Philomena Duffy. Is this Miss Cordelia Mirafiore?'

'Yes,' Cordelia said, her heart beating fast. 'That's right.'

'And you called about my cousin Frances?'

'Yes.' Cordelia cleared her throat. 'My mother was called Frances and she was from Dublin, and she was sixty-two when she died, and...'

'Oh!' Phil exclaimed. 'How extraordinary. But... she's dead?'

'Yes. She died two years ago. Lung cancer.'

'I'm so sorry. How sad for you, my dear.'

'Thank you.' Cordelia was about to say goodbye and hang up when Phil spoke again.

'But you are also a cousin, aren't you? My second cousin?'

Cordelia hesitated. 'I guess I could be.'

'That's wonderful,' Phil said, sounding happy. 'I would love to meet you.'

'That would be nice,' Cordelia heard herself say.

'How?' Phil asked, sounding excited. 'And when?'

'There's a little café near the hotel where I work in Miami Beach. It's called the Coffee Pot. Could we meet there? Tomorrow morning at ten?'

'That sounds perfect,' Phil replied. 'I'm staying at my editor's apartment quite close by. See you then, dear little cousin.'

Cordelia hung up, wondering if she was dreaming. Was this really happening? She was tempted to call Philomena back and explain her own doubts. Phil hadn't questioned anything. She had felt the name and age was was all she needed. But then the thought of meeting this woman and the idea of feeling, somehow, that they were related, was too lovely to resist.

Cordelia had gone to the café the next morning, butterflies churning in her stomach. She had dressed carefully in a green linen shirt and black slacks, feeling that somehow the green of her shirt would make her look more Irish. So many thoughts went through her mind as she waited nervously for Philomena to arrive; should she confess straight away that the only things her mother had had in common with this Irish cousin was her first name and the time and place of her birth? Or should she pretend all was well and she was a hundred per cent certain that they had been the same person? Or...

Cordelia checked her watch. Philomena was over twenty minutes late. Should she leave right now and forget the whole thing? She was about to do just that when the door to the café opened and a tall, dark-haired woman dressed in a white ankle-length linen dress sailed in, looked around, brightening when Cordelia's hand shot up in an involuntary wave.

Philomena hurried to the table and stopped, smiling at Cordelia. 'There you are, Cordelia.' She held out her hand. 'Hello, I'm Phil. How wonderful to meet you.'

'Hello,' Cordelia said shyly, shaking Phil's cool hand, breathing in the light scent of Chanel No. 5 and returning the warm smile. 'Lovely to meet you too.'

Phil eyed Cordelia's empty mug. 'I'm so sorry I'm late. It took me ages to get dressed, as usual. I always dither a bit when it comes to choosing an outfit. But then I thought this dress would be simple, cool and not too ageing. What do you think?'

'You look amazing,' Cordelia replied, taken aback by the older woman's charm and charisma. There was something about her that made you want to be her friend, Cordelia thought, something warm and friendly. Her intelligence and empathy shone through her brown eyes and it was obvious she looked at the world with humour and a touch of mischief. She was simply irresistible.

Phil sank down on the chair opposite Cordelia while she studied her intently. 'You don't look much like Frances, apart from those blue eyes,' she remarked.

'My father is Italian,' Cordelia replied.

Phil nodded. 'Ah, such good luck. That explains your black hair and the golden skin. That's a very pretty combination.' Philomena paused and waved at the waitress. 'Yoohoo,' she called across the café. 'Be a dear and bring me a tall iced latte and a croissant.'

The order arrived within seconds and Philomena beamed at the waitress, thanking her profusely, and then paid for both her own and Cordelia's order, adding a very generous tip, which made the waitress smile. The she turned to Cordelia while she sipped her iced latte delicately through a straw. 'So… where were we?'

'Uh… Frances. My mother…'

'Oh yes,' Phil replied. 'Of course. What a fabulous coincidence. There I was, talking about my life and my family on a TV show and you were watching and then you called, and here we are. Together.' She put her hand on Cordelia's arm. 'I'm so very sorry about your mother. It must have been so hard to lose her like that.'

Phil's sympathy made tears well up in Cordelia's eyes. There was something about Phil that reminded her of her mother, something in her voice and her eyes. Maybe they were related after all? She suddenly wanted it to be true so badly her doubts melted away. It had to be true, and that small detail of the last name didn't really matter. Not right now, anyway. She pushed it all away and smiled through her tears. 'Thank you,' she said. 'It's hard and I do get lonely sometimes.'

'But now I'm here and we'll be friends, won't we?' Phil said, her beautiful eyes glinting with tears. 'I'm very lonely too, you know. I miss my nieces and my lovely house. America is grand and exciting but it's not like Ireland.' She straightened up and smiled brightly.

Cordelia told Philomena about her darling mother to whom she had been so close. She told her all about her childhood that had been so happy, despite not having a father, about all the things they had done together, about the music that constantly flowed through the little house, about weekends in the mountains and trips to the seaside, all on a shoestring budget which didn't matter at all. 'She made my childhood fun and happy,' Cordelia ended with a wistful smile.

'How lovely,' Phil said, looking as if the story had moved her profoundly. 'I'm glad you have such happy memories. They help a lot, don't they?'

'Yes, of course,' Cordelia replied, feeling suddenly she had met a kindred spirit. They sat in the café for a long time, sharing their life stories, both comforted by each other and forming a bond that would grow stronger and stronger. They met often after that, mostly in the same little café, or on the beach for a walk in the evenings.

Cordelia was mesmerised by Philomena: her charm, her warmth and wit and her offer of friendship. It was as if all her wishes had come true and her lonely, desperate life was changing. She suddenly had a lovely kind of aunt who had the life most women could only dream of. And when Philomena asked if Cordelia could possibly take on the job of personal assistant, she found herself accepting at once.

Forgetting all her doubts was astonishingly easy. Cordelia quickly settled into Betsy's condo near Miami Beach. There was plenty of room as the apartment had three bedrooms and when Philomena's publisher came down from New York the following week, Cordelia was already established as Philomena's assistant and stylist. Having a flair for style and fashion, Cordelia had suggested that Phil should stop dyeing her hair and keep the natural silver colour, which was more becoming and softer than the fake-looking dark brown. Phil's lovely dark eyes and luminous skin were enhanced by the natural grey and the new colour scheme for her clothes that Cordelia had suggested worked beautifully, giving her a touch of glamour as an older woman who wore her years with panache. Betsy approved wholeheartedly and the three women quickly bonded during their first long weekend together.

Betsy had given her blessing and praised Cordelia for having had the guts to come forward and contact Phil. 'You were the missing piece in our partnership,' she'd said before she'd left to go back to New York. 'I know Phil will be in safe hands and her writing will be even better now that you're taking on the chore of dressing and make-up and the whole boring shebang of looking good at book talks and signings and so on.'

The weeks had flown by, all full of different engagements, until it was time for Phil to go back to Willow House. But when she returned to the apartment after the final event in the publicity campaign, Phil announced that she would like to stay on in Florida a while longer. She felt too tired to get organised to go back to Willow House, where they were so busy with the new guesthouse and Maeve was about to have her first baby.

'I'll only be in the way,' she'd said. 'Roisin and Cian will run the guesthouse beautifully and won't want me interfering. I'll go then and stay for a while to see the baby and attend the christening. Here, I can write in peace while you look after me.'

Cordelia had agreed, thinking Phil did look tired. The past weeks had been hectic and even someone half her age would have found it exhausting. And this way she didn't have to say goodbye to Phil, who had become so dear to her. Looking after her had been a joy, the best time in her life, she realised, were it not for the niggling feeling that they had never actually confirmed that they were related, nor had she admitted that her mother's name was O'Brien. But she brushed away these thoughts and concentrated on the positive: that Phil appreciated all Cordelia had done and declared that she couldn't manage without her. It seemed less and less important that Cordelia might not be who Phil thought; what mattered more was the closeness and love that had grown between them ever since they first met. The pain of losing her mother eased while Cordelia cared for Phil and the long, lonely months had finally come to an end. They were family, whatever their real relationship, Cordelia felt.

'Where have you been all my life?' Phil had said with a sigh one day as Cordelia brought her a tropical fruit juice while she sat at her computer working on her next novel. 'You seem to read my thoughts as well. I was just thinking that I'd love something cool to drink, and there you are with one before I had a chance to ask you.'

'I thought you needed a break. You've been writing for over an hour.'

'I'm in the zone,' Phil said and sipped her drink. 'This new novel is fun to write. I have a new heroine called Monique. She is a Creole woman from the French West Indies. But…' She paused and put down the glass. 'I'm not sure about the hero. How should he look? What should he do?'

Cordelia sat down on the edge of a stool near the desk. 'Maybe a contrast to this Monique? I suppose she is a brunette with dark eyes?'

'Yes.' Phil laughed. 'A bit like you, with golden skin. I can't have a heroine who gets bright red after only ten minutes in the sun.'

'Definitely not,' Cordelia agreed. 'But the man in her life… Maybe he could be a contrast? Fair hair and blue eyes…' Cordelia half-closed her eyes as she conjured up the face of the new hero. 'His hair should be short, and he should have a beard. Not bushy, but closely cropped, as if he hasn't shaved for a week. Then he should be a little older, maybe around forty-seven or so, and be some kind of writer or war correspondent or something. He knows how to shoot a gun and fly a helicopter. An Indiana Jones type. Craggy, moody, a little angry at the world. Suspicious of women perhaps? A real cynic.'

'But then he softens little by little as Monique tames him,' Phil filled in. 'Oh, that's brilliant. And I think I'll make him… Irish. I haven't had any Irish heroes yet. What do you think?'

Cordelia nodded. 'Yes. Good idea. Irish men are all the rage these days. I mean, that *Poldark* actor is Irish. And then there's Colin Farrell and Liam Neeson and…'

'That's true.' Phil put down her glass and turned back to her laptop. 'I'll just put down these ideas so I won't forget them and then I'll have a little nap, I think.'

'You should,' Cordelia agreed, looking at Phil's pale face. She looked exhausted although it was only eleven o'clock in the morning.

Cordelia had a niggling worry that something wasn't quite right. That pallor looked like more than mere fatigue. 'Maybe you should go and see your doctor?' she suggested. 'Just for a check-up?'

Phil got up. 'No, it's just old age, darlin'.' She walked slowly to her bedroom door. 'Wake me up when lunch is ready.'

The following days had been very similar. Phil's fatigue never got better, and after the summer when it was time for her to go back to Ireland, Cordelia bid her a fond farewell wondering if Phil would make it back to Florida after Christmas like she planned. But she never did.

The campaign for her next book had been shaping up well and Cordelia was preparing the final details, including the wardrobe for Phil's return and the start of the book tour. But then she'd had a phone call from Phil early one morning.

'Sweetheart,' Phil started. 'I'm afraid I've had a little setback. So silly of me, but I seem to have contracted something quite serious. I'm in hospital and they're doing tests. Nothing to worry about, but it means I can't come over as planned. Not for a while, until they have sorted it all out. I'll keep you posted. So sorry if this upsets everyone.'

'Oh no,' Cordelia exclaimed. 'How awful. Just look after yourself, OK? Rest and take it easy and don't worry about a thing. I'll come over if you want.'

Phil sighed. 'No need, sweet girl. Maeve and Roisin are here, fussing like a flock of hens. I want you to stay and look after things for Betsy. And maybe you could run my online stuff for a while? The website and the Facebook page and all that. Look after my readers for me. They are very dear to me.'

'Of course,' Cordelia had promised, with a sob. 'I miss you so, Phil. Do take care.'

'I will, darlin'. And you could perhaps come here when I'm a little better. I'd love to show you Willow House. It's wonderful in the summer...'

That was the last time they had spoken. A month later the terrible news came that Phil was gone and Cordelia was alone once more.

Chapter Three

Light rain fell as they neared the village of Sandy Cove. 'This must be that "nice soft day" Phil used to talk about,' Betsy said with a laugh, looking up at the rain. 'We're going to have to get used to it. In fact, maybe it's good for the complexion. Phil had wonderful skin for her age – it might have been the soft Irish air and all the moisture.'

'Probably,' Cordelia replied, slowing down at a crossroads. 'Left or right?' she said, studying the area. 'There's no road sign.'

Betsy looked out the window. 'I'd say right. The left road is narrower and seems to lead straight to the ocean. We need to get to the village, drive down the main street and then take a left down a lane to Willow House, Maeve said.'

'Oh. OK.' Cordelia turned into the road on the right. *Maeve*, she thought as she increased the speed. *Maeve and Roisin, sisters and Phil's nieces...* How would they greet her, the supposed second cousin? She hoped they'd accept her as easily as Phil had done, delighted to have found a relative so far from home. But they would be on their own patch and wouldn't need her as Phil had. And then the rest of the family, Patrick McKenna, their father and their mother, Anne-Marie, who hadn't been very close to Phil. How would they greet her? Cordelia's stomach churned as she considered the situation. She'd have to think of an explanation for her mother's maiden name if it ever came up. But why would it?

'Can't wait to see Willow House,' Betsy prattled beside her. 'And meet the nieces and the brother. So kind of them to let us stay there. Maeve said Roisin has closed the guesthouse to visitors for the next two weeks, which must have been difficult for them as this is the busiest season. But I suppose they needed the peace to grieve. Poor girls, they were so close to Phil.'

'I know,' Cordelia mumbled as they reached the outskirts of the village. 'Phil was always on the phone to them and they skyped regularly when she was in Miami. It must have been such a shock for them that she was so sick and then died so soon after the diagnosis.'

'Cancer,' Betsy said, taking a tissue from her handbag. 'And it all happened within a month. But they told me she died holding their hands and smiling, saying she would see them all in the next life, happy to be with her husband, the love of her life.' Betsy sobbed loudly, then stopped, blew her nose and put away her tissue. 'Enough. We have to be strong.'

Cordelia blinked away tears. 'Yes, we do. I've cried for days, so now I must be brave and get through this. Phil would want us to celebrate her life, not mourn her death. She didn't believe in death, she used to say.'

'I know.' Betsy looked out at the street for a moment. 'It's a gorgeous village. I love the little shops and that quaint pub. And look –' she pointed at a little house near the end of the street '– that must be Paschal's bookshop. He's Maeve's husband.'

'Ah yes, but I think someone else runs it now.'

'Really? But what a great shop. It's closed, though. Probably because of the funeral. But I'm looking forward to browsing there when he opens. I'd love to bring a souvenir home with me.'

'Here's the lane now,' Cordelia interrupted and drove down the narrow lane, coming to a stop in front of a pair of wrought-iron gates. 'The gates are closed. There's a sign. Can you see what it says?'

'*Closed until 17th July for family reasons*,' Betsy read. 'But Maeve said to toot your horn three times and they'd open from the house. The family are all there for a lunch.'

Cordelia nodded. She tooted three times and, when the gates slid silently open, drove across the gravel, pulling up in front of the steps that led to a heavy oak door. She glanced up at the house, awestruck by its old-world elegance. Here she was at last. At Willow House, Philomena's home that she had talked about so often. It had seemed like something from a fairy tale, but now Cordelia saw that it was every bit as beautiful and welcoming as Phil had described.

Betsy opened her door and got out. 'I'm glad we got here safe and sound. Great driving, Cordelia. I couldn't have done it better. Or at all, really.' She laughed. 'Let's go and meet the family.'

'OK.' Cordelia nodded, wiping her clammy hands on her jeans. Here we go. She had to face the family with confidence. Attend the funeral and then she could go back to her old life. A life without Phil, who had meant so much to her. Or a new life in a way. Betsy had offered her a job at the publishing house in New York in their marketing department. She thought it could be a fun job and it was well paid. But first things first.

Cordelia got out of the car just as the front door swung open and two women came into view, one of them short and blonde, the other tall with dark red hair holding a toddler on her hip. Betsy rushed forward. 'Darlings,' she shouted. 'We meet at last.'

The women smiled and held out their arms, enveloping Betsy in a group hug, until the child let out a loud cry. They laughed and broke apart. The red-haired woman glanced over Betsy's shoulder at Cordelia. She came down the steps and held out her free hand.

'Cordelia? I'm Maeve. Welcome to Willow House,' she said.

Cordelia shook her hand and looked into the kind green eyes, smiling. 'Hello, Maeve. So lovely to meet you.' She touched the child's cheek. 'And who is this?'

'This is Aisling, who has just turned one,' Maeve said and jiggled the baby up and down, which made her laugh, showing two bottom teeth. She had dark hair and her mother's green eyes. 'Aisling means "dream" in Irish. But she is teething now so there's not much dreaming in our house at the moment.'

'Oh.' Cordelia shook the baby's hand. 'Hello, Aisling, I'm Cordelia. Nice to meet you.'

Aisling peered suspiciously at Cordelia. Then she reached out and grabbed the strap of Cordelia's handbag.

Maeve removed the baby's hand from the strap. 'No, Aisling, don't touch. We'll go in and find some toys for you instead.' She smiled and nodded at Cordelia as she walked into the house. 'Lunch in the garden,' she said over her shoulder. 'But Roisin will show you to your rooms first so you can settle in.'

Cordelia turned as Roisin tapped her on the shoulder. 'Hi, Cordelia. I'm Roisin,' she said, looking curiously at Cordelia. 'So you're the mysterious cousin, eh? Phil talked about you all the time. She was very fond of you. It seems you took very good care of her.'

Cordelia smiled at the pretty blonde woman. 'Thank you, Roisin. Taking care of Phil was a great pleasure. She told me all about you. I nearly feel I know you and Maeve already.'

'Only the good things, I hope,' Roisin said and let out a little sigh. 'Oh, it makes me sad to talk about her in the past tense.' She shook herself. 'But let's try not to be too gloomy. Phil would hate that. Come on, girls, grab your bags and I'll get you settled.'

They got their bags out of the car and followed Roisin into the bright hall. Cordelia looked at the polished wooden floor and the beautiful staircase that rose in a graceful curve to the next floor. This house had been lovingly restored to its original features. She lugged her suitcase up the stairs, breathing in the scent of rose petals and beeswax with a feeling she had been transported to another era.

They arrived on the top landing and Roisin walked down the corridor and opened the first door on the right. 'You're in here, Cordelia. It's a small room, but you have a view of the ocean if you hang out the window. Betsy, you're opposite. No sea view but your bathroom is bigger. I have to go downstairs and help out with lunch but do give us a shout if you need anything and we'll see you on the back lawn in half an hour. You'll meet the whole family then. My husband and the lads, and also my parents who arrived from Spain last night. Dad is dying to meet you, Cordelia. He remembers your mother very well.'

'Oh,' was all Cordelia managed before Roisin ran down the stairs. She shot Betsy a pale smile. 'See you later, Betsy.'

'Cheerio,' Betsy said and opened the door to her room. 'See you at lunch. Must freshen up. You must be looking forward to meeting the dad. He was your mother's first cousin, right?'

'Yes. Really looking forward to meeting him,' Cordelia replied.

She went into her room and closed the door behind her, leaning against it while she tried to steady herself. Philomena's brother. Oh God, how would she handle meeting him? Would he ask questions about her mother's maiden name and maybe wonder if she truly was the real Frances? No, maybe not. He hadn't seen the real Frances since she was nineteen and left for America and had no contact with her. Phil had shown her a family photo, taken a year or so before that, where Frances had been standing in the background. With her light brown hair and slim frame, she could easily be Cordelia's mother, who had had similar looks and build. Both very Irish-looking girls in those days. A very young Phil had been in the foreground, sitting between an attractive woman and a very handsome man who had been her parents. Phil had obviously got her looks from her father. That was the only photo she had of Frances, but she had said there were others in an old box somewhere.

Cordelia glanced around the pretty room, barely noticing the gorgeous wallpaper and the big bed stacked with embroidered pillows, the matching curtains billowing in the warm sea breeze that blew in through the open window, or the soft sage-green carpet under her feet. Then she put down her suitcase and wobbled to the bed, where she collapsed, staring up at the ceiling. Jetlag and nervous tension made her stomach churn and the poached egg on toast she had enjoyed only an hour ago suddenly seemed like a very bad idea.

She got up and tottered across the room on legs that felt like jelly and opened the door to a lovely bathroom with light blue tiles on the walls and a white marble floor. How gorgeous. If she wasn't so tired and tense, she would have enjoyed the comfort and luxury of the exquisitely decorated bedroom with its pretty en suite and lovely views. She went inside and sat on the edge of the bathtub, wishing she had the time to sink into some warm water and use the luxury toiletries on the shelf over the sink. But there was less than half an hour before she had to go downstairs and face the family.

Fighting a wave of nausea, she tried to gather her thoughts. What could she do? Nothing, of course. She had to go down there and be who they thought she was – the daughter of Phil's first cousin. Phil had accepted her story without question. So why wouldn't her brother, who hadn't seen that woman since she was nearly a child? Feeling slightly better, Cordelia splashed some cold water on her face, washed her hands and ran her fingers through her short curls. She looked at her ashen face in the mirror and pinched her cheeks. 'You will get through this,' she said to herself. 'You *can* do it, and you will. There is no other way.'

Cordelia went back into the bedroom, grabbed her handbag from the bed and walked to the door. OK. This was it. Time to go down there and face the family. This would be the hardest part. The rest wouldn't be easy but once she had been accepted, she could breeze through and then go back to America and pick up her life. She needn't complicate matters; she was only there to say goodbye to Phil as her friend just as much as her relative. No one need know of her doubts, and she might never meet them again. She straightened her shoulders, stuck a cheery smile on her face and went downstairs.

Chapter Four

Cordelia walked through the house, glancing into rooms, wondering how to get out to the back lawn. There had to be a door or a French window somewhere. She went down a corridor lined with paintings, and Persian rugs on the polished oak floor. Glancing into what seemed to be a library, she found no way out there; then she discovered a large dining room on the right-hand side, with an enormous mahogany table and a bay window overlooking the back lawn, where she could see a group of people gathered near a table where a buffet had been laid out. They were talking to each other and a tall man with white hair had his arm around Maeve. Betsy was chatting with Roisin and another blonde woman. But even here there was no way out. Opposite the dining room, she discovered a large, bright room with beautiful Donegal carpets, two large yellow sofas flanking the period fireplace, and other comfortable chairs scattered throughout the room.

Cordelia spotted an open French window at the far end, and walked towards it, stopping to look at the painting over the fireplace. It was a portrait of a beautiful red-headed woman wearing a yellow floaty dress and a pearl choker, her hooded green eyes looking at Cordelia as if she could read her mind and didn't like what she saw. Cordelia tore her eyes away from the portrait and told herself not to be silly. That must be Maureen McKenna, the first lady of this house, who had lived here over a hundred years ago. Phil had told Cordelia about her. 'Feisty and maybe a little scary,' Phil had said with a laugh. 'Not at all the demure, gentle soul we see in that portrait. An iron fist in a velvet glove, I suspect.'

Feeling relieved that this woman wasn't here today, Cordelia stepped out through the French windows and slowly walked towards the group at the end of the lawn. She was momentarily distracted by the stunning views from this side of the house and had to stop to look out over the intensely blue ocean, the rugged coastline and the outline of the two craggy islands she could see shimmering in the distance. The famous Skellig Islands, where *Star Wars* had been filmed, but also the islands of the ancient monastery that had stood there for more than a thousand years. There was a sense of mystery and magic about those islands and she wished she could go there right now, and not have to face the family and get even more deeply mired in this nightmare of lies. But it was only for a few days, she told herself and put on her sunglasses, as if they could shield her from the probing looks.

Betsy spotted Cordelia as she neared the group. 'Hi, Cordelia!' she shouted, waving. 'Come and meet the family.'

As Cordelia drew closer, the tall older man left the group and walked towards her, holding out his hand. 'Cordelia?' he said. 'How lovely to meet you at last.'

Cordelia smiled and shook his hand. 'You must be Mr McKenna, I mean Patrick,' she mumbled through stiff lips.

He smiled and nodded. 'Yes. I am he. Phil's baby brother. Not so baby now, of course. More like an old man.'

'Not that old,' Cordelia replied, smiling into his green eyes. He had white hair and freckles all over his face and looked a lot younger than his seventy years. 'Maeve looks just like you,' she added, feeling a little less scared.

'And you are Frances' daughter,' he said, peering at her. 'She was my first cousin.'

Cordelia nodded. 'I know. Her mom and yours were sisters.'

'That's right. But they were not close, as far as I can remember. I always had a feeling there was some kind of hostility between them. But we never knew what it was about. I have a vague memory of Frances as a skinny girl with serious eyes, but I think we only met once when I was ten and she was around seven. I've seen a photo somewhere but that's all. She looked like her mother, I believe.' He studied Cordelia for a moment. 'You're not very like her with the black hair and golden skin, but there is a family resemblance all the same, and those blue eyes. You're tall and slim, just like I remember her.'

'Yes, she was tall,' Cordelia replied. 'But my hair and skin are from my dad's side of the family. His ancestors came from Italy.'

'A very nice mix, then.' He smiled at her. 'So amazing that you met Phil over there and that you became friends. It's as if it was meant to happen,' Patrick said with a warm glint in his kind eyes. He took her hand. 'Come, let's meet the others and then have something to eat. You must be a little tired after the trip across the Atlantic.'

'Just the jetlag,' Cordelia confessed, feeling relieved that he accepted her so easily. 'It's making me feel a little dizzy.'

'Have a bite and then go and lie down. There's plenty of time before the removal, which is at six this evening. And then there's a party in Phil's honour at the Harbour Pub.'

Cordelia stopped. 'Oh God,' she exclaimed. 'I should have said how sorry I am about the loss of your sister. I was so bowled over by meeting you that I nearly forgot.'

He patted her hand. 'That's OK, my dear. It was a shock to hear she had died, of course. And it's sad to lose a sister. Very sad. But we hadn't been in touch much the past few years, what with us living in Spain and she being off on a book tour around the US. She didn't tell anyone about her illness and maybe that's what she wanted? To just slip away in her sleep and not go through painful treatments that wouldn't have worked anyway. So, while I'm sad, I'm also happy for her. She's at peace at last and with Joe, who was the love of her life.'

'That's lovely.'

They had reached the group and Patrick let go of her hand to join his daughters while Betsy introduced Cordelia to Roisin's husband Cian, a tall man with light-brown hair and kind eyes, then Paschal, a handsome man with wild dark hair and a lovely smile. Roisin's three sons, all tall teenagers, shook Cordelia's hand then sidled off to look at their phones.

Then the blonde woman approached and looked at Cordelia curiously. 'Cordelia,' she said. 'The daughter of the elusive Frances.' She held out her hand. 'Hello. I'm Anne-Marie, Maeve and Roisin's mother.'

'Hello. So sorry about your loss,' Cordelia said as she shook hands with Anne-Marie, slightly chilled by the older woman's probing pale blue eyes.

Anne-Marie nodded. 'Thank you. Phil was wonderful and will be missed by many, especially my daughters. I believe you were very close to her during the past year?'

Cordelia nodded. 'Yes. I didn't know her long, but we became close.'

'I heard you looked after her very well. She said she didn't know how she had managed without you all these years. So we are very grateful that you were such a huge support to her while she did all that publicity. Must have been gruelling for a woman that age.'

Cordelia was surprised by the kind words. Phil had told her she and Anne-Marie had never been close; Anne-Marie, being a career woman, had looked down her nose at Phil, whose only work had been to look after her husband and help out support him in his career in international law. It hadn't been easy to constantly move to a new country and learn a foreign language, not to mention entertain at executive level and host posh dinner parties, smiling and looking good even if you were sad and lonely inside. But Anne-Marie had never understood that. The only thing Phil said she had been grateful for was that the girls had been allowed to spend their summer holidays with her from early childhood to their teens. This helped Phil to cope with her sorrow of not having been able to have children. Maeve and Roisin were her daughters for the summer and they had been all so happy together, running wild on the beach and swimming in the ocean.

Cordelia nodded and smiled. 'Yes, it was. Especially the last few months before she left to go back to Ireland. She seemed so exhausted. I thought it was something more than just fatigue and suggested she see a doctor, but she refused. Maybe if…'

Anne-Marie shook her head. 'No. It was inoperable. It wouldn't have helped to see anyone. This way she had some quality of life the last few months. She spent the days with Maeve and Roisin at

Willow House and then, six weeks before she died, she had to go into hospital to help with the pain. She didn't even want Roisin to close the guesthouse and she asked for detailed reports on all the bookings. It has only been open for a year, so it's important to keep it running and to get repeat business. That's what she said, anyway. I think she might have hoped she'd get better and come back and run it with Roisin, but it was not to be.' Anne-Marie sighed, looking sad. 'We weren't close, as she might have told you. My fault, I suppose. I should have made more of an effort, but I was so focused on my career. But I was grateful that Phil gave my girls such wonderful summer holidays in this beautiful part of Ireland. You must spend a few days exploring now that you're here.'

'Oh, I'm only staying until after the funeral,' Cordelia replied. 'I'm going back with Betsy the day after tomorrow.'

'I see. But maybe you'll be back on another occasion? In happier circumstances, I mean.'

Cordelia squinted in the sun as she looked out at the stunning view from the back lawn. 'I would love to come back and explore this gorgeous country.'

Anne-Marie smiled and nodded. 'Of course. You'll always get a warm welcome here. You're family, after all. Aren't you?' she said, looking intently at Cordelia, making her squirm.

'That's right,' Maeve interrupted, stepping forward. 'Come and have some food and sit with Roisin and me. Aisling is having a nap, thank goodness, so I can take a break.'

Cordelia immediately warmed to this lovely woman. There was a touch of pain and sadness in her eyes that moved Cordelia. She knew how close Phil and Maeve had been and it must be hard for

Maeve to deal with everything so soon after Phil's death. 'I'm so sorry,' she said to Maeve as they approached the table. 'This must be so sad for you. I'm sure you'll miss Phil terribly.'

'So will you,' Maeve replied. 'Phil told me you had been so close during the year after you met. And how you looked after her every need. It must have been a little like having a family again. And now she is gone as well.'

'Yes,' Cordelia said hoarsely, blinking back tears. 'I can't believe she's passed away.'

'Neither can we. She was such a life force. Lived her life to the full and everyone she met adored her. I still expect her to walk through the French doors wearing some fabulous vintage outfit, laughing at us and telling us it was all a mistake and she was only joking.'

Cordelia smiled wistfully. 'I know what you mean. She is still so *present* somehow. Her readers are devastated. Especially those who used to chat to her on social media. It was awful to have to make the announcement. The outpouring of grief was incredible.'

'But she is not really dead,' Maeve declared. 'She will live on in the memories of those who loved her. And through her books. What will happen with the novel that was ready to be published?'

'There were two,' Cordelia replied. 'She managed to finish the first draft of the second book in the new series before she left. Betsy says they will publish them both. Not because of the money, but because that's what Phil would have wanted.'

Maeve nodded and glanced at Betsy, who was talking to Roisin and Cian. 'Betsy is an astute businesswoman. I think the new books will be huge bestsellers, too, and she knows it. But I know they were close, so I can't criticise her. She has a good heart under that hard business shell. Dead honest too. You'd never catch her doing anything shady or telling lies.'

'No.' Cordelia cringed as she listened to Maeve's words. Betsy was as honest as the day is long. What would she say if she knew Cordelia wasn't? That she had doubts about her right to be here and she wasn't saying a thing? She'd eat her up and spit her out in no time. Cordelia shivered despite the warm sunshine. This family gathering suddenly felt oppressive and threatening. But she only had to get through the service this evening, the wake, where she could excuse herself and plead jetlag, and then the funeral tomorrow. She had to make herself believe she really was the long-lost cousin.

Maeve tapped Cordelia's arm. 'I have to get something to eat before her nibs wakes up. The daughter of a friend is keeping an eye on her, but once she's up, we'll all have to chase her around the place. She only just started walking, but she races about and gets into everything now with astonishing speed.'

'She's a gorgeous little girl. I love the name too.'

Maeve smiled fondly. 'Yes. We called her Aisling because of its meaning in Irish. And it was our dream to have this baby and then it came true. Quite miraculous considering my age. I'm forty-three. My doctor says I probably won't have another one.'

'Oh. What a pity.'

Maeve shrugged. 'Yes, but I'm so happy to have her. More children might be too much for me to handle.'

They made their way to the table and started helping themselves to cold meats and salads. 'Just a simple lunch,' Maeve explained. 'We'll be fed royally at the pub tonight. Thank goodness for Nuala and Sean Óg. They're the owners of the Harbour Pub and our best friends here. Nuala is the salt of the earth and Sean Óg is the most dependable, kindest man I know. Lovely couple. They're nearly like family.'

'I'm looking forward to meeting them,' Cordelia said, feeling quite the opposite. She sat down on a wrought-iron garden chair near the edge of the lawn, balancing her plate on her lap and putting her glass of water on the grass. Slowly eating and drinking, looking out at the sea and the beach below, she started to feel better and enjoy her surroundings. The air was full of the scent of flowers mixed with a salty tang of seaweed, and swallows flew around emitting high-pitched tweets. She looked up as Roisin arrived, carrying a plate in one hand and a rickety garden chair in the other.

'Hi,' she said, setting down the chair. 'Thought I'd join you. I need a break from the men. And I thought you looked a little lonely there by yourself.'

Cordelia smiled. Roisin had a warmth that was hard not to like. 'I just wanted to catch my breath and look at the view. This really is a stunning place.'

'It's heaven.' Roisin sighed and started picking at the food with her fork. 'But right now it feels a little sad. As if it has lost its soul. The end of an era, really. Phil loved this village. Especially the house. It was her special place on earth, she used to say.'

'Yes. She told me. She was always longing to go back and always talking about the two of you and how she was looking forward to running the guesthouse with you.'

'I know,' Roisin said wistfully. 'She loved the idea of the house being filled with people from all over the world. But she never got to see that.'

'She would have been the best hostess.' Cordelia smiled at the thought. 'I can see her welcoming guests wearing her vintage fashion. What a blast that would have been.'

Roisin laughed. 'Oh yeah, she would have been *magnificent*. I can tell you knew her very well.'

Cordelia nodded. 'I did. I thought she was fascinating. I'm so happy to meet you and Maeve, even if it's a sad occasion.'

'Me too. I was dying to meet you after all the nice things Phil said about you.'

'Oh, that's lovely.' Cordelia glanced back at Patrick McKenna. 'Nice to meet your dad. Is he as fond of this house as Phil was?'

'Not really. Dad's more of a city person and Phil loved Willow House and their father was sure she would be happier being the sole owner. So he left this house to her in his will and Dad got the house Grandad owned in Tralee.' Roisin squinted at Cordelia in the bright sunlight. 'Didn't you know all this?'

Cordelia stiffened. 'I don't know much about the McKennas. Phil didn't mention them often. She talked more about her mother's family and how they hadn't been in touch with them.'

'I think there was some kind of row between Granny and her sister a long time ago. But I don't know much about that side of the family either. The McKennas were a dominant bunch. They had all the money and the status. That old Kerry kingdom arrogance, if you can call it that.'

'Kingdom?' Cordelia asked. 'How do you mean?'

'There is an old saying in Kerry that goes something like, "there are only two kingdoms, the kingdom of God, and the kingdom of

Kerry." Referring to Kerry as a kingdom goes back to ancient times, when the O'Sullivan clan ruled over Kerry. It's been called that ever since, which makes us very proud and maybe a little arrogant. The McKennas are all such Kerry patriots.'

'Oh. That's interesting. I don't know much about ancient Irish history. Mom only talked about the rising and the Civil War afterwards. And she told me a little about Dublin and the mountains behind it. She used to walk there with her dad when she was a kid.'

'Oh yes. Jimmy Fitz. I've heard of him. He was quite strict, I believe.'

'I think so.' Cordelia looked away from Roisin's probing gaze which made her feel slightly uncomfortable. But it was just her own nerves playing tricks. Why would Roisin not believe her mother had been the real Frances? Yet Roisin was hard to figure out. She seemed fun and bubbly but there were undertones of scepticism, as if she didn't take people at face value.

They were interrupted by Patrick, who walked towards them, his phone in his hand, looking slightly shaken. 'I just had a call from the solicitor. Phil made a will. He wants everyone who is a beneficiary to come to his office on Thursday. That means you, Roisin, and Maeve. And you too, Cordelia. You have to be there, he said.'

'Me? Why?' Cordelia asked, alarmed.

Patrick shrugged. 'He didn't say. Something to do with you being mentioned in Phil's will. I think she left you something, so you need to be present.'

'To sign the forms?' Cordelia asked.

'Yes, maybe.' Patrick nodded. 'Just a formality. But you also need to confirm your identity.'

Cordelia felt her hand lose all strength and she dropped the glass she was holding onto the grass. *My identity*, she thought. The word made her flinch. She had no real evidence that she and Phil were related, even if she felt it in her bones. How long would it be before they discovered the truth?

Chapter Five

The wake was not as sad as Cordelia had expected. She should have been standing in a corner crying into a glass of port, but instead she was given her first ever glass of Guinness. She listened to haunting Irish music played on the tin whistle by Paschal that then swiftly changed to a lively jig as he was accompanied by a man with a banjo and a woman playing the fiddle. She watched as Maeve and Roisin started to dance, joined by Cian and their sons, all accomplished Irish dancers.

Cordelia carefully sipped her drink which was not like any beer she had ever tried. It had a bittersweet taste that wasn't at all unpleasant but would take a little time to get used to. She glanced across the pub at the chatting, drinking crowd and knew that this was what Phil would have wanted. A party to celebrate her life, not a quiet gathering at home where everyone was sobbing into their cups of tea and nibbling at cakes, like when her mother had died.

It was nice to let out a little steam after the gruelling afternoon that had ended with the brief, beautiful service in the little village church. She had looked at the coffin and suddenly realised that Phil was truly dead and would be buried the next day. She would never see that beautiful smile again or hear the melodious voice. Never chat and laugh together on the balcony in Miami, enjoying the cool evening breeze from the sea. *Never again*, Cordelia thought. A beautiful voice rang out in the church, singing 'On Eagle's Wings', and that's when the tears came. All the pent-up grief and sorrow suddenly came out. Unable to stop, Cordelia cried all through the rest of the ceremony with Maeve at her side holding her hand, comforting Cordelia although she was grieving herself.

Cordelia shivered at the memory and sipped the strange-tasting drink. All around her, everyone was talking about Phil and what a wonderful, fascinating woman she was. There was such love for her and great sorrow of her passing but still an acceptance that death was a part of life. There was a comforting feeling of her life not ending, just of her having left this life for the next one, a consoling thought even if Cordelia wasn't quite sure she believed in it.

As she stood there, she suddenly felt like someone was looking at her. She looked around and then across to the other side of the pub where an open door led to the restaurant and discovered a man standing there, leaning casually against the doorframe sipping from a pint of Guinness. Dressed in a white shirt and jeans, he was tall and very handsome with short fair hair and a neatly trimmed beard. His luminous grey eyes framed by black lashes were clearly noticeable even from a distance. Then he looked straight at her. As their eyes met, Cordelia felt a kind of electricity shoot through her. She stiffened as he made his way through the throng towards her, her hand holding the glass shaking slightly. Then he was at her side, smiling into her startled eyes.

'Hello,' he shouted over the din. 'I know we haven't been introduced, but I know who you are. I saw you standing here all alone. Are you OK?'

'Yes, I'm fine, thank you,' Cordelia replied, her vocal cords straining to speak loudly enough for him to hear. 'But sad, of course,' she added, touched by the kindness in his eyes. He strained to hear her, and brushed her elbow, steering her across the floor through the crowd out to the terrace where it was blissfully quiet and much cooler.

'There,' he said, standing back to look at her. 'I could barely hear you. Now we can talk. I'm Declan, a refugee from Dublin, otherwise known as the blow-in. And you're the American cousin, right? But what's your name?'

'Cordelia Mirafiore,' she replied. 'And yes, I'm from America.'

He nodded. 'I just knew you were the woman they've been talking about.'

'They talked about me?' She suddenly realised that he was the embodiment of that hero she and Philomena had conjured up when she was working on what would be her last book. Fair hair, close-cropped beard, blue-grey eyes. It all fitted in a surreal way. 'Are you a war correspondent?' she asked. 'And do you know how to fly a helicopter?'

He laughed and shook his head. 'Uh, no. Neither of those things, I'm afraid. Why?'

She smiled. 'No reason. It was just something Phil and I were talking about a while back.' She sighed as a wave of sadness hit her when she said the name.

He looked at her with sympathy in his grey eyes. 'I'm very sorry about your loss. Phil was a remarkable woman.'

'Did you know her well?'

'No. Only slightly, I'm sorry to say. I was actually interviewing her for a feature just before she was admitted to hospital. It'll be an obituary now,' he added, looking sad. 'I'm a journalist,' he explained.

'I thought you might be,' she said, smiling. 'I have a feeling Phil liked you.'

Cordelia looked at Declan, wondering if Phil had been inspired by him when she created her latest romantic hero. 'I hope she did,' he replied. 'But as I said I only met her a few times. I feel I missed out on knowing someone really special.'

'Oh, yes, I think you did,' Cordelia agreed. 'She was amazing.'

'Much sadder for you and the rest of the family, of course.'

'Thank you.' Cordelia sighed and brushed away a lock of hair falling into her eyes. 'But she wouldn't want us to be sad. She loved parties and fun and telling jokes and chatting to people and…' Cordelia drew breath.

He touched her arm. 'That's how you should remember her. I'd love to talk a bit more about her. For the obituary. Maybe you could tell me about her writing career and all her book talks and media appearances in the US? And how her readers reacted to her?'

She suddenly felt overwhelmed by the look in his eyes. 'Of course. But not now.'

'Of course not.' He laughed. 'There's no rush. I love your name by the way. Cordelia Mirafiore. So poetic. Cordelia,' he repeated. 'What does it mean?'

'I… I don't really know.'

'I must look that up. And Mirafiore… Italian, right?'

'Yes.' Cordelia couldn't stop looking at him. Up close he was even more handsome than from afar and there was a touch of wariness in his eyes, as if he had been through a lot of hardship and heartbreak and come out of it not trusting anyone. But his kindness came through in the way he was looking at her as if he was trying his best to cheer her up. He looked to be in his early forties, or maybe even a little older, with lines around his eyes and a mouth that only made him more interesting.

'Ah!' he suddenly exclaimed. 'I have it now. Cordelia was King Lear's youngest daughter and his favourite. Were your parents into Shakespeare by any chance?'

'No idea. Don't think so.'

'Maybe you should ask them?'

'That's not possible. My mother died three years ago and my dad…' She shrugged. 'I don't even know if he's still alive. My parents split up thirty years ago, when I was only three. I haven't seen my father since.'

'That's tough,' he remarked, his eyes full of empathy. 'Having lost both parents must make you feel quite alone in the world.'

'Losing my mother was hard. But my dad?' Cordelia shrugged. 'I never felt that sad as I didn't know him at all. I only wished I had a father because everyone else had one. But my mom was wonderful and we were happy together.'

He nodded. 'I know what you mean. I was brought up by a single mother, too. No big deal, really. Tougher for her to be all alone than for me.' He looked at her intently. 'But your story is fascinating all the same. Your mother being from Ireland and you finding a member of her family after all those years, who happened to be a famous author. That's incredible. Roisin told me how you found each other. Maybe you should go to Dublin and do some research and see if you can find anyone else related to you? I could help you if you like. It'd make a fantastic story for a Sunday edition in one of the national newspapers.'

'No,' Cordelia said, alarmed. 'I mean, that's very kind of you, but I don't want to be in any newspaper. I'm going back to America soon. I've had to delay my trip for a day or two because of the will, but once that's settled, I'm off back home.'

'The will?' he said with a glint of excitement in his eyes. 'Phil included you in her will? Does that mean…?'

'I don't know,' Cordelia snapped, suddenly annoyed at his probing questions. Was he about to ask her if she was inheriting? 'And that's none of your business anyway,' she added, knowing she sounded rude. But he had touched a very raw nerve when he probed her about the will. It had been niggling at her ever since she heard about it, and his question had brought it out in the open.

He put his hand on her arm. 'Of course not. I'm sorry if I upset you.'

'That's OK. I'm sorry I snapped at you like that.'

'No offence taken. I shouldn't have asked that question.' He looked at the glass in her hand. 'You're not enjoying that, are you?'

'Not really,' she confessed.

He took it out of her hand. 'I'll get you something better. What would you like?'

'A vodka and tonic with a slice of lemon,' she said. 'If that's possible.'

'Don't move. I'll be back in just a second with that. Anything to eat?'

Cordelia suddenly realised she was starving. 'Oh yes. Some of that grilled lamb and salad would be great. But I can go and get that myself.'

'No need. I'll see what I can rustle up. Promise not to leave before I'm back.'

'I won't budge,' she said with a laugh, her spirits lifting. He was so beguiling, the way he cocked his head at her and looked at her pleadingly. She forgot her worry about the funeral the next day and the visit to the lawyer as she smiled back at him and saw the admiration in his eyes. It was a long time since a man had looked at her like that.

'Sit here and enjoy the view while I'm gone,' he ordered. 'Won't be long.' He smiled warmly at her and left.

Cordelia sat down at one of the tables and relaxed for the first time since that morning. Some of the guests wandered outside with plates, sitting down at the tables. They smiled and nodded at her and she smiled back, then turned her back on them and gazed out over the harbour where the sun was low in the sky, casting a mellow buttery light over the blue water. Small colourful fishing boats at anchor swayed gently on the slight swell and seagulls flew silently over the sea, dipping and rising then disappearing further out. The air was still warm with a soft breeze that felt like a caress cooling her hot cheeks. What a magical place this was, so peaceful and soothing. She closed her eyes for a moment and took a deep breath, letting it out slowly as her body relaxed. Then she opened her eyes and smiled at Declan, who was coming towards her with a loaded tray.

'Drinks and food,' he announced, setting down the tray on the table. 'I should have asked one of the staff to take it out for us, but they're so busy serving and clearing tables. And this way I could sneak out without replying to questions from your family. Or maybe you want to sit with them?'

'No, this is fine,' Cordelia replied, feeling she needed a break from all of them, including Betsy. 'I'll go and talk to them when I've eaten.'

'Great.' He handed her a plate. 'Here. Lamb, salad, potatoes and some soda bread topped with smoked salmon. No vodka tonic I'm afraid, as they were so busy at the bar. I just grabbed a bottle of wine for us to share. A nice, light Chianti. Hope that's all right.'

'Lovely.' Cordelia attacked the food with gusto, stuffing her mouth with succulent lamb, crisp lettuce and potato salad flavoured with chives. 'This is great,' she mumbled through bites. 'I hadn't realised how hungry I was.'

'Must be the air,' he said, picking up a cutlet and biting into it. 'Sea air improves the appetite. And it soothes the spirits.'

'I suppose,' she replied. 'But right now, food is all I want.'

'Of course,' he said. 'You need to eat.'

'I'll try.' She picked up her wine glass and took a sip. 'Nice wine.'

'Yes. Italian. Like you.'

'I'm American,' she corrected and he looked up, bemused. 'Nothing more or less.'

'Of course,' he said sounding contrite. 'I didn't mean… I was just so taken by your name. We forget sometimes over here that America is such a melting pot and that despite all the different names from all kinds of countries, everyone is simply American and proud of that.'

'Exactly. My mother was Irish, but she was very anxious to be as American as possible. She loved our country and was very happy there, despite all the struggle. Especially Morristown, where I grew up. Small town in New Jersey,' she explained.

'She sounds like a real trouper.'

'Oh, she was,' Cordelia said wistfully. 'The best mom ever. We were very close.'

'Just like Phil. You were close to her, too, I suspect.'

'Yes. Very.' Cordelia picked at the rest of her food. 'And now I'm all alone.'

Declan looked surprised. 'Really? No husband or partner?'

'No.' She sighed. 'I haven't had much time to socialise. I was looking after Mom for nearly two years before she passed. After that, I didn't feel much like going out on dates or partying. And then, when I found Phil, working with her took up a lot of my time. I tried dating a few times, but I never found a man I could stand for longer than an hour. Phil urged me to go out and have fun, so I joined a dating site. The guys looked great on screen but in real life…' She shook her head and laughed. 'Total nightmares, most of them.'

He smiled and let out a chuckle. 'I know what you mean. I've been on a series of blind dates that have been so awful they would make you laugh.'

'I bet mine were worse.'

'We could have a competition sometime. I'll tell you mine if you tell me yours.' He touched her arm. 'Ah, but you're an attractive woman. That special someone will come along one day. I can't see you being left all alone for very long.'

She tried not to blush but felt the heat creeping into her face. 'Maybe,' she mumbled and nibbled at the slice of smoked salmon, once again enjoying the smoky, salty taste. 'This is delicious,' she said to change the subject.

'Kerry produce,' he said, picking up his own slice of salmon-covered bread. 'There is a smokery in Killorglin not far from here.'

Cordelia gestured at her empty plate. 'Everything was fabulous. The lamb, the vegetables and the potatoes. Even the butter. Never tasted food that fresh before.'

'Irish cuisine is excellent,' he replied, looking proud. 'Especially here and especially in the summer. Local new potatoes with Kerrygold butter and a little salt. That's the food of the gods.'

'Wish I could stay and have a vacation here.'

'Why can't you?' he asked.

'I'm moving to New York to take up a new job. Betsy, Phil's publisher, has offered me a really good position at their headquarters in New York. It's the chance of a lifetime, so I really can't take any time off.'

He nodded. 'Of course. Congratulations.'

'Thank you.'

'Yoohoo, Cordelia,' Betsy chanted, coming towards them, waving. 'There you are,' she called.

'Hi, Betsy,' Cordelia said and gestured at Declan. 'This is Declan. He's a journalist.'

'Oh?' Betsy pushed her glasses up her nose and peered at Declan. 'Hi, nice to meet you.' She turned to Cordelia. 'I changed your booking so you can stay for the meeting with the lawyer. I'll be going back the day after tomorrow, but you're now going back on the Friday morning flight. I'll email you the details so you can check in yourself. Then you'll have the weekend to pack and lock up the condo. And I'll see you at the office in New York on Monday morning. I've booked you a room at a hotel that's quite reasonable on Thirty-Fifth and Seventh. Within walking distance of Penn Station. Then you have to look for an apartment as soon as you can.'

Cordelia nodded. 'Great. Thank you so much for organising my trip back, Betsy.'

Betsy patted her arm. 'You're welcome. I'm going back to the house. I'm exhausted and tomorrow will be quite an ordeal, I'm sure. See you in the morning, honey.' She nodded at Declan and disappeared into the throng of guests.

Declan looked at Cordelia and laughed. 'That woman doesn't hang around. Was that Betsy?'

Cordelia smiled. 'Sure was. I like her a lot, but she's a real dynamo. Typical New Yorker, works eighteen hours a day. Everything has to happen yesterday and she doesn't take no for an answer. Can't wait to work with her.'

'I'd be terrified.' He paused. 'Do you think she might be interested in my novel?'

'Only if it's a red-hot romance.'

Declan's face fell. 'Not really, no. It's more literary fiction set in the world of journalism. I forgot Red Hot Romance was the name of Phil's publisher.'

'They're planning to publish new genres. Romantic suspense is one of them. Maybe you could rejig your book and make it more romantic and add a little suspense?' She laughed.

'I'm afraid that would be impossible.' He sighed. 'Ah well, I'll have to look elsewhere, then.'

Cordelia suddenly felt a wave of fatigue hit her and she stifled a yawn. 'Sorry. I'm very tired. It's been a long day and my body clock is still on American time. I think I'll follow Betsy and go to bed.'

He jumped up. 'I'll walk you home.'

'Oh,' Cordelia started but was interrupted by Roisin, who had just arrived at their table.

'There you are,' she said, glancing at Declan. 'I see Declan looked after you. But we're all going back to the house and I thought you might be tired.'

'Oh yes.' Cordelia sighed. 'I was just about to leave.'

'OK. I'll just get the boys and Cian and we'll be off. See you tomorrow, Declan.' Roisin walked away and Cordelia picked up her tray, but Declan stopped her.

'I'll look after that. You go on.' He smiled, looking into her eyes. 'It was lovely to meet you, Cordelia Mirafiore. I'll see you at the funeral, but I don't suppose we'll have a chance to talk again like this.'

'No,' Cordelia replied. 'I enjoyed our chat.'

'Me too. Good luck with the new job. And with the family. I have a feeling you'll need it.'

'Thank you,' Cordelia said, knowing he was right. She would need some very good luck in the next few days. That, and a cool head.

Chapter Six

The solicitor's office in Killarney was bare and cool, with white walls, a huge bookcase crammed with legal books and a desk covered with stacks of papers. There were three chairs in front of the desk, waiting for the three beneficiaries. A tall man with a balding head and glasses rose as Maeve, Roisin and Cordelia filed in. He shook hands with them and asked them to sit down. 'I met you at the funeral,' he said. 'But let me again express my sympathy on the death of your aunt. She was a formidable woman. Very nice, too. Knew what she wanted until the very end.'

Maeve nodded. 'Thank you. Yes, Phil was amazing. We miss her terribly.'

Roisin sniffed and blew her nose. 'I still can't believe I'll never see her again.' She dabbed at her eyes. 'Sorry, but I'm not feeling so well after everything.'

Cordelia said nothing, just sat there gripping the armrest of her chair, waiting to hear what Phil had left her. She was one of the beneficiaries, Patrick had said, so there must be something. What could it be? A little money, perhaps. Or a piece of jewellery. It would be lovely to have a memento of that happy year during which she and Phil had become so close. But sitting here waiting was nerve-racking. She hadn't slept well, waking up several times, staring into the darkness, wondering what would be revealed at the lawyer's office. Had Phil had some kind of inkling that she wasn't related to this family after all? Would the lawyer reveal something Phil had said that would confirm the truth about that last name? But Cordelia had never mentioned any of her concerns to Phil, so…

She jumped as the lawyer cleared his throat and started reading from a piece of paper in his hand.

'To my nieces Maeve and Roisin, and my cousin Cordelia Mirafiore, I bequeath my whole estate, to be split in three equal parts so that they will all be owners of Willow House together. They will also share equally whatever money is in my bank account after my death. They shall also own and share the rights of my work and the income thereof.'

There was a gasp then a shocked silence in the room as Maeve and Roisin looked at each other, then at Cordelia, who tried her best not to faint. She gripped the arms of her chair so hard it hurt. This was earth-shattering, impossible to take in all at once. It couldn't be true. She was one of the main heirs to Phil's estate?

'There must be some kind of mistake,' she said, barely able to talk. 'I can't believe Phil would…'

'No mistake,' the solicitor replied. 'Phil knew what she wanted.'

'I can't believe it,' Roisin muttered. 'Was she really all there when she signed all this? I mean mentally?'

'Roisin,' Maeve chided. 'That's not very—'

'I know,' Roisin interrupted, avoiding Cordelia's eyes. 'But we have to be sure that Phil was mentally stable when she signed that will. Was she?'

'Absolutely,' the solicitor replied. 'And I will have to remind you that a person's will is just that: the wishes of the deceased, which have to be respected to the letter. This was what Phil wanted, how she wished her estate to be distributed after her death.'

'Of course,' Maeve mumbled.

'And,' he continued, 'this is all subject to probate, so the inheritance will not be handed over until that is settled.'

'Probate?' Cordelia asked. 'What does that mean?'

The solicitor cleared his throat. 'Probate is when we establish who has ownership of a property and if there are any claims from other people. It has to go through a probate court before we can pay out the inheritance. It's just a formality but all wills have to be cleared in this way.'

Cordelia nodded. 'I see. Thank you.'

'You're welcome,' the solicitor said. 'All I need for now is your signatures that you have read and understood the will. I will also need your proof of identity. Maeve and Roisin, if you have a driver's licence or some other identity card with your PPS number, and Miss… Mirafiore, I'd like your passport, please. We'll make photocopies of all of these so we have them on file.'

They all dug in their handbags and handed over the required documents, which a secretary took away at the request of the lawyer. Then he slid three sheets of paper over the desk with figures and columns.

'This is what's in her various bank accounts and the income she was receiving from her royalties and her foreign deals. It's quite substantial. Please sign where marked. I will need your bank details and perhaps you could decide between you how the income will be handled when it comes to the royalties, which are paid twice a year. You will have to set up an account for the incoming money and then perhaps distribute it in three parts every month. It's up to you. Talk to your bank about it. The inheritance tax will also have to be dealt with, but according to Irish law, you can inherit a certain amount without paying tax. Anything after that is taxable as income.' He drew breath. 'Is that all clear?'

They nodded and signed their papers in silence, still shocked by what was in the will. Roisin and Maeve glanced at each other again and Cordelia could feel negative vibes against her. But that was a normal reaction. They must be shocked and bewildered that Phil had bequeathed an equal part to her, their second cousin who they hadn't known existed until recently, and she could understand that. But it wasn't her fault. Phil had obviously wanted this, had wanted Cordelia to be a beneficiary and to have the same amount as her nieces. It didn't seem fair, somehow. Cordelia hadn't done much to deserve such a legacy. She had looked after Phil full time, that was true, but she had loved every minute of it. Phil had been a fascinating, intelligent, fun woman with a charisma that was hard to resist. Cordelia had felt happy in her presence and loved all the intimate moments when they had talked late into the night when Phil couldn't sleep, or when they had been out shopping for clothes and giggled like schoolgirls at silly outfits. All this flitted through her mind as she looked at the figures on the paper in shock. This was a lot of money, more than she had ever earned in her entire life.

And then the house... Willow House, a third of which would now be hers. It was unbelievable, like a dream she would soon wake up from. But the edge of the chair dug into the back of her legs and she felt cold sweat in her armpits. This was real and she didn't know what to do. The doubts she'd hidden seemed a thousand times worse now that this had happened, and she knew she should say something. But then what? Would they call the police? And what would Betsy say? She'd be furious and fire her before she had started the new job. She might even sue.

Cordelia swallowed noisily and knew that she had to carry on being who they thought she was: the daughter of Phil's first cousin.

Before they left, the solicitor handed them each an envelope with their name in Phil's handwriting. 'She asked me to give you these after I read the will. I think it will explain her decisions.'

Maeve put her letter in her handbag. 'Thank you. I'll read it when I get home.'

'Me too,' Roisin said and stuffed her envelope into her tote, while Cordelia followed their example. She'd read it in the privacy of her room at Willow House.

When they left the solicitor's office, Maeve suggested they have lunch before setting off back to Sandy Cove. 'It's actually a lovely day,' she said, looking up at the blue sky. 'Why not have lunch at Muckross Park? They have a nice outdoor café there where they serve salads and sandwiches.'

'I couldn't eat a thing,' Roisin said, looking pale.

'You must,' Maeve insisted. 'And Cordelia, too. We need to talk.'

Roisin sighed and nodded. 'You're right. We have to decide what to do about Willow House.' She glanced at Cordelia. 'And you need to be in on everything, Cordelia, as you're now part-owner with us.' Roisin shook her head. 'What on earth was Phil thinking? It's probably explained in the letters, but she must have known it would be complicated to say the least.'

Maeve smiled. 'Of course she did. It's her little joke on us. I can hear her giggling in heaven, sitting on a cloud with Uncle Joe. "Life shouldn't be too easy," she used to say, remember? She thought wrestling with problems keeps us young. And maybe she was right.'

Roisin shrugged. 'I could do without this particular problem.'

'Not your fault, Cordelia,' Maeve cut in with a warning glance at Roisin. 'You couldn't have known this was going to happen.'

'Or did you?' Roisin interrupted, staring at Cordelia.

'No,' Cordelia replied. 'Of course not. I thought I was going to faint when I heard.'

'Me too.' Maeve took her car key out of her bag. 'I'm parked down the street and Roisin came in my car. How about you, Cordelia?'

'I parked in the car park opposite Killarney House. Let's meet up at this Muckross Park place. I passed it on the way here.'

Maeve nodded. 'Great. Just drive in through the main entrance. The café is just before the big manor house. We'll see you there.'

'OK.' Cordelia left them and walked the short distance to her car.

Maeve had asked if she wanted to come with them, but Cordelia had explained that she wanted to explore the Ring of Kerry on her own afterwards, not knowing she would be standing here trying to recover after the shock of her inheritance. She looked around and noticed what a nice town this was, the main street lined with shops and pubs, where traditional music could be heard through the open windows. Tourists thronged the street, buying souvenirs in the many craft shops that sold everything from tweed jackets and hand-knitted sweaters to postcards and mugs covered in shamrocks. It could be argued that it was too touristy and a little too commercial but it still had that higgledy-piggledy charm of all small Irish towns: old houses mixed with new, their façades painted in vivid colours and the street lined with hanging baskets crammed with flowers, like something from a storybook.

When she reached the car, she felt a little better, although the letter in her bag seemed to weigh it down, demanding to be read. But no, she couldn't take it out now, she had to go and meet Maeve and Roisin for lunch and that talk, which would probably be fraught with emotion.

Why now, she wondered, and why here? Couldn't they just as easily talk when they got back to the house? Maybe Maeve was anxious to set some boundaries straight away, or establish who was boss? Would she and Roisin turn against Cordelia and see right through her deceit? Would it be best to give up her inheritance and sign it all over to them and then leave never to come back? It would be the most honourable thing, of course, and the one thing that would save her from serious trouble and possible lawsuits. But something told her not to give up what she had been given. It was Phil's wish that she should have it, wasn't it?

Cordelia drove the short distance to Muckross Park with butterflies twirling in her stomach, wondering what on earth she was going to do. While she drove, she remembered what Phil had told her about her two nieces:

'Maeve is thoughtful, kind and very empathetic. Hard-working and a bit of a perfectionist. Roisin is more hot-tempered and very ambitious. Give her a project and she sees it through to the end, even if it kills her. Very loyal once you have earned her trust. I always think that if I need comfort, I'd go to Maeve, but if I need something done, Roisin is your man, I mean woman,' she had ended with a giggle. 'I'm so proud of them both,' Phil had said. 'You'll love them and they'll love you. We'll all be together one day, when I move back to Ireland. Promise you'll join me there and stay.'

Cordelia had promised without really meaning it, not thinking this would ever happen. But now it had, in a very sad way and not at all how Phil had predicted.

Muckross Park was enchanting. Cordelia drove through the imposing gates past a cute little gatehouse with a slate roof and leaded windows and continued down the narrow lane that wound itself through woods where tall pines were mixed with rhododendron bushes, palm trees and other subtropical trees and shrubs that shaded the road and filtered the sunlight, giving the air a slightly misty, magical light. Cordelia slowed the car and looked around, nearly expecting fairies to appear from behind the trees. Pity there was no time to get out and walk through these woods, planted in the Victorian era. She could nearly see the ladies in long skirts carrying parasols, wandering through these woods and gardens on their daily walks.

As she drove up to the restaurant, she could see the old manor house on the edge of a large lake with majestic mountains rising steeply on the other side. The restaurant was modern, but the surrounding rose garden still held that atmosphere of the old days, with the lovely conservatory and glasshouses still intact beyond the flowerbeds and fountains.

Cordelia walked through the entrance and out the other side, where she found Maeve and Roisin sitting at a round table shaded by a large white umbrella.

'Hi,' Maeve said. 'We just got here.'

'Lovely place.' Cordelia pulled out a chair and sat down. It was cool under the umbrella and she was grateful for the breeze on her hot face. 'It's getting really warm now,' she remarked.

Roisin fanned her face with the menu. 'I know. We're due to have a heatwave, they say. I can feel it already.'

Maeve took the menu from Roisin and opened it. 'We're not used to hot weather. But I'm sure you are.'

Cordelia nodded. 'Yes. After six years in Florida, the heat here won't bother me. Not that I like very hot weather, though. I'm glad I'm moving to New York. I like real winters.'

Roisin sat up. 'You're moving to New York?'

Cordelia nodded. 'Yes. Betsy has offered me a job and I accepted. I will be assisting their marketing manager and I'll also be organising book tours and all kinds of publicity campaigns for their authors. They're hiring more staff now that they're expanding.' She drew breath, wondering when the small talk would end and they'd start discussing the inheritance and how to manage everything. 'That was my plan, anyway,' she continued. 'But now…'

'Now?' Roisin filled in. 'What are you going to do?'

Cordelia looked back at her. 'I don't know. What are you going to do? Both of you? I mean, things must look very different now that I'm one of the beneficiaries of Phil's will. I'm sure you had other plans before this happened.'

Maeve sighed. 'We had no plans at all. All we could think about was Phil and that she was dying. She left us long before we had expected. She seemed to want to let go.' Her eyes filled with tears. 'It was so hard to just sit there and watch her fade away.'

Cordelia felt her own eyes well up and she put her hand over Maeve's. 'Sorry. I didn't mean...'

Maeve nodded and took a tissue from her handbag and dabbed her eyes. 'Of course you didn't. We're all sad and shaken still. You too, Cordelia. I know you and Phil became close during the past year. She said you saved her life and helped her carry on when she was beginning to feel ill. She managed to write, which she loved and then you did everything for her, even got up during the night to sit with her when she couldn't sleep. She told us how you used to watch the sunrise together. That must have been exhausting.'

'It was beautiful, and I'm glad we had those moments,' Cordelia replied.

Roisin got up. 'It's self-service here. If you tell me what you'd like, I'll get it.'

'Thanks, Roisin,' Maeve said. 'I just want something light. Maybe an egg salad sandwich on brown bread and some water.' She smiled at Cordelia. 'Sounds dreary but an Irish egg salad sandwich is delicious.'

'Then I'll have to try that,' Cordelia replied. 'I'll go with you if you like.'

'No, you stay with Maeve. I won't be long,' Roisin promised and walked into the restaurant.

Maeve sat back and looked around. 'The gardens are beautiful this time of year.'

'Gorgeous,' Cordelia agreed, breathing in the rose-scented air. 'So lovely that they managed to keep the Victorian period atmosphere here.'

'You can imagine the ladies walking around, their long skirts trailing on the ground,' Maeve said dreamily.

'I know.'

Maeve sighed and sat back in her chair, fanning her face. 'It's very hot.' Her eyes focused on Cordelia. 'You're going back tomorrow?'

'Yes. Betsy rebooked my ticket.'

'Are you sure you should? I mean maybe you should stay for a while now that you've found out about the will. In fact, you should perhaps think about staying for a longer period. I mean the three of us are partners now. We have to decide what to do about the house for a start. And organise the sharing of the money and the royalties. It's a lot to consider and it would be easier if we didn't have to do it long distance.'

'Oh.' Cordelia looked at Maeve. 'I hadn't thought about all of that.'

'Of course not. It's all been so overwhelming. Really life-changing for you. But we've only just found out so we'll all have to try to get used to the idea. I'm still in shock, to be honest.'

'Yes. Me too.' Cordelia thought for a while. 'I have to think about this. It could mean giving up that new job in New York. I need to know what kind of income I'd have and all kinds of things like that. And staying here for an extended period… I don't know if… Well, it depends on the visa, too.'

'What visa?' Roisin interrupted, putting a loaded tray with sandwiches and a carafe of water on the table. 'You don't have an Irish passport?' She sat down and helped herself to one of the sandwiches.

'No,' Cordelia replied. 'How could I? I'm an American citizen.' She reached out for a sandwich and bit into it, enjoying the taste of egg mixed with mayonnaise, chives, tomatoes and lettuce. 'Mmm, delicious,' she mumbled through her bite.

'An Irish classic,' Maeve declared as she picked up her sandwich.

Roisin swallowed her large mouthful and turned to Cordelia. 'Didn't you know that you can get Irish citizenship if one of your parents or grandparents were born in Ireland? All you need is their birth certificate and yours and then a completed application form. Easy-peasy. Doesn't take long, I've heard.'

'Oh.' Cordelia stared at Roisin. 'I had no idea. My mother didn't say anything about this. But she didn't want to go back to Ireland and didn't actually have a passport. She became an American citizen just after she married my dad, and she was very proud of that.'

'So she never went back even for a visit?' Maeve asked. 'Or travelled anywhere else?'

'No. We travelled a bit around the US, but never went abroad. I only got a passport myself last year, when Phil told me to get one in case I wanted to go with her to Ireland.' Cordelia put her sandwich on her plate and wiped her fingers with a napkin. 'But my mother never wanted to go back to Ireland. We couldn't afford it in any case. After my dad left, she worked as a music teacher in the local high school and gave piano lessons in her free time. I worked, too, when I was old enough. Babysitting, stacking shelves in the supermarket, that kind of thing.' She looked at their surprised faces and smiled. 'But you know what? We were happy. It was just the two of us and we managed fine. We lived in a rented house in Morristown, which is a lovely little town in a beautiful part of New Jersey. I had a friend who lived on a farm in the countryside nearby. They had ponies and we used to have so much fun riding in the forests. And we skated on the lake in the wintertime. I don't actually remember feeling poor or that I needed anything other than what we had.'

Maeve smiled. 'Sounds like total bliss. Your mum must have been a special person.'

Cordelia nodded, feeling a surge of love for her mother. 'Yes, she was. And she was fun and loved to joke and laugh. She used to tell me she was once a "bold girl" but she grew up when she had me. My dad leaving was probably awful for her, but she never showed it.' Cordelia shrugged and picked up her sandwich. 'I was only three when this happened so it didn't have much impact on me. He wasn't a hands-on kind of dad, and he wasn't around much anyway.'

'What about your friend?' Roisin asked. 'The one with the farm? Are you still in touch?'

'No. She married a man from Illinois straight after graduation and moved to Chicago. I trained as a beautician and then worked in New York for a bit before I moved to Miami.'

'And then your mother died and you met Phil,' Maeve said.

Cordelia smiled as she chewed on her sandwich. 'The story of my life in a nutshell,' she said when she had finished.

Roisin took a sip of water. 'What about men?' She smiled with sudden warmth in her eyes. 'Sorry. I know that's a bit of a personal question. But I'm interested. You're very pretty, so I thought you might have an interesting love life.'

Cordelia blushed at the compliment, feeling more relaxed. 'Thank you. I never thought of myself in that way. I was a bit of an oddball at school.' Encouraged by the friendly look in Roisin's eyes, she continued. 'Men have never figured much in my life. I had a boyfriend in New York. Doug. A stockbroker. We met when he brought his mother to the beauty salon where I worked.' She smiled dreamily as she thought of him. 'We dated for over a year.

He was cute, sexy and rich, so what's not to like? I thought. But as time went on I discovered he was a real mommy's boy. Couldn't do a thing without asking for her approval.' Cordelia rolled her eyes. 'He was on the phone to her all the time, even when we were out on a date. I started thinking she was in bed with us too, and that really turned me off.'

Roisin laughed. 'Sorry, but it sounded so funny the way you said it.'

Maeve joined the laughter. 'I can imagine. His mother giving him pointers on how to make love or something.'

Cordelia grinned. 'That's how it felt. It's funny now, but at the time it felt kind of sad. He was a really nice guy, only he never grew up. It finally got so much on my nerves I broke it off to everyone's relief, including mine. I bet he's still the same, calling his mother every day and driving women away in droves.'

'And you didn't have any men in your life after that?' Maeve asked.

Cordelia sighed. 'No. I did go out on dates and went out on Friday nights with my workmates but I never found anyone I wanted to stay with. Men in New York are… Well, not really husband material. Most of them are only looking for a quick fling or even just a one-night stand.' She sighed and made a face. 'I tried online dating but…'

Maeve laughed and shook her head. 'If it was anything like what I experienced in London, you don't need to explain. Tried that once or twice, but the men who turned up weren't exactly true to their profile photos.'

Cordelia giggled. 'To say the least. One guy had put his height at six feet, but he was more like five feet three and that was probably his waist measurement too. And I think he must have been at least ten years older than the age he had posted. He picked his teeth all through the meal. Ugh.'

'Dream date, compared to some of mine,' Maeve joked.

'What about you?' Cordelia asked in order to turn the spotlight off her non-existent love life. 'You must have had a very exciting life in London.'

'Not really,' Maeve said with a sigh. 'It was work, work, work until I came here for a rest when I was on the brink of a nervous breakdown. There was a man in London who seemed perfect, but he turned out to be quite the opposite.'

'Then she met Paschal, who rescued her,' Roisin cut in. 'And now they're living happily ever after in their lovely little cottage by the sea.'

Maeve shot Roisin a smile. 'Sounds clichéd, but yeah, that's it in a nutshell. I had to kiss a lot of frogs before I found my prince. Unlike Roisin, who didn't have to kiss anyone before her very own prince winked at her across a crowded lecture hall and they got married when they were still nearly teenagers. Nobody thought that would last, but it did.'

'Yeah,' Roisin said with a happy sigh. 'And here we are nearly twenty years and three kids later, still together.'

'It's been a happy twenty years,' Maeve remarked. 'Apart from that little episode last year.'

Cordelia's eyebrows raised while Roisin threw a crumpled-up napkin at her sister.

Roisin turned to Cordelia. 'Cian bought a campervan against my wishes last year and took off up the west coast with it.' She drew breath. 'But back to you and your life. You lived in New York for a while, didn't you?'

Cordelia nodded. 'Yes. Then I moved to Miami to look after my mom, and during that time I wasn't really in the mood for dating, even if I used to dream of finding that perfect man one day and have a family. The strange thing was that it was then I discovered Fanny l'Amour's books. I used to binge read them. It was a wonderful of way of escaping from the sadness to all the exotic locations she described. And the romantic parts... Wow.'

'She was an amazing writer,' Maeve said.

'Wonderful,' Cordelia agreed. 'And I couldn't believe it when we met in person and she turned out to be... who she was.'

'Your mother's cousin,' Maeve said with awe. 'What an amazing coincidence.'

'Yes. It was like a dream come true,' Cordelia said with a sad little sigh. 'And we clicked straight away.'

'Looking after Phil was a full-time job, though, I can imagine,' Roisin cut in.

'Yes.' Cordelia smiled wistfully. 'But I did go out on dates. Phil nearly forced me to. She even fixed me up with some of the men at the radio and TV shows she appeared in from time to time. She said I was young and pretty and should have fun rather than staying in to look after an old woman. So I did and she stayed up and asked me to tell her every detail. It was as if she was living vicariously through me. She even picked my outfits, which was a huge help. She had such an eye for style.' Cordelia blinked away tears that threatened to well up.

'She did,' Maeve agreed and patted Cordelia's arm. 'I know. The memories make us sad. But hey, what if we didn't have them? What if we'd never had Phil in our lives? We wouldn't be sad right now, but we wouldn't have had the joy of knowing her.'

'Or the money,' Roisin said. She put her hand to her mouth. 'Oops. Me and my big mouth. It just came out. I didn't mean it the way it sounded. It's not about the money, really.'

'No,' Maeve filled in. 'It's not the money. It's the house. That's going to be a bit of a headache if we don't agree.'

'I know,' Roisin replied. 'But it's too soon to talk about it. I just—' She stopped. 'I'm sorry, Cordelia, but I was so shocked when I heard about the inheritance. I couldn't understand why Phil wanted you to have a third of Willow House. You're not even a McKenna.'

Cordelia felt a dart of fear. What did she mean? Had she… Then she breathed out. Of course. Frances, the real Frances hadn't been a McKenna, as her mother had been born Brennan and then married to a Fitzgerald. 'I know. It is strange. Maybe it's explained in the letters she wrote?'

'I'm sure it is,' Roisin replied. 'But now you've told us all of this, I realise how important you must have been to Phil. So I'm not shocked any more. We'll work it out, I'm sure. And I want to go back and read my letter in peace and quiet.'

'Yes.' Maeve nodded and got up. 'I think we should go home and read our letters and then meet later and talk about it. I'm sure Paschal is a little worn out after chasing Aisling around all morning, too.'

'Good idea.' Roisin picked up her handbag. 'Let's go. It's too hot here anyway. We'll talk over dinner. Mum and Dad are leaving at five to catch the evening plane to Málaga from Cork. I want to spend a little time with them. We were going to take the boys to Spain in August to stay with them, but I'll cancel now that I have to stay to run the guesthouse.'

'Yes, for now, anyway,' Maeve agreed. 'Until we decide what to do. In any case, we should run it through to next year, because we have bookings until the end of this season. Phil wouldn't want us to disappoint these people.'

'Yes,' Cordelia said, having finished her sandwich while she listened. 'That's a good idea.'

'I agree,' Roisin said. 'But now I just want to get back.' She walked swiftly ahead of them through the rose garden on her way to the car park.

Maeve and Cordelia trailed behind her. 'Are you still leaving tomorrow morning?' Maeve asked her.

'I think I have to. Perhaps I'll call Betsy and tell her what's happened. She might give me a little extra time.'

Maeve laughed. 'I doubt it. From what you've said about Betsy, she'll want you to stick to the schedule she decided. There's no waiting around or extra time with Betsy.'

'No. That's true,' Cordelia agreed, not looking forward to breaking the news. 'I'm not sure what I want to do, to be honest.'

'Of course we'd like you to stay. It would be great to have you here to run the guesthouse with us. But you have to decide what's best for you, of course,' Maeve said, putting her arm through Cordelia's.

Cordelia nodded. 'Yes. I know. But it's hard. I've been doing whatever someone else wants for so long, I think I've lost the habit of thinking of myself.'

'I have a feeling you never had it.'

'Oh.' Cordelia stopped in her tracks and pulled her arm from Maeve's. 'I never thought of it that way.'

'Some people just are that way. Unselfish and giving, always thinking of others first.' Maeve started to walk again. 'Not a bad trait but it could turn you into a doormat and then you're your own worst enemy.'

'Yes, maybe,' Cordelia replied, wondering what Maeve would say if she knew how selfish she'd been coming here in the first place.

'I suppose you have to go back to sort things out and pack up in Miami,' Maeve said, cutting into Cordelia's thoughts. 'And maybe even go to New York and see what you feel about working there.'

'That's what I'm planning to do. But then…'

'God knows, we could do with an extra pair of hands during the busiest time of the year,' Maeve said with a smile. 'But maybe that's selfish of us. I don't want to put any pressure on you at all.'

'Oh,' Cordelia said, looking up at the green hills. 'I don't think it'd be a hard choice at all. But I have to go back home for a bit to sort out my feelings – and my life.'

'That's the hardest bit, isn't it?' Maeve said. 'Sorting out your life.'

Cordelia laughed. 'Oh yeah. It sure is.' She increased her pace as she spotted Roisin by Maeve's car, waving them on. 'But we'd better get going. Roisin's getting impatient.'

'Yes. She wants to get back to Cian and the boys. They're planning to take off in the campervan for the weekend and she wants to make sure they have all their gear. Then she can put her feet up for a bit before the guesthouse opens again on Monday.'

'She works hard.'

'She does, but she thrives on hard work.' Maeve laughed. 'I used to be very driven, too. But then I became more laid-back when I moved here, and now with a wild one-year-old, I have little time for that.' She quickened her pace.

They got into their cars and drove off through what felt to Cordelia like an enchanted forest and out the gates onto the main road and the way back, Maeve and Roisin chatting animatedly in their car, Cordelia in hers, deep in thought.

Chapter Seven

Once back in her lovely room at Willow House, Cordelia opened the window to let in the cool breeze from the sea and took the letter from her bag. She stacked a few of the lace-edged pillows on the large bed, kicked off her sandals and lay down, holding the letter against her chest, trying to stay calm. Whatever was in there, she had a feeling it would dictate the rest of her life. This was the last message from Phil, her very last thoughts and feelings before she left this life for the next. Her heart beating, her stomach full of fluttering butterflies, Cordelia tore the envelope open and started to read.

Dearest, darling Cordelia,

It breaks my heart to think that when you read this, I will be gone. It makes me happy to know that I will be with my darling Joe in the next life, but I'm sad to think you will be all alone, left to grieve with no family or a home to go to. I know that dear Betsy will look after you. She promised me when we spoke last that she'd offer you a position with her firm with a good salary. But this is not your only choice, as you will by now know the details of my will.

I have left you and my nieces equal shares of all that I own and any income thereof. This includes my lovely Willow House, which might have come as a surprise to you all. I can imagine Maeve and Roisin are by now a little shocked to have learned that they have to share everything, including the house, with you. You might ask yourself why I am doing this, as the house is McKenna property and had nothing to do with my mother's side of the family. But you are as much of my blood as they are. And you, as I said above, have no family and have never had a real home. Maeve and Roisin are privileged and have had everything anyone would want: a happy childhood, a good education and now husbands and children. You have none of these things and never did. Whatever happened between Frances and her family drove her away from Ireland into a life of hardship far away from home. I don't want that to happen to you.

You gave me so much during this last year in Miami: love, companionship and your tender care when I needed it the most. You always thought of me first, you were always there at my side. I cherish the memories of our time together and felt I needed to give something back. Money would not have been enough, but this way I can give you a home and maybe even a family, if they have the heart to take you to their bosoms, which I'm very sure they will.

It will be up to you how you deal with this gift, and you should think carefully about what you do with it. I'm sitting here, in my bed, imagining you staying at Willow House at least for the summer to get to know your mother's country, the lovely friendly village where I grew up, and the house that has been part of my family since it was built over a hundred years ago. But it is your choice and your inheritance, so you must do what your heart tells you. But whatever you choose, you will have some money and the income from my royalties, as long as the books keep selling. This gives you the freedom to follow your own star and do whatever you wish. Choose wisely, darling Cordelia, and don't worry about whatever anyone else wants or thinks. You have spent your young life caring for others. Now it's time to think only of yourself.

I wish you the very best of luck and much happiness. Look up at the stars on a clear night, and find one that winks. It will be me, smiling down at you, enjoying your happy moments.

Yours forever,

Phil

Cordelia read the last lines with tears running down her cheeks. Oh, what a darling Phil was. Trying to give her the gift of family and home, something she had never had. But now she did. If only she could be sure they really *were* family. There had been that strange feeling of connection with Phil the moment they met. Looking into Phil's beautiful dark eyes, she had felt a tug somewhere inside, something that didn't come from her mind, but her heart and her soul. Were they kindred spirits? Or did it come from somewhere in their DNA? Did they share the same genes?

Cordelia had felt the same strange vibes when she met Maeve, and to a lesser degree with Roisin, but it was still there, like a tiny quiver as they said hello. And she was sure they had felt it, too. If only she could find out more about her mother and her early life in Dublin. If only she could be sure. What was it that Phil had written about her mother? Cordelia skimmed the tightly written page and found it: *Whatever happened between Frances and her family drove her away from Ireland into a life of hardship so far away from home. I don't want that to happen to you.* So Phil hadn't known what made Frances leave Ireland… What could it be? Had Phil known but decided not to tell Cordelia because she thought it might be too painful? But it could have been a great help and maybe even given her a clue to who her mother really was. The real Frances – or someone with a similar story?

Cordelia sighed and put the letter carefully back into the envelope. She would never know what the big secret was. But she might be able to find out if her mother was the real Frances. Somehow, some way… She simply had to start digging into the past, if only to find out for herself.

But first things first. Cordelia sat up in bed and picked up her phone. She had to decide what to do. A plan slowly developed in her mind and she scrolled through her contact list and found Betsy's number. It was time to get going. One step at a time…

Betsy gasped when Cordelia told her about the will. 'Holy mother. I had no idea. You're sharing her entire estate with Maeve and Roisin?'

'So it seems,' Cordelia said, sitting on the edge of the bed, her phone pressed to her ear.

'Gee, that's a real bombshell, honey. What are you going to do? Does this mean you won't be coming to New York?'

'No. I am. I'll be on that flight to Miami tomorrow morning. Then I'll spend the weekend packing up. I'll have to pack what Phil left behind, too.'

'I already did that. Took me a full day before I caught the evening flight to New York. It'll be shipped to Ireland next week. So all you have to do is pack and sort your own stuff and get your ass to New York. If you still want the job, of course. But you have to tell me quick, so we can look for someone else if you don't. We need more staff immediately for the new imprints.'

'I know. But… I thought I'd work with you for a while, and then go back here once the will is out of probate.'

'How long will that take?'

'Two months or so, I think. Would that be OK?'

'I don't like it, but sure, why not. Better to have you for a short while than not at all, I guess. You can help us find someone to take over during the two months. But I warn you that it'll be busy around here.'

'When is it not?' Cordelia quipped.

Later that afternoon, walking onto the beach dressed in a swimsuit that had belonged to Phil, Cordelia spread a towel on the warm sand, and walked to the water's edge. The view across the blue waters of the bay was stunning and the islands shimmering in the far distance added a touch of magic to the scenery. The sun warmed her back and the waves lapped at her toes and she felt a surge of well-being as she waded into the crystal-clear water, colder than the sea in Miami where she had swum nearly every day during her years there.

Swimming had been one her favourite sports, better than hours in the gym. She was a true water baby, her mother had said when they went to the Atlantic coast for their summer vacations during her childhood. But here, on Ireland's west coast, the scenery was wilder, the water colder and the air much fresher. Swimming here would be both a treat and a challenge, Cordelia thought as she tried to gather enough courage to go in. Then, without further hesitation, she threw herself in with a splash, and started to swim with slow steady strokes, straight out towards the glittering horizon. The cold water made her gasp but it didn't take long for her to get used to it and she began to enjoy the feel of it against her hot skin. Halfway out, she turned on her back and floated, closing her eyes against the sunlight. How lovely it was to just float here in a weightless state, away from the house and the family who had gathered for tea under the large sycamore.

'Your shape is the same as Phil's,' Maeve had said when Cordelia had complained that she hadn't brought a swimsuit, and then they had gone to find the suit among Phil's clothes hanging in the wardrobe in her room downstairs. 'Must be the Brennan genes,' she had added, handing Cordelia the suit. 'Phil and Dad's mother,' she explained when Cordelia stared at her with a confused expression. 'Our grandmother, and your mother's aunt. They were sisters, of course. Olive and Clodagh, the Brennan girls. Then Olive married Brian McKenna and they had Phil and Patrick. Clodagh married Jim Fitzgerald about ten years later and they had little Frances, who became your mother.'

'Oh yes. Of course,' Cordelia said casually, taking the swimsuit. She glanced into the wardrobe, where a long line of clothes in beautiful colours hung in a tidy row. 'That's some wardrobe,' she remarked. 'I knew Phil had a lot of vintage clothes, but not this many.'

Maeve smiled and touched the sleeve of a Chanel jacket. 'Yes. She had an amazing collection. We'll go through them later and see what we want to keep. Not that I have the kind of lifestyle for such clothes, but it would be fun to have something as a memento.'

'I don't think I want anything,' Cordelia said with a tiny shiver. She held up the swimsuit, a one-piece in shimmering turquoise. 'This is great. I remember her buying it in Miami. That would be enough for me.'

'Yes, you keep that one,' Maeve agreed and closed the wardrobe. 'There are beach towels in the hot press, I mean linen cupboard, in the corridor upstairs. I'll go and get Aisling and Paschal. We're having tea in the garden with Mum and Dad before they leave. You're welcome to join us, of course.'

'Thanks, but I think I'll go for that swim. I'll leave you to visit with your parents before they leave. I already said goodbye to them when we got back. Your dad was very sweet to me by the way. He said he was happy for me.'

Maeve nodded. 'I think he meant it. He likes you, he said. Mum, too, of course. But she can be a little stand-offish at times.'

'I'm sure she doesn't mean it,' Cordelia soothed, remembering Maeve's mother's cool farewell. 'I think she might have been a little shocked by the news of the will. But that's OK. I'm sure it was a real bombshell.'

Maeve shrugged. 'In a way, but not really. Dad knew he wouldn't inherit anything. Phil and Dad had talked about that a long time before she got sick. But maybe Mum felt that Roisin and I should have been left the house.' She shrugged. 'It is the way it is. Phil's wishes have to be respected and followed.'

Not knowing quite what else to say, Cordelia left to change into her swimsuit and find a beach towel.

Now floating in the cool water, she blinked and looked up at the blue sky and wondered what Maeve was really feeling. She seemed so warm and empathetic, but maybe she was hiding feelings of resentment and distrust? Roisin was easier to read, being more open and direct, often blurting out what was on her mind without thinking. But one thing was clear: the sisters formed a united front that nobody would ever be able to break. They were nice to Cordelia, and after the shock of the will, had been ready to accept Phil's final wish. But how would they get on in the long run? They were sisters and Cordelia was just a second cousin. She could never be as close to either of them as they were to each other.

Cordelia swam slowly back to shore, mulling over the problems. How on earth was she going to handle sharing the house with the sisters? Should she give up, hand her part over to them and confess? Or come back when the probate had been sorted out and run this little hotel with them? Or…

Another solution popped into her head. She could ask them to buy her out, take the money and go back home to her new life in New York. She'd have a nest egg and an income from the rest of the money. She could buy her own apartment, maybe go to university and get a degree and then start a whole new career… The latest solution seemed too good to resist, but maybe difficult to realise. It would be unfair to ask Maeve and Roisin to pay that amount of money for her share of a property that seemed very valuable. And it would cut her off from this family that had accepted her so readily. A family that Phil had wanted her to be part of. The dilemma seemed suddenly impossible to solve.

Cordelia waded onto the beach and sat down on the towel, staring out over the shimmering water across the bay and the craggy outlines of the islands through the heat haze. Above her seagulls glided around, their plaintive cries the only sound in the still air. The soft wind gently lifted her hair, and as she turned and looked at the pink house standing proudly on the green hill, the windows glinting in the sun, she suddenly knew what she had to do. It was Phil's wish that she should come here and be a part of this house, this village.

It was more than an inheritance, it was part of her heritage, her Irish roots. Her mother had lived in denial, trying to forget her true self. She had to find out what had happened to the real Frances, who she was now beginning to believe was her mother. She just had to prove it, not only to this family, but to herself. Phil had, through her legacy to Cordelia, given her the chance to have a family, to belong in a way she had never experienced before. She had watched families together as she grew up, wishing, longing to be part of one, to have sisters and brothers, aunts and uncles, cousins and grandparents. It was a dream she never thought would come true. But here it was, within her reach.

As she wandered slowly across the beach and started up the steps, Cordelia could hear voices from the tea party that was winding up on the back lawn. She was nearly at the top when she heard the words that made her freeze.

'We're going to investigate,' Mary-Anne said. 'We have hired someone to do some research both in America and Dublin.'

'Is that really necessary?' Maeve asked. 'I'm sure Phil would have—'

'Phil was such a romantic. I'm sure she didn't ask too many questions. She wanted to believe this woman was her cousin, so she did. It was lovely that she had someone like that to look after her during that time when she was not well. But now it's a whole different matter. It's about property and money. We have to be absolutely sure she is who she claims to be.'

'I'm sure you'll find that she's telling the truth,' Maeve replied. 'But go ahead, if that makes you happy.'

'We want what's best for you and Roisin and your children,' Patrick cut in. Then he said something in a low voice Cordelia couldn't hear and she had the impression they were saying goodbye. They all walked off after a while, but she stood there, shivering, until she heard the car drive off.

When she was sure they had all left, she made her way across the lawn and into the house. Once in her room, she had a hot shower and slowly dressed, her mind on the conversation she had just overheard. The fact that there were doubts about her identity didn't surprise her, but Mary-Anne's words had startled her and would have hurt had Maeve not stood up for her. That had been both surprising and sweet. Maeve was obviously both fair and kind, and that made Cordelia like her even more. But the parents were going to start digging into her mother's past – a worrying thought which made Cordelia even more determined to get her own answers. And it would be better to be ahead of the posse. Unlike them, she knew where to start.

Cordelia turned on the small radio on the bedside table. It seemed to be tuned to a local radio station, and soon classical music wafted through the room, making her feel more relaxed. Then, after a short news bulletin, the programme changed to something called 'The Late Afternoon Show'. The male presenter's deep slightly gravelly voice made Cordelia blink. She had heard that voice very recently. Was it? Yes, his next words confirmed it:

'Hello, all you people going home after work. This is Declan O'Mahony with some soothing music to drive home to after a day at the office. I will start with Mozart's "A Little Night Music", followed by one of Chopin's "Nocturnes". Then if you're still awake I have a dedication and something more modern. Sit back, relax and let all the stress float away…'

Cordelia smiled as she lay on her bed and let herself nearly drift off as the music started. When "Nocturnes" began, she lay there, remembering her mother playing these pieces on their piano in the little house in Morristown. She had such happy memories of that time; her mother had filled the house with music and given her a happy childhood. They had struggled to make ends meet but it had made them both strong and resilient. Cordelia felt a surge of love and gratitude as she listened.

'Nocturnes' ended, its last notes hanging in the air before the presenter spoke again. 'Now wasn't that lovely? But I would like to change tack a little and go for something more modern, like Frank Sinatra. His voice is perfect for relaxing later tonight, with maybe a glass of wine and someone special by your side, looking at the stars that are spectacular in my neck of the woods. Yes, I am speaking to you from County Kerry, in that magic place where there is no light pollution and the stars are brighter than anywhere else in Europe. No special someone beside me, and no glass of wine, but…' He paused. 'I have the image of a beautiful woman I met very recently that won't leave my mind. She was here for a brief visit but it was one of those encounters that are so special because you know that you might never meet again. I would like to dedicate the next piece of music to her. This one's for you, Cordelia. Have a wonderful trip back home.' Then Frank Sinatra's velvety voice filled the air as he sang 'Strangers in the Night'.

Wide awake, Cordelia sat up on the bed, listening to the song. When it ended and the commercials came on, she turned off the radio, got out of bed, tiptoed to the window and looked out. The sun was setting into the still water of the bay, bathing it in a magical golden light. A warm breeze softly ruffled her hair. She suddenly felt a dart of joy, knowing that even if she was leaving the next day, it wouldn't be long before she came back.

Chapter Eight

The trip back to Miami was tiring but uneventful. No first class this time, and Cordelia found herself sitting in the middle seat, squashed in between a large man who chewed gum, laughing loudly at whatever he was watching on his TV screen, and a woman who chatted non-stop about her Irish trip and how she had found the Irish so 'cute' and the houses 'so quaint' and the whole country so 'darling' as if she had just been visiting Disneyland. Cordelia pretended to go to sleep, but it was difficult to keep that up during the seven-hour flight, so she turned on the TV screen and watched two movies she had seen before while she tried to sort out what she would do when she got back. First, she had to pack her things in Betsy's condo and then get on that flight to New York on Sunday evening. She'd need to start work on Monday morning, but she would go to Morristown the following weekend and start her research into her mother's past. There were a few leads and she could try to contact some of the people she was planning to meet ahead of time. When the plane landed in Miami, the plan seemed promising and she felt a lot more positive than when she had left Ireland. She would be way ahead of the McKennas by the time they started digging.

On Monday morning in New York, Cordelia walked the short distance from the hotel to the Red Hot Romance office, on the twentieth floor of a tall building only two blocks away. Betsy was already at her desk, talking into her phone and typing on her laptop at the same time, a cigarette dangling from her red lips. She looked up as Cordelia hovered in the door.

'There you are. It's past eight o'clock. Did you oversleep?'

'No, eh… I thought you said nine, but I wanted to be here early. Sorry.'

'Got to go,' Betsy said into her phone. 'Talk later.' She hung up and took the cigarette out of her mouth and stubbed it out in her coffee mug. 'Not supposed to smoke here, or at all really. But I'm a little stressed right now. We usually start at eight, but you'll need to be here a bit before that so you can get coffee at Starbucks across the street.' She sat back and looked approvingly at Cordelia's black linen shift. 'Great dress. OK, so your job here will be assisting our marketing manager, who will be very busy as we kick off our new romantic suspense imprint. We have named it Red Hot Suspense. Head of Marketing is Dorothy Fassbender, Dotty for short. She's in her office waiting for you.'

Cordelia nodded. 'I'll go straight away. Thanks for giving me the job and letting me work for only a short while. I need the money while I wait for the probate. And I need to be in New York to…' She was going to say 'to get to Morristown easily', but she didn't want Betsy to know there was any doubt about her mother's identity. No need to spread it around.

Betsy made a shooing gesture. 'Go. I'll see you around.'

'OK,' Cordelia said and hurried across the lobby to the marketing manager's office. Dotty was a pleasant blonde in her fifties and she soon had Cordelia busy at a small desk beside the window with her own laptop and a list of tasks, including updating the new website and setting up social media accounts for both the new imprint and some of the authors they had just signed. The job was easy for Cordelia, who loved this kind of thing. The graphics were already there in a folder in the computer system, so she didn't have to worry about making up images. There were other jobs that consisted mainly of administrative tasks and also making phone calls to bookstores that would be willing to host book signings for authors. All things she had done for Phil, but on a larger scale.

At the end of the day, Dotty declared she was very pleased with Cordelia and, as she had heard that she was staying in a hotel, offered her a room in her large apartment on the Upper East Side. Cordelia accepted at once and they came to an agreement about the rent.

Cordelia grinned. 'It sounds perfect to me. Thanks, Dotty.'

'You're welcome. I'll get the room tidied up and you can move in on Wednesday.'

'Great. I'll get my stuff over that evening,' Cordelia said, feeling everything was falling into place. A temporary job and now a room for a fairly reasonable rate in a very select part of town. The Upper East Side, no less. Her mother would be impressed. Now she could concentrate on the most important task: looking for her Irish roots.

The following Saturday, Cordelia sat in a cab on her way to the parish church in Morristown, feeling a pang of nostalgia as she looked out the window. She'd stayed in a cheap hotel near the train station and was heading to the little parish church just outside town where her parents had been married and where she herself had been baptised and received her first communion. She had already made an appointment with the parish priest, who, to her disappointment, was not the priest she remembered from her childhood. But he had seemed nice and helpful and promised to assist with the parish records. They'd look at them together, he said.

There was her school, which looked a little more rundown but nearly exactly the same as when she had graduated fifteen years ago. The shop where she had worked during weekends had been closed and the house where they had lived stood empty with a 'For Sale' sign outside. Everything looked a little shabbier and more neglected and she was glad her mother wasn't here to see it. They turned the corner and drove down the next street where, at the end, the steeple of the white church could be seen above the treetops. Her stomach churned as they pulled up in front of it.

She paid the taxi driver and walked through the gates and down the gravel path to the doors that stood open. Inside, the church was exactly the same as it had been when she was a child and they had gone to Mass there every Sunday. Even the faint smell of candles and incense was just as it had always been. She walked up the aisle, touching each pew, feeling the smooth wood under her fingers and looked up at the stained-glass windows with the Holy Family and the dove above it that she had gazed at during many Masses and ceremonies. Her mother's ashes were buried in the graveyard, and the memory of her funeral was suddenly painfully vivid. Cordelia stood there for a while, looking at the altar, numb with sorrow. Then she heard someone walking behind her and she turned around and saw a priest in a dark suit and dog collar coming towards her.

He was tall and fairly young with kind eyes behind steel-rimmed glasses. 'Cordelia Mirafiore?' he asked.

'Yes?' Cordelia replied. 'Are you Father Richards?'

'Yes.' He came closer and shook her hand. 'I have the parish records in my office. It's in the building next door. If you come with me, we can take a look together.'

Cordelia followed Father Richards to the parish office in the small house next door to the church, where he took out a thick leather-bound ledger from a cupboard and laid it on the desk. 'Here it all is,' he said, and opened the ledger. 'Births, marriages and deaths since this church was built in 1852. As you can see there were a lot of them. Your mother's maiden name seems to be a different one from what you told me. But I think I have found her.'

'Oh. It's not O'Brien?' Cordelia asked, her heart beating.

'Could be. Similar but with a strange spelling. I think it's in Irish. Didn't you know?'

'Yes,' Cordelia replied. 'I knew it was in Irish. It would be O'Brien in English, I always thought.'

'You weren't quite sure what the English version was?'

'No. Well, you see, she never told me anything about her past or her family back in Ireland. She said it was too painful and that she wanted to be truly American. Some kind of family feud or something, I guess. She used her married name at all times.'

'I see.' He flicked through the pages until he came to a page bookmarked with a slip of paper. 'Here we are,' he said, running his finger down the line of names. 'Fifth of May, nineteen eighty-six. Marriage between Gino Mirafiore from Brooklyn, New York and Frances…'

'Frances – what?' Cordelia whispered.

Father Richards turned the ledger around for her to see and pointed to name. 'Here. See for yourself.'

Cordelia stared at the name beside her father's. 'Frances… Ó Braonáin,' she read in a near whisper, stumbling over the unfamiliar letters.

'Resident in Morristown, New Jersey, born in Dublin, Ireland,' he filled in.

'That's correct. But Ó Braonáin is Irish for O'Brien,' she stated. 'Isn't it?'

The priest shrugged. 'Could be. I'm not familiar with the Irish language, but you could ask old Mrs Donovan. She does the flowers in the church. She's from Ireland and might know the old language. She's eighty-two, but still very active in the parish.'

Cordelia brightened. 'I think I remember her. She knew my mother, too. They both sang in the choir when I was small.'

'Did they? How lovely.' The priest closed the ledger. 'Is there anything else I can help you with?'

'Yes. I'd like a copy of my parents' marriage certificate, if that's possible? I'm looking into getting an Irish passport, you see.'

The priest nodded. 'Of course. I can send it to you if you give me your address.'

Cordelia gave him the address to Dotty's apartment. 'Thank you so much.'

'You're welcome, my dear. I'm sorry I couldn't help you more than that. But maybe Mrs Donovan can fill you in.'

'Where will I find her?'

'She should be in the church right now, or about to arrive. She'll be putting in fresh flowers today for the Masses tomorrow with the ladies from the parish council.' He rose. 'I'm sorry, but I have to go. I have a number of house calls to make, and then there's the retirement home.'

'Of course.' Cordelia got up and shook his hand. 'Thanks again for your help.'

When the priest had left, Cordelia walked back to the church, taking the path to the graveyard, where she found the grave and its simple granite headstone with *Frances Mirafiore*, the dates of her birth and death and then the inscription, *Proud to be American* underneath, according to her wishes. Cordelia placed the flowers she had brought on the grave and stood there in silent contemplation, a wave of sorrow welling up inside her.

Oh Mom, she thought, *you took so many secrets with you when you left me here, all alone. I wish you had told me…*

Cordelia shivered despite the warm day and turned away from the grave, walking back to the church, saying a silent prayer to whomever was up there that she would find out about her mother one day.

In the church, the dim light was pierced by a shaft of sunlight through the window over the altar. Cordelia spotted a woman with white hair dressed in loose slacks and a blue linen top sorting out flowers at a table near the little side altar. She walked closer and cleared her throat. 'Hello? Mrs Donovan?' she said, her voice echoing in the empty church.

The woman turned around and looked at her over the rim of her glasses. 'Yes?'

'I don't know if you remember me, but my name is Cordelia Mirafiore and I think you knew my mother.'

'Oh!' the woman exclaimed and dropped the flowers she was holding. 'Cordelia! Is it really you?' She took Cordelia's hands in both of hers, tears welling up in her myopic brown eyes. 'Frances' daughter. Oh my word, how lovely it is to see you. I remember you as a little girl with those serious blue eyes and the curly dark hair. Do you remember?'

Cordelia smiled and shook her head. 'I'm afraid I don't remember much about that time. I was so young.'

Mrs Donovan patted her hand. 'It was a long time ago, that's for sure.'

'Yes,' Cordelia said, wishing she could remember. 'Mom did talk about doing the flowers and playing the organ here, which she loved. Did she ever talk to you about her parents back in Ireland?'

Mrs Donovan shook her head. 'Not much, I'm afraid, we weren't that close. But I know that there was something sad in her past. Something that made her flee her family and her country. She was happy here in America, she said, despite life being a little difficult. But she never minded the hard work and she loved this town and her life here. Then she went to Miami because of her health and I heard she had passed away. So sorry, my dear. It must have been so hard for you.'

Cordelia nodded. 'Thank you. Yes, it was hard. She died far too soon.'

Mrs Donovan smiled sympathetically. 'You'll always miss her. But don't forget that there is love in your grief, too. Remember her with love and treasure your memories.'

'I will. Thank you,' Cordelia replied, thinking that it had been the same with Phil. So much love and such happy memories.

'So,' Mrs Donovan said, turning back to her flowers. 'Is there anything else I can help you with?'

'Yes. It's about my mother's maiden name. I didn't know the Irish version until I saw it in the marriage records just now. It said O… Branoin, or something. O'Brien in English, right?'

Mrs Donovan shrugged. 'I have no idea. I never learned Gaelic. Sounds like O'Brien, though, so that must be it.'

'I'm sure you're right.' Cordelia let out a sigh. 'But why…' She stopped. No use asking the old lady any more questions. 'No, never mind. It's all a bit strange, that's all. I thought I'd find answers to some of my questions here, but instead I found more questions that nobody can answer.'

'I'm sorry,' Mrs Donovan said sympathetically. 'But maybe the answers are not here, but across the Atlantic, in Ireland? I have a feeling you must go there and continue to search.'

Cordelia nodded. 'Yes. You're right,' she said. 'I have to go back to Ireland.'

The following evening Cordelia was watering Dotty's plants and nipping off dead leaves, trying to figure out what to do, when her phone rang and she stared at the caller ID: Maeve. What did she want?

'Hi, Maeve,' she said. 'How are things?'

'Terrible,' Maeve said.

'Oh? What's up?'

'Chicken pox,' Maeve groaned.

'Oh no! Are you all sick?'

'Not me, but Aisling came down with it yesterday and now Roisin has just got it, too. She never had it as a child, strangely enough. I did and Paschal, too, thank goodness. Roisin is very sick with it though.'

'Oh that's terrible,' Cordelia said, pressing the phone to her ear to hear better as a police siren screeched outside. 'I'm in the middle of Manhattan, so it's a bit noisy. Could you speak up, please?'

'OK,' Maeve shouted. 'Is this better?'

'Yes, fine.'

'Great. I'll make it short. We desperately need someone to run things while this is going on. And…' Maeve paused. 'We were wondering, as we discussed the possibility of you running the guesthouse with us when you've sorted things out over there, if…' She stopped. 'Well, you see where I'm going with this, don't you?'

Cordelia laughed, a dart of excitement shooting through her. 'Yeah, I get it. And I've had chicken pox, actually.'

'Great. So… would it be at all possible for you to come over here right now? I mean as soon as you can? I know you're over there starting that new job and trying to sort out things but… The house is full of guests, Roisin is very sick and Aisling isn't much better. The probate will come through in a month or so, our lawyer said, so you'd have to come anyway in a couple of weeks. Would it be possible at all for you to come right away? We need you badly and as it'll be part yours soon, I thought…'

'Oh, but… I thought… your mother… I mean, proof of my identity,' Cordelia rambled on, the words tumbling out in no particular order. 'I heard what she said before she left, you see.'

'Oh no!' Maeve exclaimed, sounding horrified. 'I'm so sorry you heard that. But you can forget it. My mother has nothing to do with the will. Nobody else has contested it and never will. Please,' Maeve pleaded. 'Can you come? We need you.'

'OK. I'll come as soon as…' Cordelia paused. As soon as she could tell Betsy she was leaving before she had even started, and pack her things and let Dotty know she'd have to look for another tenant and book a ticket, and… She stopped herself, realising Maeve was probably holding her breath and crossing her fingers over there in Sandy Cove. Her heart sang at the thought of going back to Ireland and of digging deeper into her mother's past. The answers lay there like Mrs Donovan had said and now she had a good reason to go as soon as possible. 'I'll get on it straight away. See you in a couple of days.'

'Brilliant,' Maeve said as wailing could be heard in the distance. 'There she goes again. Poor thing, she's in an awful state. I have to go. Thanks a million for coming over. You're a total brick and an angel from heaven. Bye for now.'

Cordelia smiled as she hung up despite all the problems she knew she'd have to face. Maeve's voice had hurtled her back to Ireland, to that lovely place where, after only a few days, she had felt instantly at home. *Sandy Cove*, she thought, *my new home and my new kind-of family*. A family she felt she belonged to, if only in spirit. But maybe also by blood? What she had learned at the parish office had given her some strong clues. But she needed to continue her search in Ireland and now, with Maeve's phone call, there was no reason to stay or to try to make a new life in New York. Her mother's past – and her own future – lay on the other side of the Atlantic.

Chapter Nine

The flight landed at Shannon at 7.30 a.m. It had been a long uncomfortable night as Cordelia tried to sleep but found the events of the past few days whirling through her mind. The thought that she was on the cusp of a new life in Ireland was both exciting and frightening. She couldn't believe she had left everything behind so quickly. But things had fallen into place neatly. After her phone conversation with Maeve, Cordelia had booked herself on a flight to Shannon that would leave the following night and then called Betsy, trying to explain what had happened. Betsy had grumbled at first, but then softened and said she understood completely. 'This is what Phil wanted,' she said with a little sob. 'And who am I to stop you fulfilling her wishes? I'm sorry to lose you but I had a feeling that was on the cards anyway. Remember you're welcome to come back whenever you want. There will always be a job here for you.' She promised to sort things out with Dotty and said she'd come over to Sandy Cove for a visit when she could.

Cordelia hung up with a light heart and tidied up Dotty's apartment, said goodbye to the plants and left a thank you card on the hall table, as Dotty was away for the weekend. She looked around the elegant apartment and thought that although Dotty seemed to have all a woman could want in life – a career, plenty of money and this lovely place – there was something missing, something very important. A family and someone to love.

It felt good to close the chapter in America, even if it might not be for good. Whatever happened, she would go over to visit her mother's grave from time to time. Betsy would be happy to give her a job again, she had said, so in a way Cordelia hadn't burned all her bridges. If and when she came back, she would have the answers to all the mysteries and feel very different about her own life and her future. Cordelia had looked into applying for an Irish passport before she left, and all she needed was her own birth certificate, her mother's Irish one and her parents' marriage certificate. Then it would take two to three months before she could pick up her Irish passport at the nearest passport office in Ireland. She immediately applied for her mother's birth certificate to be sent to her at Willow House, and dug out her own, which she found in an envelope with all her other important papers. She then sent an email to the parish office in Morristown, thanking Father Richards for his help and asking him to send her parents' marriage certificate to her new address in Ireland.

After a sleepless night, Cordelia went through passport control in Shannon and collected her luggage. She loaded the two heavy suitcases onto a trolley and pushed it slowly through the doors into the arrivals hall, where she was greeted by a familiar face smiling at her.

'Paschal?' she said, confused. 'Why are you here?'

He grinned and took the trolley from her. 'Maeve's orders. "Give her the star treatment," she said. "Then she'll never want to leave."'

I'm supposed to turn on the charm, too, but I'm not sure how to do that. So all you get is my lame attempts at the Irish welcome.'

Cordelia laughed. 'That's more than enough,' she said, looking up at his handsome face with the velvet eyes and sweet smile. 'I couldn't cope with any more. But I said to Maeve I'd rent a car from Hertz.'

'I know. I asked if you could cancel and they said yes. You don't need to hire a car. We'll fix up something when we get to Sandy Cove. In the meantime, you can use Roisin's car. We'll organise the insurance for you. And you might have to get an Irish driving licence if you're going to stay.' He looked at her. 'Are you?'

Cordelia shrugged. 'I'm not sure yet. There are so many things to sort out before I decide where I want to live. So we'll see. I've applied for an Irish passport in any case.'

'OK, that sounds good. The car rental desk is across the arrivals hall. You just have to give your name and sign a form to say you've cancelled the rental. Then we're on our way.'

Cordelia nodded. 'OK.' She yawned. 'I'm sorry but I'm whacked.'

Paschal smiled. 'Jetlag and lack of sleep must be a killer. Why don't you try to have a nap while I drive? We can stop in Adare and have something at one of the cafés if you get hungry. It's an hour away.'

'Sound like a perfect plan.'

When Cordelia had cancelled the rented car, they made their way out of the terminal building to the parking lot where they loaded Cordelia's luggage into Paschal's four-by-four.

'You obviously didn't come for just the weekend,' Paschal joked as they heaved the two heavy suitcases into the back.

'I brought all my clothes and some other stuff,' Cordelia confessed. 'Just in case I decide to stay a bit longer. I quit my new job before I even started, though, which wasn't a good move.'

Paschal opened the passenger door. 'Oh? What did Betsy think of that?'

'She was disappointed but very nice about it in the end,' Cordelia replied. 'And to my relief she said she'd always have a job for me if I want to work in publishing when I get back.'

Paschal nodded. 'I see. Great that she took it on the chin. She's quite sweet behind that tough façade.'

'Yes, she is.' Cordelia climbed into the car and leaned her head against the headrest. 'I just want to forget about everything over there now.'

'You sleep, I'll drive and I'll wake you up when we're in Adare. Pretty village. You'll like it.'

'Not as pretty as Sandy Cove, I bet.'

'Not by far.' Paschal got into the driver's seat. 'Adare is a chocolate box. Sandy Cove is our very own Tír na nÓg. A kind of paradise in Irish mythology,' he added as Cordelia looked confused. 'The land of joy and happiness and all kinds of other delights.'

'Sounds wonderful,' Cordelia mumbled and closed her eyes.

'Well, not quite the truth but it has some of those elements.' He started the engine, turning on the car radio at the same time. 'Some soothing Irish music to help you relax,' he said as a woman's voice singing a ballad in Irish filled the air.

'Thank you.' How kind, she thought drowsily, to come and pick her up so early in the morning. And how lucky Maeve was to have such a handsome, sweet husband. Would she ever find someone like that? Someone to care for her and watch over her and love her until death did them part? It didn't seem possible but you never knew. Maybe things like that could happen in Sandy Cove, the land of youth and joy… She smiled and drifted off to sleep to the sound of Irish music and the soft rumbling of the engine.

What seemed like only minutes later, Cordelia woke up to find them driving down a street lined with thatched cottages and Victorian houses. She sat up and rubbed her eyes. 'Where are we? Is this Adare?'

Paschal laughed and pulled up outside a shop. 'No, my dear, we're in Sandy Cove, the Shangri-La of Ireland's west coast.'

'Oh? But…' Cordelia stared at him through the haze of sleep and jetlag.

He grinned. 'You were conked out so I didn't want to wake you. Thought I'd let you get as much sleep as possible as you'll need all your strength when you face the bedlam at Willow House.'

'Bedlam?'

'Yeah, well, it's going to be hard work to keep things going there. Roisin is a sick as a dog, in quarantine in the attic of Willow House, and in our house next door, Aisling has just broken out in spots all over her body and wants her mammy there 24/7. But there have been no new ones, so I'm sure she's on the mend. Maeve hasn't slept in days though. The house is full of guests who want the full Irish breakfast every day and all sorts of other services. You'll see.' He gestured at the shop outside which he had just stopped. 'But I need to pop in here for a second to talk to the new owner and sign something. Do you want to come in with me? Used to be my shop but I sold it to this great woman who will turn it into the most popular book-and-curiosa shop in Europe. She hopes. She's great craic, anyway.'

'Oh. OK,' Cordelia replied and got out as Paschal opened the door for her. 'It'll help me wake up.'

'She certainly will,' he said with a wink, indicating inside.

Cordelia followed Paschal into the shop and looked around in delight at the books, antiques, handcrafts and souvenirs organised in a colourful array that invited browsing. A woman with wavy light brown hair dressed in a dark green handprinted shirt, black jeans and platform sandals was crouching in front of the bookcase, sorting books and muttering to herself.

'Sally?' Paschal said.

The woman jumped up and clasped her hand to her heart. 'Paschal! Ohmigod, you gave me a fright. There hasn't been anyone in here since this morning and here you are bursting in like a cannonball.'

'Sorry about that,' Paschal said, shooting her a disarming smile. 'Didn't mean to frighten you.'

The woman caught her breath and smiled. 'It's OK. I think my heart just about managed to cope.' She turned her attention to Cordelia. 'And who is this lovely creature? Have we met before?'

'This is Cordelia Mirafiore,' Paschal replied. 'Maeve's second cousin from America who's come to rescue us in our hour of need.'

'That's very brave.' Sally beamed at Cordelia, her lovely hazel eyes flashing. 'Nice to meet you, Cordelia. I think I saw you at the funeral.' She held out her hand. 'I'm Sally. The new owner of Paschal's magic cave of delight.'

Paschal laughed. 'It'll be your cave of delight now, Sally. Happy to hand it over to you, my dear.'

'I'm sure you are. But just you wait. I will shake this place up in no time.' She winked at Cordelia. 'I'm going to bring it into the twenty-first century and make it the go-to gift shop in all of Europe.'

'I don't doubt that for a second,' Paschal replied.

Cordelia couldn't stop looking at Sally. She appeared to be in her late forties and had an irresistible charm. With a slim figure, hazel eyes that sparkled with humour and warmth and a face full of freckles, she gave the impression of an indomitable spirit combined with great empathy and kindness.

Sally met her gaze. 'You look a little jetlagged. I bet you'd love to collapse into bed. I'll just give these papers to Paschal to sign and then you can be on your way.' She went to the counter and handed Paschal a large envelope. 'It's all in here. All we need is your signature and maybe Cordelia can witness it? And then I think you should take her to the house and feed her and give her a chance to rest.'

'Will do.' Paschal extracted a document from the envelope, fished out a pen from his breast pocket and scribbled his name at the bottom. He handed the pen to Cordelia. 'Here. Could you sign on the line where it says "witnessed by"?'

Cordelia nodded and signed, feeling a dart of excitement as she put her address as Willow House, Sandy Cove, County Kerry. This was the first time she'd written it down on paper. Her new home, even if it was a hotel. She smiled at Paschal. 'It feels strange to see it there in black and white. The address, I mean.'

'Are you moving here, then?' Sally asked. 'For good?'

'I don't know,' Cordelia replied. 'But for now, that's my address.'

'Aha.' Sally winked and took a pack of cards from a stack on the counter. 'I had these made up. Maybe you could put them in the reception area or something?'

Cordelia looked at the cards with the logo and 'Sally's Curiosa' written in curly letters at the top. 'No problem.' She put the cards into her bag while she glanced around the shop. 'This reminds me of a shop near Morristown in New Jersey where I grew up. It's called The Magic Shop and it's incredible. Everyone goes there for a browse on Sundays. Weekdays too, if they can. It has everything, from elegant knick-knacks for the house to custom jewellery and accessories. Books, toys, you name it. The owners go into New York City regularly and buy up things in markets and all kinds of little boutiques. End of lines, sales, whatever. Then they sell it on in The Magic Shop. Maybe you could do something like that here? On a smaller scale, of course.' Cordelia drew breath and laughed. 'Sorry. Didn't mean to tell you what to do. It's just that this space looked similar and it has the same feel, somehow.'

Sally, who had been staring at Cordelia while she spoke, nodded. 'You know, that's a fantastic idea. Truly fabulous. I will think about this very seriously and see if I couldn't implement some of those ideas here. In a way that would suit this place, of course. Thank you.'

Cordelia smiled. 'You're welcome. And hey, why don't you look up their Facebook page? It has pictures of the interior of the shop so you can see the layout.'

'I certainly will,' Sally said. 'And maybe we can meet for coffee sometime? Or even a drink?'

'That'd be great,' Cordelia replied.

Paschal pulled at Cordelia's arm. 'I think we should get going. You need food and rest and Roisin and Maeve need *you*. See you, Sally.'

'Bye, lads.' Sally waved as they left, promising to be in touch.

'You've made a friend for life,' Paschal remarked as they got into the car. 'Sally is great craic and a grand woman.'

Cordelia put on her seat belt. 'Is she from here?'

'Born and bred. But she's been away for a long time. She left for Dublin to study art and design when she was in her late twenties, then went to Paris to work at one of the fashion houses there. She met Phil there and they became friends, even though Sally's many years younger.'

'How old is she?'

'She doesn't look it, but I think she must be mid-fifties. Looks after herself and she has great genes. Her mother was one of the old ladies who used to read Phil's novels before they were published.'

'I heard about that,' Cordelia interrupted. 'What happened to the old birds?'

'All sadly dead. And Sally owns the bungalow now. Her mother left it to her in her will. Anyway, Sally married a Frenchman about thirty years ago, but the marriage didn't last. I think she had a string of lovers after that, but now she's given up men, she says. She came back here only last year and then she ran my shop until she bought it. I think she'll make it work. She's one of those people who never give up.'

'I had that impression, too.'

'But here we are. Ready to face reality?' Paschal turned the car into the lane that led to Willow House, drove through the tall gates and pulled up in front of the house.

'Oh yes,' Cordelia said and looked up at the house. It looked lovely in the sunshine, with the windows glinting and the front door open, as if inviting her in. She jumped down from the car and walked up the steps and into the hall, where she was met by a dark-haired young girl in a white apron over a summer dress. 'Welcome to Willow House,' she said, smiling. 'I'm Kathleen. Can I help you with your luggage?'

'Oh.' Cordelia laughed. 'I'm not a guest. I'm Cordelia Mirafiore. I've come to…'

'To take over?' Kathleen said with a happy sigh. 'Oh thank God you're here. It's a bloody madhouse, to be honest.'

'Kathleen, please get Cordelia something to eat in the kitchen,' Paschal panted behind them, a heavy suitcase in each hand. 'I'll put these in your room. You're to have Phil's old room beside the kitchen, Maeve said. Roisin has been locked up in the attic and will only be allowed out when the spots have gone. Cian and the boys have departed in fright up the west coast in that campervan. I don't blame them. Right now she looks like something from a horror movie, she says herself.'

'She does,' Kathleen said with a little shiver. 'She has it worse than any kid I've ever seen. Even the doctor backed away at first when he came to check on her. But he said she has to drink loads and rest and use calamine lotion and she'll be right as rain in about a week or so. I brought her some of my mum's barley water she made especially for Roisin.'

'That's very kind,' Cordelia said, following Paschal into the bright, airy bedroom just off the kitchen that was to be hers.

He put the suitcases on the floor beside the large wardrobe. 'There. I think Maeve said to push Phil's fashion collection to the side and try to find space for your clothes. She has already cleared most of the chest of drawers. Phil never threw anything out, so there was a lot.' He drew breath. 'OK. If you can manage now, I'll go and see what's going on at home. Hopefully they'll both be asleep.'

Cordelia smiled at him. 'Thanks for picking me up, Paschal. I really appreciate it.'

'You're welcome. Kathleen will fill you in on the routine here. Give us a shout if you need anything. Maeve will pop over when she gets a chance.' With that he was gone, leaving Cordelia to settle in and catch her breath.

She sat down on the big white Victorian bed and looked around. The room was lovely, with wallpaper covered in tiny white flowers against a yellow background, white muslin curtains and a light blue rug on the wooden floor. All the furniture was painted a distressed white and the whole effect was light and airy and wonderfully cosy at the same time. Cordelia could picture Phil sitting in the blue velvet easy chair by the window reading a book, gazing out at the view of the garden and the blue ocean glinting behind the shrubs, warmed by the sun streaming in through the window.

She sighed and felt a dart of sorrow at being here, in this room, this house. She also felt her stomach rumbling and realised she hadn't eaten anything since the night before. She got off the bed and went through the small sitting room, which now doubled as an office, into the kitchen, where, in the middle of the mess of breakfast dishes, Kathleen was frying eggs and bacon at the electric cooker beside what looked like an old wood-burning stove. She looked around as Cordelia came in.

'Hi. I'm frying up some eggs and rashers for you. That OK? I made tea and there's soda bread in that basket and butter and marmalade on the table. Put it all on a tray and take it out to the garden. I'll bring you this in a minute.'

'Rashers?' Cordelia asked.

Kathleen laughed. 'Bacon to you Yanks. We call them rashers here. Should have made you the full Irish but we ran out of mushrooms and black pudding. Everyone was starving this morning for some reason.'

Cordelia found a tray and put the bread and tea on it. 'I can imagine. But hey, don't go to any trouble for me. I can manage on my own. I'm sure you have a lot to do.'

'Yeah, I have to clear up this mess, and then go and make the beds. Twelve today and a load of towels and sheets to wash. But it's OK. No big deal to fry a few rashers and eggs for ya.' She smiled and put the food on a plate and handed it all to Cordelia. 'Here you go. I'll put everything in the dishwasher and then make the beds. Maeve said to let you have a nap and then she'll be around later.'

'OK. Thanks, Kathleen.' Cordelia put the plate on the tray and wandered slowly outside and found a garden table and chairs where she sat down and dug into her very late breakfast.

As she savoured the crisp bacon, the fresh eggs and the homemade soda bread, she tried to gather her thoughts. She was excited at the thought of running the guesthouse, even if it meant having to work hard, as Kathleen seemed to be the only other person employed there. She hoped it wouldn't be that hard to get into the swing of things, as she desperately wanted to get deeper into the search for her mother's identity and early years in Ireland before that dramatic flight to America. Frances had cut all ties with her family and Cordelia was determined to find out why. But was her mother the real Frances? That was the biggest question and the one that simply had to be answered.

It was a warm, sunny day with a strong wind from the south-west, which Paschal had told her was the norm around here. She could tell from the shape of the trees that this was the case, as they were all leaning slightly towards the north-east. Finishing her tea, she blinked in the bright sunlight as a wave of fatigue overtook her. Time to lie down, she told herself and carried the tray back in through the door and into the now clean and tidy kitchen, where a large dishwasher droned on. Kathleen was obviously a fast worker.

Cordelia walked into her bedroom, glancing at the two suitcases and decided to tackle them later. She closed the door and took off her shoes, collapsing onto the large bed, her head sinking into the soft pillow. She closed her eyes and drifted off, dreaming of her mother and Phil and those happy days that now seemed so long ago.

Chapter Ten

Refreshed after a short nap, Cordelia had a shower and changed into a blue skirt and a white linen shirt. She pulled a brush through her short curls and swept some powder blusher over her cheeks. If she was to greet guests, it would be a good idea to look her best. She checked the time on her phone and discovered it was already two o'clock. Leaving her unpacked suitcases still on the floor, she went out into the kitchen to see if Kathleen was around to explain the routine of running this guesthouse. But the kitchen was empty and as neat as a pin.

Cordelia looked around, thinking what a nice room it was with the old beige enamelled wood-burning stove she knew was called an Aga, the original cupboards painted white and the big pine table with its scrubbed top where generations of women had served family meals through the years. The flagstone floor was polished by many feet and blue china plates lined the plate rack over the sink. The dishwasher and the industrial-size electric cooker were the only modern equipment. Whoever had done the restauration of this house had a very gentle touch and a keen eye for a period feel.

But there was work to be done, and the first thing was to check on poor Roisin in her attic room, away from the guestrooms on the first floor. Cordelia walked through the kitchen and down the corridor that ran through the middle of house and glanced at the pictures on the walls – mainly watercolours and seascapes with the odd oil painting here and there, depicting cottages and larger houses surrounded by trees, a hunting scene and portrait of a man in a ruffled collar looking at her haughtily.

She glanced into the dining room and noticed the big dining table was set for breakfast the next day, and the sideboard equipped with packets of cereal and bowls of nuts. What a nice idea to have all the guests sitting together for breakfast, Cordelia thought and walked on, peeping into the lovely, bright drawing room where, she supposed, guests could sit in the evenings with the fire lit if it was chilly. They would all be out discovering the delights of the area during the day, or busy hiking, swimming or surfing and would then gather in this welcoming room, talking about what they had seen and done or simply relaxing with a cup of tea or a glass of wine. She wasn't surprised that the guesthouse was so popular as it was truly a home away from home where guests from all over the world could mingle and meet up. Unusual but very charming.

Cordelia walked softly up the curved staircase and onto the landing and then up the next staircase, steeper and narrower, that led to the attic rooms. Up here, the skylights cast a bright light onto the pine floorboards of the landing, where there were three doors. Cordelia opened one of them and discovered a large bright room with three beds, a TV and two chests of drawers. Must be the boys' room, she thought and closed the door. The middle door revealed a bathroom with a Victorian roll-top bath and a power shower in the corner. The final door had to be Roisin and Cian's bedroom. Cordelia knocked softly.

'Who is it?' a hoarse voice croaked.

'It's me, Cordelia.'

'Oh. Uh, come in, but don't scream when you see me,' Roisin said.

Cordelia opened the door and walked into a bright bedroom with a large double bed, where Roisin lay, supported by a stack of pillows. She looked awful, her face covered in spots and a crust of pink calamine lotion, her eyes red and streaming and her hair stuck to her head. 'Oh, God,' Cordelia exclaimed without thinking.

'I know,' Roisin muttered and pulled the duvet up to her chin. 'I'm a horrible sight.'

'You poor thing,' Cordelia soothed and walked closer. 'Can I get you anything?'

'No, thanks.' Roisin closed her eyes. 'This is the worst phase, the doctor told me. It'll last another few days, he said. Then I will slowly get better. I take paracetamol to keep the temperature down and he gave me something to help me sleep. And then calamine lotion. But it doesn't seem to help much.' She opened her eyes and peered at Cordelia. 'But what are you doing here? I thought you'd gone back to the States and wouldn't be back for a couple of months.'

'Maeve asked me to come and help out. And she said the probate won't take as long as they thought. Only another three weeks or so, she said, so I'd have to come soon anyway.'

'Oh. Good,' Roisin mumbled. 'Thanks for coming. Great that you're here to take over. Maeve's exhausted and Aisling is at that needy stage. Just my luck not to have had the chicken pox when everyone else did. You've had it, I take it?'

'Yes. When I was six. I still remember how itchy it was.'

Roisin squirmed in the bed. 'Please don't mention itchiness. Makes me want to scratch.'

'Please don't,' Cordelia urged. 'If you do, you'll get marks that never go away.'

'So I've been told.' Roisin looked thoughtfully at Cordelia. 'But you're a beautician. You must know something about skin and stuff. Maybe you could give me a facial when I get better? Just to make sure I don't look too bad when Cian comes back.'

'Of course I will,' Cordelia promised. 'I'll get some soothing stuff at the pharmacy and make up a lotion for you.'

'Oh, brill,' Roisin mumbled, suddenly looking exhausted. 'That would be so kind.' She sighed and smiled wanly. 'I'm sorry. I'm not very good company right now. I just feel like sleeping all the time.'

'Of course,' Cordelia soothed. 'You must feel awful. Can I get you anything before I go?'

'No… yes… maybe some of that soup Kathleen made?'

'Of course.'

'Not too hot. Just lukewarm. And some iced water. And ice cream. Vanilla. I'll phone you when I wake up.' Roisin let out a weak giggle. 'That was quite a tall order, wasn't it?'

Cordelia joined in the laughter. 'Yeah, but I got it. Call me when you need it and I'll get it all for you.'

'Thank you so much.' Roisin turned onto her side. 'Sorry if I'm grumpy. I'm so glad you're here. I feel so relaxed now that I don't have to worry about the guests or breakfast or anything.'

'I'm glad to help. And I'm really sorry you're so sick.'

'Thanks,' Roisin replied in a sleepy voice. 'Would you mind closing the window before you go? And pulling the curtains. The light hurts my eyes.'

'Of course.' Cordelia closed the window, admiring the sweeping view of the back garden, the beach and the cliffs. Up here, she could see far out to sea and the outlines of the Skellig Islands shimmering in the distance. 'Fabulous view from here,' she said.

'Yeah, lovely,' Roisin mumbled. 'I wish I wasn't sick so I could enjoy the nice weather.'

'You'll feel better soon.' Cordelia pulled the curtains across the window and tiptoed out. Roisin was obviously very uncomfortable. Just as she was about to close the door, Roisin said something.

Cordelia stopped, her hand on the doorknob. 'What?'

'I said that… Mum said something about a test we should have you do. I can't remember what it was. Ask Maeve.'

'Thanks, I will.' Cordelia left, softly closing the door, her heart beating like a hammer. Maeve and Roisin's mother hadn't given up. She walked down the stairs, mulling over the problem. Mary-Anne McKenna was obviously trying to find out the truth. Cordelia felt a cold spike of fear going up her spine. But Maeve had said to forget it and that neither she nor Roisin were listening to their mother. But what if they changed their minds? What if… Cordelia tried to push away her fears as she made her way downstairs. She'd better come up with something before Mary-Anne did.

Back in the kitchen, Cordelia found a pale and frazzled-looking Maeve sorting through a pile of envelopes on the kitchen table. 'Today's post,' she said as Cordelia walked in. 'Mostly junk mail but two bills that have to be paid. Don't know why Roisin hasn't organised direct debit for those. But I'll show you how to do it online.'

'Great.' Cordelia smiled. 'Hi, Maeve. How's Aisling?'

Maeve laughed and put her hand to her forehead. 'I'm sorry. Where are my manners? I hadn't a clue who I was talking to.' She gave Cordelia a hug. 'Hi, how are you? Thanks for coming so soon. Aisling's asleep and Paschal has taken over for a bit.'

'You look exhausted,' Cordelia remarked when she had hugged Maeve back.

Maeve sighed and pushed her hair out of her eyes. 'I know. I didn't get much sleep last night. I'm really sorry to have landed you with all this when we should be welcoming you with open arms. I'm sure Roisin was really grumpy, too. She's a terrible patient.'

Cordelia smiled. 'A little grumpy, yes. But she's feeling awful. How's little Aisling?'

'She is still covered in spots and they're very itchy. But there have been no new ones, so maybe it'll get better soon. Paschal's amazing with her.'

'It was kind of him to meet me.'

'That was my idea. Thought it was the least we could do when you were such a brick to come over like this.'

'My pleasure,' Cordelia said politely. 'No problem at all.'

'I hope it wasn't a major hassle.'

'No, well, yes. In a way. Betsy was a bit shocked when I told her I wasn't staying. But she'll get over it. Not sure she'll offer me a job again, though, despite her promises. She might just have said it to be nice. But it doesn't matter. I'm happy to be here.'

'And so are we, believe me,' Maeve said with feeling. 'I know you might think it was a bit weird to ask you to come back so soon. But under the circumstances, there was nobody I could ask to help out so quickly, and Paschal said it would be good for you to get used to running this place.'

'I'm glad to help. And I was ready to leave in so many ways.' Cordelia started to walk to the large fridge beside the window. 'Do you mind if I get myself something to eat?'

Maeve put the envelopes back on the table. 'Of course not. I'll have something myself. I didn't get much breakfast. Aisling was really fretful all morning and then I thought I'd catch half an hour's sleep when she settled. Let's make a sandwich or something and we'll have it outside, under the sycamore.'

'I'll make it,' Cordelia offered and took an array of lettuce, tomatoes, ham and mayonnaise from the fridge. 'Maybe you could take some soup to Roisin? She wants it not too warm and toast and ice cream.'

Maeve rolled her eyes. 'She's like a five-year old. OK, I'll take it up to her while you make the sandwiches. Bread in the breadbin over there. See you outside in a few minutes.'

Later, as they sat under the sycamore eating sandwiches and looking out over the quiet beach, Cordelia finally plucked up the courage to ask about Mary-Anne and her investigation: 'Roisin mentioned that your mother had said something about me and some kind of test.'

Maeve put her half-eaten sandwich back on the plate. 'Oh God. I wish she hadn't told you.' She looked at Cordelia and frowned.

'Mum is being a bit of a pain, I'm sorry to say. She seems to think you're some kind of impostor. She says we have to make sure you really are the granddaughter of Granny's sister. But of course you are. In any case, this is none of Mum's business. She wasn't related to Phil by blood and she wasn't mentioned in the will, neither was Dad. He didn't object at all. He thought Phil should be left to do what she wanted with her property. Mum has sent us a DNA kit, but we're not going to do it. So please don't worry about it.'

Cordelia worked hard to swallow the bite of her sandwich in her suddenly dry mouth. 'But why does she think this? Has she found something out about my mother?'

Maeve shrugged. 'I don't know. I didn't really listen. She was going on about it so much that I stopped paying attention. Roisin and I both feel that Phil's will was her last wish and we shouldn't contest it in any way. But Mum won't stop. She said something about your grandparents, but she wasn't sure. She said she'll be in touch when she knows more.'

'Oh.' Stuck for words, Cordelia sipped water from her glass. She met Maeve's kind eyes, knowing that she had to tell her the truth about her own doubts and what she had found out about her mother's last name. But she first she needed to ask a question. 'Was… were your granny and mine good at Irish? I mean, were they fluent Irish speakers?'

'Irish?' Maeve thought for a while. 'Not Granny as far as I know. Everyone spoke a bit of Irish in those days, though. It's still a compulsory subject in school here but most of it doesn't seem to stick. Depends on where you live, too. Kerry people are generally quite good at it. Granny and her sister lived in Dublin, so maybe they didn't speak Irish that well when they were young. At least my granny didn't. But your granny Clodagh taught Irish in a girls' school before she was married.' Maeve nodded. 'Yes, now that I think about it, she was supposed to have been a real champion of the Irish language and culture. But as I never met her, I can't swear she kept it up or anything. Your granny was married to Jimmy Fitz, but she died when your mother Frances was in her teens so Jimmy brought her up. The Brennans were total strangers to us. It was all about our grandfather and the McKennas when I grew up.' She stared at Cordelia. 'Why did you ask about their knowledge of Irish?'

'Because I have just found out that Mom's maiden name was Ó Braonáin, not Fitzgerald. It says so on her marriage certificate.'

'What? Ó Braonáin? Well, that's Brennan in Irish, but…'

Cordelia gasped, her heart doing a flip in her chest. 'Brennan?' she exclaimed. 'It means Brennan and not O'Brien? Are you sure?'

Maeve laughed. 'Of course I'm sure. Didn't you know? That was our grannies' maiden name.'

'I…' Cordelia stopped, not knowing what to say. *Brennan*, she thought, *my mother's last name was the same as Maeve's grandmother… Which has to mean… Oh, God it's true, my mother was the real Frances.* 'I… Oh, this is so confusing.' Cordelia tried to steady her breathing.

Maeve looked bewildered. 'It sure is. Why would she call herself by her mother's maiden name and not her own?'

'I don't know,' Cordelia whispered. 'I… I didn't even think she was called Brennan.'

'How do you mean?'

Cordelia cleared her throat. 'I… Well, you see I was a little doubtful whether my mom was *actually* that Frances Phil was talking about. I thought her name meant O'Brien. That was the only thing that didn't fit with Phil's story.'

Maeve stared, horrified, at Cordelia. 'Does this mean that… when Phil was talking about Frances Fitzgerald on that TV show…'

'She might have been talking about someone else,' Cordelia filled in, feeling miserable. 'I know what you're going to say. That I told a huge lie and pretended to be someone I'm not. But everything else fitted so perfectly. The first name, the date of birth, the town she came from, everything. Except that last name, of course. Which now fits. But I didn't know that at the time.'

'Holy mother,' Maeve whispered, her face ashen.

Cordelia leaned forward and fixed Maeve with her eyes. 'I wanted it to be true so badly that I made myself believe it. Phil did too. When we met…' Cordelia's eyes filled with tears. 'It was like I was meeting someone I had known all my life. Phil said the same thing. She said… she said that… that she felt she had been waiting for me and that Frances meant for us to meet, to be together.'

'She was lonely and homesick,' Maeve murmured. 'She needed you – or someone like you. And then there you were, and you just fell into her life and became her constant companion. A wish come true. How perfect,' she ended with a touch of venom in her voice.

'You make me sound like some kind of con artist.' Cordelia grabbed Maeve's hand. 'Please. Try to understand. I was so lonely after Mom died. She was all the family I had. I didn't know how to start living again. When I met Phil… she was so fabulous and sweet and fun and… Well, you know.'

Maeve nodded. 'Yes.'

'And then she started talking about her family back in Ireland and that cousin called Frances who had been born in Dublin and went to America when she was nineteen. Just like my mom. Everything fitted.'

'Except the last name,' Maeve reminded her, a chill creeping into her voice.

'My mother was born on Christmas Eve, too,' Cordelia said, ignoring Maeve's remark. She let go of Maeve's hand and leaned back in her chair, exhausted. She stared out over the glittering water of the bay and breathed in the sweet salt-scented air, trying to pull herself together. How could she ever explain to someone like Maeve what it was like to be all alone in the world? To have no family or relatives and very few friends. Maeve had a husband and a child, a sister, nephews, parents. She was surrounded by family. Cordelia turned to look at Maeve. 'Now that I know my mother's last name was Brennan, I feel I'm getting closer to knowing for sure that my mother was the real Frances.'

'Brennan is quite a common name,' Maeve remarked.

'I suppose,' Cordelia said bleakly. 'But…'

'And you must have known that not all the facts were true when you picked up the phone.'

Cordelia nodded. 'I knew her last name wasn't Fitzgerald.'

'I see. And when you met Phil, you didn't tell her this?'

Cordelia twisted her hands in her lap. 'No.'

'You lied by omission.'

'Not really,' Cordelia stated. 'I… I believed it to be the way—'

'The way you wanted,' Maeve said sternly. 'And then you inveigled Phil to employ you and made her love you.'

'I loved her, too.'

'Of course you did.' Maeve looked at Cordelia for a long time without speaking.

Cordelia looked back at Maeve, knowing that if she was told to go, she would. What she had done was wrong and now she would have to suffer the consequences. She knew what was going through Maeve's mind. Cordelia had befriended Phil under false pretences and kept up the lie for a whole year. But Maeve didn't know the depth of the love Cordelia had felt for Phil, or the hours she had spent looking after her, or the peace of mind she had given Phil during that year. 'I'll leave if you want,' she whispered. 'I know I don't deserve Phil's gift to me. She said in her letter she wanted to give me a family, but that was because she believed…' She got up and took her plate and glass.

'No,' Maeve said, looking as she was waking from a trance. 'Sit down. I'm thinking.'

Cordelia sat down again, her legs shaking, waiting for Maeve to speak.

After a long pause, Maeve looked at Cordelia thoughtfully. 'Do you know what I've just done?'

'No?' Cordelia replied, confused.

'I've walked a mile in your shoes, as the saying goes. Phil always told us to do that with other people. She was the most empathetic person I've ever known. She always seemed to know other people's feelings and where they were coming from. That's what she said to me in her letter. "Try walking a mile in Cordelia's shoes," she wrote. Didn't know what she meant at the time, but now I do. I can't imagine what it would be like to have no family whatsoever, to be all alone in the world like you. You must feel so horribly lonely.'

'Sometimes, yes,' Cordelia whispered.

'Phil knew that. But she also believed you to be her cousin's daughter. I know you had doubts, but as you say, everything except that last name made sense. And now that might fit too, in an odd way. Of course you didn't know that at the time, but now we both do. So… I think we must carry on and try to find out more.'

Cordelia's eyes filled with tears. 'You do? So you can forgive what I did? And you believe that my mother was the real Frances?'

'There's nothing to forgive. You did what you did, and that was not right. But heck, would I have done the same thing if I were you? Maybe. It's not for me to judge. When I put all the facts together, I begin to understand what happened.' Maeve paused and swallowed. 'Phil's letter hinted at all of this and I understand what she meant now. So, let's take it from here and not worry about right or wrong. Phil gave you this gift because she loved *you*, not some distant cousin she didn't know. Her last wish was for you to be here and for us to accept you and we must honour that wish. You did so much for her and made her happy. So I'm sure it was of no importance if you were the real cousin or not. She loved you for who you are and what you did for her. So in that way, there is no real problem. Not for me anyway.' She smiled and patted Cordelia's arm. 'I like you a lot already. I'm sure Roisin does, too. But this has to stay between you and me for the moment. Until you can find out more.'

'What about your mother?'

'We'll just ignore her.' Maeve sighed. 'My relationship with my mother is complicated to say the least. She has always been so bloody ambitious for us. It was as if we had to earn her love and attention by doing well in school and later in our careers. Phil was the one who gave us that unconditional motherly love with hugs and bedtime stories and fun and games. Dad did too, when he could. But Mum was… Oh, I don't know. I suppose her way of showing love was to make sure we did well. She was so proud of Roisin, but being an interior designer wasn't as good in her eyes. I should have aimed for something more academic, she thought.' Maeve shrugged. 'But whatever. That's not important now. Don't worry about Mum. I'll deal with her. I'll tell her not to bother us with that right now that we're dealing with the chicken pox.' Maeve stopped as her phone pinged twice. She checked it. 'Roisin wants more ice cream. And Aisling is crying, so I have to go. Kathleen is on her break, but she'll be back later and we'll go through the drill of the running of the guesthouse.' Maeve got up. 'See you later.'

'OK. Thanks, Maeve. For being fair. And for understanding.'

'I don't really understand anything right now,' Maeve replied. 'But I'm doing my best.' She made a face as a distant wail could be heard from the direction of the cottage. 'I'm being called back to duty. Poor little thing, she's really sick.'

Maeve smiled shyly and ran off down the path along the cliff, leaving Cordelia sitting in the shade of the sycamore going over what she had said. She seemed to have been wavering in her belief about the true identity of Cordelia's mother. Maeve's remark that Phil had loved Cordelia for herself and not for her family connections was a beacon of light over the otherwise bleak truth. Cordelia realised that Maeve was now her ally and wouldn't share her guilty secret with anyone, not even her sister.

With a feeling of hope and optimism, Cordelia got up and gathered the plates and glasses. She was here to help out, to get to know the house and to be part of a team. That was a thought she wanted to hang on to. She looked at the house, standing there on the hill, its windows gleaming in the sunlight. Deep within her, there was a dart of something new and comforting: a feeling of belonging.

Chapter Eleven

It didn't take Cordelia long to get the hang of the running of Willow House. With the help of Kathleen and Maeve, she soon figured out how to manage the accounts, purchases, bookings and the roster. The guesthouse seemed to be staffed entirely by Kathleen and members of her family. Mrs Donelly, Kathleen's mother, did the cleaning of the bedrooms and downstairs rooms, as well as the washing of all the bedlinen, towels and tablecloths in the laundry in the rebuilt shed at the back of the house. Kathleen's brother Paddy tended to the garden and the vegetable plot, and even looked after the hens in the new henhouse behind the greenhouse, which a delighted Cordelia discovered when a brown-speckled hen had startled her by wandering into the kitchen one morning. Kathleen had laughed and shooed the hen out again, saying that Paddy should train 'the chooks' better. 'The hen house is a new feature,' she explained. 'Maeve's idea to have fresh eggs. And the guests adore them.'

'It's a lovely idea,' Cordelia agreed when she had got over the shock. 'Sorry, but I'm a city girl. I'm not used to hens in the flesh, so to speak.'

'They're great creatures,' Kathleen said, still laughing. 'I could watch them forever. I grew up with animals, you know. We have a farm up in the hills with cows and sheep. My older brother runs it now. But I grew up there and love helping with the animals. Especially the hens. They all have their own personalities. That was Clara you just met. She's very social and a real chancer. Always looking for a treat. I'll introduce you to the others later. They're in a special pen, but Clara always manages to escape.'

'Can't wait to meet the rest of the girls.' Cordelia turned back to the frying pan on the cooker, where she was making blueberry pancakes. 'I'll have these ready in a second. I'll just flip them over. Did you put the maple syrup on the sideboard in the dining room?'

'I did,' Kathleen replied, picking up two plates crammed with sausages, bacon, eggs and all the rest of what made up a full Irish breakfast. 'The blueberry pancakes are huge hits with the Yanks. I told them they were cooked by a real live American. But they said they already met you yesterday when they checked in. The couple from Texas and that woman from Chicago.'

'Yeah, they're very nice. I'll go out and say hi and serve them these,' Cordelia promised. 'Is that it?'

'Yes. No more cooking today, thank goodness.' Kathleen pushed the door open with her hip and disappeared.

Cordelia smiled and turned back to the pancakes. She had only been here ten days but she was now so familiar with the house and the routine of running the guesthouse, she felt as if she had always been there. Maeve was delighted to have a break after the tiring few weeks of the chicken pox. Baby Aisling was better and now back to her usual lively self, but Roisin was still feeling poorly and had been told to rest. The doctor explained that chicken pox could be a lot more serious for an adult and a long convalescence was often necessary. But Roisin was not contagious and was improving, slowly, and she was still listless and tired, spending her days sitting on the beach or lying on the couch in the small sitting room-cum-office beside the kitchen.

Cordelia looked up from her task as Roisin wandered in through the kitchen and after a brief 'good morning' disappeared into the sitting room to watch the early morning news on TV. Cordelia promised to bring her tea and toast and was rewarded with a wan smile.

'Come in and sit here for a while when the breakfast rush is over,' Roisin said. 'I think we need to talk.'

Talk about what? Cordelia wondered as she flipped pancakes. Roisin didn't know anything about Cordelia's doubts and fears. Only Maeve knew and she had sworn she wouldn't pass it on to Roisin or anyone. 'It has to stay between us,' she had said. 'No use sharing it with anyone else until we have more facts.' Cordelia was deeply grateful for Maeve's loyalty and felt that she more than anyone had inherited Phil's kind heart and empathy. But as she waited for her mother's birth certificate to be sent to her, she felt increasingly uncertain. What would she do if it turned out that she wasn't related to the McKennas after all? Cordelia shivered and pushed the thoughts away. She'd deal with that when she had to.

Cordelia put the pile of pancakes on a plate and went into the dining room, where the guests were sitting around the big table chatting and laughing and making plans for the day. It had turned a little cooler with a promise of rain so most of them were in jeans and sweaters and discussing the historical sites they might visit, or a trip into Killarney and maybe even a hike in the mountains. There was so much to do in the area, they agreed, and so many quaint little shops to browse in. 'One right here in this cute little village,' a woman with a Texas accent remarked. 'Something Curiosa, isn't that right?' she asked, looking at Cordelia.

Cordelia put the plate of pancakes on the table. 'Yes. It's called Sally's Curiosa. Well worth a visit. You can buy all kinds of crafts and home-made jams too. She's recently updated the shop, I hear.' She smiled at the woman. 'Hi. I'm Cordelia. We met yesterday. You're from Houston, right?'

The woman smiled back after helping herself to two pancakes. 'Yes. My name's Liza. You're from New York?'

'No, Morristown, New Jersey,' Cordelia corrected.

'And now you run this place?' her husband asked. 'Great little guesthouse. Well run, very comfortable. Much better that one of those big hotels.'

'Yeah,' another woman cut in. 'We love it. This is our second visit. This time, the American touch with the pancakes is so great. Makes us feel even more at home.'

'That's wonderful,' Cordelia said, smiling. 'I'm glad you like them. Have a great day.'

'See you tomorrow,' the woman said. 'And then we'll be back next year for sure.'

'That's great,' Cordelia replied, beaming at the woman as she left. 'We'll be happy to see you again.'

Back in the kitchen, she started to help Kathleen wash the frying pans and put the dishes in the dishwasher, but Roisin sticking her head through the door of the office interrupted her. 'Phone call,' she said. 'Sally O'Rourke. And there's something in the post for you.'

'OK.' Cordelia hesitated, a dish in her hand.

'Go ahead,' Kathleen said and took the dish from her. 'I'll take care of the rest.'

'Thanks, Kathleen.' Cordelia walked into the office and sat down at the desk, picking up the phone. 'Hi, Sally.'

'Hi there, stranger,' Sally replied. 'Thought I'd see you around but you haven't been around the village much, I take it.'

'Not really,' Cordelia admitted. 'But it's been quite crazy here with a packed house and Roisin sick and everything. And little Aisling demanding her mom with her at all times.'

'So you've been running the ship single-handed? That must have been a little rough when you just arrived and everything.'

'I've had Kathleen and her mom to help me. It's been very busy though. I've managed a walk on the beach and a swim most days, so I can't complain.'

'How are the patients now?' Sally asked.

'Nearly all better,' Cordelia said and smiled at Roisin sitting on the sofa. 'Not contagious in any case. Right, Roisin?'

'Tell her I'm beginning to feel nearly human,' Roisin said. 'And I'm not dangerous to be around any more.'

'In that case, why don't the two of you come for a drink at the Harbour Bar,' Sally suggested. 'We could even stay on for a bite to eat there. They have fresh crabs tonight, they said.'

'Hold on, I'll ask.' Cordelia looked at Roisin. 'Sally is asking if we want to meet her at the Harbour Bar later. A drink and a bite to eat. Fresh crabs.'

Roisin sat up. 'I don't feel up to a night out yet. But you go. It'll be fun for you and you need a break. Sally will introduce you to everyone, too. Great opportunity to get to know people.'

'I'd love to go. Thanks.' Cordelia put the phone to her ear. 'Roisin's still a little tired, but I'll come. What time?'

'How about seven o'clock? We'll have a drink and a chat and then dig into those fresh crabs. I'll call my good friend Nuala and book a table.'

'Great. Thanks, Sally. See you then.' Cordelia hung up and smiled at Roisin. 'I'm really looking forward to that.'

'It'll be fun. Sally's fabulous.' Roisin got up and tapped a pile of envelopes on the desk with her finger. 'Today's post. Two letters for you. One from the States and one from Dublin.'

'Oh.' Cordelia's hand shook as she picked up the brown envelope with the Dublin postal stamp. It was addressed to Cordelia Mirafiore, Willow House, Sandy Cove, County Kerry. Her name. Her new home… This had to be her mother's birth certificate. If only… Would what was inside reveal that she had been living a lie for over a year?

'Is it something official?' Roisin asked.

'Seems like it.' Cordelia looked at Roisin and then back at the envelope, her stomach churning. She took a deep breath and ripped the envelope open. Inside, she found a birth certificate. She stared at the names and dates. At first the name of her mother's mother made her feel a deep satisfaction. 'Mother: Clodagh Brennan,' it said. There it was at last, the confirmation she was looking for. Her grandmother had been Clodagh Brennan, so her mother was the real Frances. Then she looked at the next line and her heart nearly stopped. She stared at Roisin. 'What does this mean?' she asked in a barely audible voice.

'What?' Roisin took the piece of paper from her. 'Frances Brennan,' she read. 'Mother: Clodagh Brennan, father—' she stopped and gasped. 'What? It says…'

'I know,' Cordelia whispered. 'It says "father unknown".'

'But… I mean… Her dad was Jimmy Fitzgerald. As far as I know, anyway. Jimmy Fitz, they used to call him, according to Phil. But that's all I know about that side of the family, or your grandmother.'

'My grandmother was Clodagh Brennan,' Cordelia said, staring at the names on the birth certificate. She looked back at Roisin. 'But who was my grandfather? This doesn't tell me a thing.'

'How extraordinary,' Roisin mumbled.

Cordelia swallowed as she stared at the birth certificate again. She'd got the reassurance she had been looking for, but now there was another, even bigger mystery to solve. 'Father unknown?' she mumbled, bewildered. 'That's really weird.'

'It sure is,' Roisin agreed. 'How could that be? Maybe it has something to do with why Frances left for America? What's frustrating is that there's no one to ask. There was some kind of story about Granny and her sister falling out, but I can't remember it clearly.' Roisin sighed and sat down again. 'I'll ask Maeve if she knows anything or if Phil said anything when they were talking about family matters. They were very close before Phil went to America. And of course you and she were very close, too.'

Cordelia nodded. 'Yes, we were. But Phil and I didn't talk about family much.'

'What about your mum? Did the two of you ever talk about her family in Ireland?'

'No, hardly ever. She just said there was nobody left and that she wanted to look forward, not back. She said once that her mother had died when she was young, way before she left for America and something about an aunt who didn't want to know her. She never mentioned her father. That aunt must have been your granny.'

Roisin nodded, looking thoughtful. 'Yes. I suppose it must have been. Granny died when I was fifteen, but I didn't see her much the last few years. Clodagh was younger than her, but she was already dead then. She died in some kind of car crash in the nineteen seventies, when Frances was a teenager. Must have been terrible for her. She went to America a few years after that. That's all I, or anyone knows. Not even Dad could tell us when we asked him before they left after Phil's funeral. It's sad, really, when families split up like that after some kind of quarrel.'

'Awful,' Cordelia agreed, opening the other envelope which contained her parents' marriage certificate. 'And here's my parents' marriage certificate. A marriage that only lasted four years or so.' She sighed and gathered the envelopes. 'I'll take these and send them off with my Irish passport application.'

'I hope you can get that sorted quickly.' Roisin looked at Cordelia, her eyes full of sympathy. 'I feel so sad for you, having grown up with no relatives. Not even a grandparent or an aunt. What about your dad's family? Were they ever in touch?'

'No.' Cordelia smiled. 'But there's no need to feel sorry for me. I had a happy childhood. The only thing I missed was having a father like all the other kids. And I sometimes longed to have brothers and sisters and to be part of a big family. It seemed such fun. But most of the time I felt no sadness about not having an extended family. My mother made sure my life was full of fun and laughter.' Cordelia smiled even though her eyes were full of tears. 'I treasure those memories.'

'She must have been an amazing woman.'

'Oh yes, she was. So special. In a way she was like Phil. She had this bright outlook on life and saw the positive in nearly everything. She took hardship on the chin and always rose to any challenge.'

'Sounds like they were quite similar in personality,' Roisin remarked. 'I wish I had met her.' She got up from the sofa. 'You know what? I'm going to stop being an invalid and get back to work. You've worked hard since you arrived. Now you should go and have fun. I'll do the accounts and take a look at bookings.'

'Are you sure you're up to it?' Cordelia asked, looking at Roisin's pale face.

Roisin nodded, a determined look in her eyes. 'Yes, of course. In any case, Cian and the boys will be back in a week, so then I'll have to step up to the plate. But I'll take it easy. The bookkeeping isn't too hard to manage. Kathleen needs a hand in the kitchen and with making the beds, so you can concentrate on that. I'll give you a shout if I need you to help out with updating the website and the social media stuff as you're so good at that.'

'That's a deal.' Cordelia got up to let Roisin sit at the desk. 'I'll go and help Kathleen, and then maybe I'll go for a walk around the village.'

Roisin sat down at the desk. 'Great idea. Go and have a coffee at The Two Marys'. Lovely little café, just above the main beach. Lovely walk along the coast. Sea air and sunshine, just what you need right now. Then come back here and I'll see if Maeve can join us for lunch. We have to talk about what we plan to do with the house and stuff when the probate comes through. It's time to make decisions.' She turned on the computer. 'I'll do a preliminary plan and then we can discuss it all. And there's something I need to tell you both.'

'OK. Thanks, Roisin,' Cordelia said, encouraged by the new determination in Roisin's voice. She might look pale and tired but her voice was strong and her back straight and once the computer booted up, she was inputting a spreadsheet and didn't reply when Cordelia said goodbye. She was back in the saddle and in charge again, which signalled to Cordelia that there wouldn't be much for her to do except menial tasks from now on. Would this mean she wouldn't have much say in the running of Willow House any more? At least it would give her more time to explore her surroundings and really get to know this little village and its people. And most of all, time to find out about her mother's past which was beginning to look a lot more complicated than she had thought. *Father unknown? How could that be?* she asked herself over and over again. She wouldn't rest until that mystery had been solved.

Chapter Twelve

The Two Marys' was the cutest little café Cordelia had ever been to. Perched on a cliff above the main beach, the house, a former thatched fisherman's cottage, had stunning views of the ocean and the islands. Inside, the café had retained the old interior, complete with an open fireplace and stone flagged floor. The furniture was rustic and perfectly in tune with the rough white-washed walls and old window frames. It was quiet when Cordelia arrived after a long walk on the beach; as the waves were wild, the beach was teeming with wetsuit-clad surfers, and onlookers. Nobody had time for coffee and cake when the surf was up. But Cordelia was glad to be out of the wind as she stepped inside.

Two women were working behind the counter. One of them had short red hair, the other was slightly older with greying dark hair and a sturdy frame.

'Hello,' the younger of the two said, looking up and smiling at the new guest. 'Wild out there, is it?'

'Yes, but it's lovely and the surf seems to be fantastic,' Cordelia replied, trying to tidy her hair with her hands. 'Not that I know anything about surfing, but the waves are huge so the surfing should be good.'

'So it is,' she said, peering at Cordelia with interest. 'You're the cousin over at Willow House, aren't you? The one from across the water.'

'That's right.' Cordelia walked to the counter and held out her hand. 'I'm Cordelia. Nice to meet you.'

'We're both Mary,' the woman said with a broad grin. 'But I'm Mary B, and this is my cousin Mary O. B for Byrne and O for O'Rourke, in case you were wondering.'

'I see.' Cordelia shook both women's hands in turn. 'That makes it easier.'

'Sure does,' Mary B remarked. 'A bit of a pain to have the same first names. But our parents had no imagination.'

'They named us after Our Lady,' Mary O filled in. 'Which was very popular in our day.'

'In your day, maybe,' Mary B snorted. 'Then every girl in Ireland was called Mary. But not my generation. I wish they could have called me something a bit more with it. Like Louise or Gemma. But oh, no, my mother had to ape her sister and call me Mary. I hated it when I was a teenager.'

'Me too,' Mary O confessed. 'Dreary Mary, they called me at school.'

'But now we're used to it,' Mary B cut in. 'And sure isn't the name of the café a bit of a hoot?'

'It's great,' Cordelia agreed. 'But… O'Rourke, you said? Are you related to Sally O'Rourke?'

Mary O nodded. 'Yes. She's my second cousin. Isn't that right, Mary?'

'It is,' Mary B said. 'But sure aren't we all related around here? Totally inbred, we are. It's a miracle everyone's reasonably sane.'

'Or as mad as anyone in Ireland,' Mary O filled in. 'So, Cordelia, what can we get you? Coffee or tea and maybe our special walnut cake? It's a favourite of your man over there,' she added with a nod in the direction of a table at the far window, where Cordelia spotted a man typing on a laptop. 'He's working on a novel, he says, and this is a great place for inspiration.' She lowered her voice and leaned over the counter. 'He probably listens to everything and writes it down so we have to be careful.' She winked. 'Just a tip in case you were going to give us the story of your love life.'

Cordelia laughed. 'My love life isn't interesting enough to be in any novel.'

'I wouldn't say that,' Mary B replied. 'A pretty girl like you must have a long queue of lads asking you for a date.'

'Stop blathering and let the girl alone,' Mary O ordered. 'Go and sit down and we'll bring you the cake. Tea or coffee with that?'

'A large latte, please,' Cordelia said and walked over to one of tables by the larger window, glancing at the man with the laptop, who she thought looked familiar. He looked up as she pulled out her chair. Their eyes met and she realised it was him, the man she had met at the wake and who had talked about her on that late-night radio programme. As his mouth broke into a slow smile, she felt herself blush. 'Hi,' she said and sat down.

'Hi there.' He got up and walked over to her table. 'Cordelia, isn't it?'

She looked up at him. 'Yes. And you're Declan.'

He pulled out a chair and sat down without asking if he could. 'That's right. And I didn't think I'd ever meet you again. But here you are.'

'Yes.' She looked back at him, noting every detail of his face: the luminous grey eyes, the thick black lashes, the dark beetling brows, the straight nose, full mouth, the lines around his eyes and the stubble on his square chin. He was dressed in a black T-shirt and jeans and he smelled fresh and clean as if he had just come out of the shower. She felt a rush of emotion that she couldn't quite place. What was it about this man? 'Here I am,' she said and squared her shoulders, trying to match his confidence.

'So you are. And you have to tell me why and how and if you're going to stick around.'

'I don't have to tell you anything,' she said with a laugh. 'Maybe I want to be mysterious?'

'That's a hard trick to pull off in this neck of the woods.'

Mary B arrived at the table with Cordelia's order. 'Don't you hassle that girl, Declan O'Mahony,' she said. 'Or I will throw you out and never let you back in again.'

Declan laughed. 'Thrown out and blacklisted from The Two Marys'? Now that's an achievement. I must put that into my novel, when I get started on it again.'

'Don't you dare,' Mary B snapped. 'We'll sue the pants off you and make a fortune.'

'You'd lose for sure. Hey, Mary, could you bring me another cup of coffee? I need to take a break.'

'Only if you behave yourself,' Mary B replied.

'Don't I always?'

'You do, but I don't trust that bold look in your eyes.'

'She loves me, but hates herself for it,' Declan said.

'You wish,' Mary B said with a laugh. 'I'll get you that coffee, darlin'.'

His eyes focused on Cordelia when Mary B had walked away. 'So, tell me all. You came back? Why? Just for a holiday?'

'No.' Cordelia nipped a piece of cake and put it in her mouth. 'It's a long story, but... well, I might as well tell you. Everyone knows already, I'm sure. Phil left me an equal share of her property in her will with Maeve and Roisin.'

'Oh? Phil left you part of her estate?' He looked surprised. 'How come I haven't heard about this? Perhaps I've been so into my writing lately that all of this has flown right over my head. Is this why you're here?'

'Partly. The probate hasn't come through yet, but when I had just got back to the States, they came down with chicken pox and Maeve asked me to come over and help with the guesthouse. So I—'

'You just left everything and flew back? Just like that?'

'There wasn't much to leave. I have no family over there. I had started a new job in New York, but...' Cordelia stopped, realising she was revealing a lot about herself to a complete stranger. Not something she'd normally do, but here in Sandy Cove she felt relaxed and oddly secure.

'Your heart wasn't in it?' he filled in. 'The job, I mean.'

Cordelia nodded and sipped her coffee. 'Exactly. I felt that it was time to turn over a new leaf and do something different. This –' she gestured at the window and the view '– is amazing. Such a change from city living and from America. There was only sadness and loneliness for me there.' She propped her elbows on the table and looked at him, willing him to understand. 'You know, I spent a weekend in an apartment near Central Park that belonged to a woman who had only her plants to talk to when she was at home. On the surface, she looked like she had everything I'd ever dreamed of: a lovely apartment in the best part of the city, an interesting job and financial independence. But then I realised that even though she had everything, without anyone who cares or even to talk to, she had nothing. And living in a big city was so removed from nature and the peaceful life in the country. It scared me. I didn't want to end up like her, and I didn't want to spend the rest of my life in a city like New York. OK, so she had a great career, but then…'

He nodded, his eyes serious. 'I know. I felt like that too when I came here. I lived in Dublin, which is just a small town compared to New York, but there is still that big city feel there. Here, everyone knows everyone and what they're doing before they actually do it, if you know what I mean. Can be annoying, but if you don't mind it, life's good here. Apart from the weather, but you can't have everything.'

His face broke into a smile, and when their eyes met, she had to smile back, her cheeks hot as he kept looking at her. She had liked him from the moment they first met but now she felt something more growing between them.

'But you live alone?' she asked.

'Yes. I don't even have a cat. How sad is that?'

Cordelia laughed. 'I think it would be sadder if you did. But why do you work here and not in your house?'

'I find that I work better in a noisy environment, strangely enough. At home, there is only silence and then I find myself distracted by my thoughts and feelings. Here, I create my own little bubble and I can dip in and out of it, talk to people, or just watch them and listen. Hard to explain, but that's how it is.' He looked up as Mary B placed a mug of coffee on the table. 'Thank you, Mary.'

'You're welcome. Give us a shout if you need anything else.' Mary smiled and moved away as a group of people walked in.

Declan turned his attention back to Cordelia. 'So… Where were we?'

'You were talking about you working here in the café,' Cordelia replied. 'Are you writing that novel you told me about?'

Declan picked up his mug. 'No. I've put that one on hold for now. I'm writing a series of articles for one of the main Irish newspapers. Political stuff about Ireland's role in the European Union and how it has affected the political climate here and how local politics has changed because of it.'

'Sounds interesting.'

'No, it doesn't,' he said with a smirk. 'I'm sure it's deathly boring for a fascinating young woman like you.'

Cordelia bristled. 'Actually, I *would* find that interesting, believe it or not,' she breezed on. 'Isn't it like in America, where local politicians indulge in navel-gazing instead of looking at the whole picture? They seem to ignore the fact that all politics affects the country and that they also have to look at a country's relations internationally. Trade, for example, is vital for the economy of any country, so it's important to have good relations with your trading partners. But local politics don't seem to address that.' She drew breath and ate the last piece of the walnut cake.

Declan nodded. 'Very true. Just the kind of thing my mother would say. She's a journalist like me. She's been a champion of women's rights all her life. She'd like you.'

'I'm sure I'd like her, too.'

'We might put that to the test one day. She's on a walking holiday in Scotland right now, but she'll be here for Christmas.'

'Oh,' Cordelia said. 'Christmas…'

'You'll be here then, won't you?'

'I hope so.' Cordelia realised she had been so taken up with the running of the guesthouse and her morning swims that she hadn't thought about how long she'd stay and what she'd do when Willow House was closed for the season. And most of all, she had been wrestling with her own problems and the research into her mother's past. She looked at him thoughtfully as an idea popped into her head. 'You're a reporter, aren't you?'

'Was,' he corrected. 'Now I call myself a journalist. Reporters have to do a lot of digging into people's past and reveal dirty secrets and stuff like that. Which I was good at, but it landed me in a bit of trouble, so now I write learned pieces about politics and such things. And I fiddle with my novel when inspiration hits me. Much more restful.'

'Oh, I see.' She put her elbow on the table and propped her chin in her hand. 'But you still know how to do it? Dig into people's pasts, I mean.'

He looked intrigued. 'I suppose. Why do you ask?'

'I might need help to find out something about someone.'

'I'd be happy to help if I can. Who is this person and what do you need to find out?'

'I'll let you know later on if I need you.' Cordelia sat back, not sure if she should have said anything. But the idea had come to her as he spoke and she felt sure he'd know where to look should she need his help.

'Give me a shout when you do.' He leaned forward. 'I have to tell you, I did actually know you were back in Sandy Cove. I heard it from someone in the village. So I was hoping we'd bump into each other.'

Cordelia stared at him. 'You've heard about me? From whom?'

He shrugged. 'I can't remember. Maybe it was in the little grocery shop on the corner? Kathleen Donovan was in there the other day chatting away. Or it could have been in the pub on the main street. Does it matter?'

Cordelia thought for a moment. 'Does it? Not really. Everyone will know sooner or later that I'm part-owner of Willow House and that I'm going to stay here for a while – that is, if my passport application is accepted.' She smiled. 'Then I'll have dual citizenship, so I can go back and forth if I want to.'

'Or not,' he filled in. 'I'd say you'll get enchanted by this place just like everyone else.'

'I'm enchanted already,' she said. 'And things are looking up. Roisin's better and has taken over the running of the house, so that'll leave me with more free time.'

'Bad luck for her to come down with chicken pox.' He smiled and shook his head. 'I bet that was shock to her.'

'I suppose. She seemed very annoyed that she didn't manage to catch it when she was a child. She had it bad, poor thing. But now she's better and back to normal.'

'I can see her drawing up plans and ordering everyone around in her usual fashion.'

'You seem to know her very well.'

He looked suddenly uncomfortable. 'I used to. We were friends but… Well, now we're not,' he continued, his light tone an odd contrast to the flash of pain in his eyes. 'It's kind of complicated.'

'I see. It's OK,' she added in a gentle voice. 'I won't ask you about it, or anything else you don't want to talk about.'

He touched her hand. 'Thank you. You're a balm to the soul, and a fresh wind blowing into my dusty existence.' He laughed. 'That was more poetic than I intended. You seem to inspire that sort of thing in me.'

'Do I?' She shook her head. 'Nobody's ever said that to me.'

'You've never met anyone like me, I guess.'

'That's for sure.'

'I hope that's positive.'

'Of course.'

'So I've told you all about me being a crusty, disillusioned ex-reporter trying to redeem myself by writing learned articles about Irish politics. But who are you, Cordelia Mirafiore with the blue Irish eyes?'

Cordelia felt her face flush. 'Who am I?' Then she sat up, finding the courage to reciprocate his candour. 'To be completely honest with you, Declan, I have no idea.'

'I love your fire,' he said after a long silence. 'And I'd love to see you again very soon. Would that be OK?'

'Of course.'

'How about tonight?'

'Not tonight. I'm meeting Sally O'Rourke for dinner.'

'What about tomorrow?'

'OK,' Cordelia said, her pulse quickening. 'I'm free all day.'

'What would you like to do?'

What she'd really like to do with him flashed through her mind. She looked away for a second to catch her breath. 'I'd love you to show me around,' she said when she had recovered her cool. 'To tell me about the history of this place, maybe even the history of Ireland that I only know a little about. My mom told me about the rising and the War of Independence and the famine and those things, but I'd like to know about the earlier part, about the kings and lords and clansmen of ancient times. It all seems like fairy tales to me, but I'm sure the real deal was a little less romantic.'

'Hmm, that sounds more like history lessons to me. But why not? I'm sure I can insert a little fun into the mix. So…' He thought for a minute. 'How about a boat trip? I'll see if I can get us into one of the groups going out to the one of Skelligs.'

'The Skellig Islands? I'd love to see them,' Cordelia said, trying to look cool while her heart sang.

'Great. It'll be a trip to Skellig Michael and a tour around both islands. Will you be able to take the whole day off?'

'I think it'll be OK now that Roisin's better. Could I have your phone number so I can call if something comes up?'

'I'll give you mine if you give me yours,' he replied with a suggestive grin.

'Corny but cute,' she said with a laugh as she typed his number into her phone.

'That's me in a nutshell. So it's OK for tomorrow then?'

'Yes. Pick me up at Willow House at ten o'clock. I'll have finished the chores by then.'

'Yes, ma'am.' He made a mock salute and got to his feet. 'Back to work. I have to send the article off to my editor at the *Irish Independent* this afternoon. See you tomorrow, Cordelia.'

She watched him walk back to his table where the laptop was still open with mixed feelings. She had opened up to a total stranger, a man who she found herself drawn to. Were they going on a date? Might it mean the start of some kind of relationship? She felt a frisson of excitement and a little dart of fear. What had she started? And what would it lead it to? A lot of pain or… lasting happiness? Whatever it was, she knew she wouldn't be able to resist it. *But what the hell*, she thought, getting up to pay her bill and leave. *Phil always said that life isn't about surviving the storm but about dancing in the rain.* Cordelia smiled. She wanted to dance in the rain with that handsome man. So what if it all went wrong and she got a little wet? At least she would have lived and loved and had a little fun. What was wrong with that?

Chapter Thirteen

When Cordelia walked into the Harbour Pub, she found Sally, dressed in a bright red sweater, wide-legged black trousers and silver sneakers, chatting with a tall, sturdy woman with dark hair. 'Hi,' she said, beaming a smile at Cordelia. 'I was just talking to Nuala here about you. Have you two met, by the way?'

'Yes,' Nuala said. 'Very briefly at Phil's wake. But not since then. Anyway, welcome back.' She grabbed Cordelia's hand and shook it. 'I'm so sorry about your loss. Phil was such a lovely woman. We all miss her terribly. How are you coping?'

'I'm fine. Still sad and missing her,' Cordelia replied, touched by Nuala's kindness. 'It's nice to run the guesthouse with Maeve and Roisin, the way Phil wanted. That helps a lot.'

Nuala nodded. 'I'm sure it does. But I hear the two of them have been struggling with chicken pox, so you've really had to jump in at the deep end. I'm sure that wasn't easy.'

'Kathleen's been amazing though, so it hasn't been too hard.'

Nuala laughed. 'She's a powerhouse, that girl. I'd say she could run a battleship single-handed looking cheerful while she did it. But here I am chatting when you must be dying of thirst. First drink is on the house. What can I get you?'

'I'd love a Bloody Mary,' Cordelia replied.

'Great choice,' Sally said. 'Most pubs don't do drinks like that well, but Nuala is a dab hand at the old Bloody Mary. She could whip up a Manhattan, too, if that's your cocktail of choice, and I bet she could mix a good dry Martini if pushed.'

'I love mixing drinks,' Nuala said. 'But I don't often get the chance.' She jerked her head at Sally's half-finished glass of Guinness. 'Most people go for the auld black stuff.'

'Nothing better than a glass of Guinness after a busy day,' Sally announced. 'But we'll have some wine with the crabs later, of course.'

'Gotcha,' Nuala said and started to make Cordelia's Bloody Mary. When she had made it, she pushed the tall glass across the counter. 'There you go. Enjoy. I have to go and check what's going on in the kitchen and get Sean Óg to look at the beer situation. Talk to you later, lads.'

'Sean Óg is her husband,' Sally explained.

'Why does she call him by his last name?' Cordelia asked. 'And is her name Nuala Óg, then?'

Sally laughed. 'No. Óg after a man's name means "young". It's like saying "junior" after someone's name. Or "little". It's an Irish thing.'

Cordelia laughed. 'So many sayings and expressions to learn. I love them, though. But it's like learning a new language.'

'Don't worry about it too much. It'll come all by itself. All you have to do is listen and talk to people.' Sally lifted her glass. 'Cheers. Here's to your new life in Ireland. I hope you'll feel at home here.'

'Cheers,' Cordelia said and clinked glasses with Sally. 'I feel at home already, you know. Everyone's so nice.'

'Ah well, we're a cheerful bunch and we try to make everyone feel welcome.' Sally drank some of her Guinness and wiped the foam off her upper lip with her finger. 'So I hear Roisin's better and back at the controls. It must be a relief for you.'

'Oh yes. I was glad to help out but now I'll have more time to explore this area. Roisin and Maeve have promised to let me use their cars if I want to drive down the coast or see a bit of the Ring of Kerry. But I won't have to do that on my own. Declan O'Mahony has promised to show me around.'

Sally lifted one eyebrow. 'Oh? You've managed to get him out of his shell? He's a bit mysterious, I thought. Keeps himself to himself, if you know what I mean.'

Cordelia smiled. 'Another Irish saying? But I do know what you mean. He seems a little reclusive. We met at The Two Marys' earlier today and started to chat. And then he asked me out tonight but I said I was seeing you, so we made an arrangement to go for a drive tomorrow. He's a nice man.'

'Nice and handsome and very interesting,' Sally filled in. 'I'm sure the two of you will get on like a house on fire. I have a feeling he needs a friend. He looks like a real loner. You'll probably cheer him up, if that's what he needs.'

'I'll do my best. And I need a little cheering up myself.' Cordelia sighed. 'Talking to Declan made me feel young again.'

Sally laughed. 'But you are young. What age are you? Twenty-eight?'

'Thirty-three,' Cordelia replied. 'Never found the right guy. It's been one disaster after another so far.'

'You're the same age as my daughter,' Sally said wistfully. 'But she's a lot more prickly than you. Especially when it comes to her mother.'

Cordelia noticed sadness in Sally's hazel eyes. 'I didn't know you had a daughter. Paschal said you'd been married to a Frenchman. And that you knew Phil when she was in Paris many years ago. Sorry,' she added, worried she had touched on something painful in Sally's life. 'Don't talk about it if it makes you sad.'

'Oh no, it's all right,' Sally reassured her. 'I don't mind talking about Phil or my life with you. It's good to know where people come from, don't you think? Especially if we're going to be friends.'

'I'd like that. And if you want to share your memories with me, I'd love to hear them.'

Sally smiled and nodded. 'Good. Well, Phil was my best friend in Paris in the early days. I had gone there to work at a fashion house as a designer and seamstress and Phil and Joe were there because of Joe's work. I was twenty-six and she must have been nearly forty, but we became very close.' Sally looked at Cordelia and sighed. 'Phil took me under her wing and introduced me to all her fun friends, many of them in the fashion industry. And it was thanks to her I met my husband. She felt guilty about that when our marriage broke up, but that wasn't her fault. It was ours. Matthieu and I just weren't compatible. We tried to work it out but we couldn't live together. And then he wanted to relocate to Toulouse in the South of France and I wanted to stay in Paris. Major drama and shouting matches. Jasmine, our daughter, was six then, but we finally came to an arrangement and the divorce was fairly amicable in the end.'

'Where is your daughter now?' Cordelia asked.

'She went to live with her father when she was eighteen. She did economics at university and became an accountant. She works for her dad now. Very bright girl,' Sally said proudly. 'And gorgeous too. Looks like Matthieu, who's a very handsome man in that clichéd French way. Oh, God,' she said with a little sigh. 'What is it about Frenchmen? So gorgeous and seductive and then they let you down.'

'How awful,' Cordelia said. 'I'm so sorry you had to go through that.'

Sally laughed and shook her head. 'Don't worry,' she said. 'I'm not sad or moping. I'm in touch with my daughter often and we go on holiday together twice a year. It's all very civilised in a sad way.' Sally picked up her glass. 'But I'm happy. I have finally landed back home and now I have the life I always wanted. My own shop, a little money on the side and great friends all over the place.' She drew breath. 'And now I'm going to stop talking about me.'

'No,' Cordelia said, mesmerised. Sally was a fascinating woman. With her freckly face and that wide smile that showed a gap between her front teeth, she had a wacky charm and a youthfulness that was captivating. 'Don't stop. I'd love to hear more about your life. And about Phil and all the things you did together. It's a bit like having her back for a while… You remind me of her.'

It was true, she thought. Sally had a larger-than-life personality just like Phil did, that devil-may-care attitude to life, shrugging off sorrows and hardships and looking at the bright side. It was like she accepted that life was tough and nobody owed you a living and that you had to count your blessings and carry on. Not that Phil hadn't been sad at times, but that was also something she had accepted and tried to cope with. Cordelia had a feeling Sally was the same: going through the heartbreak of divorce and then her daughter going to live with her father, leaving Sally all alone. She looked like someone who had been through a lot but had come out smiling.

Sally nodded. 'Yes. I know what you mean. Phil is with us still and always will be. I have a feeling she is smiling down at us right now, nodding and approving and wanting us to be friends.' She sighed. 'Oh, she was such a strong, brave woman. I think it was because her mother was such a tower of strength. Independent during a time when women were supposed to be submissive. Maybe that was why…' Sally paused and leaned forward. 'Her dad was a bit of a lad, as we say around here,' she said in a conspiratorial voice. 'Brian McKenna had an eye for the women, in other words. I think he had affairs and flings all over the place. The marriage wasn't happy, I believe. Could have been because Phil's mother was such a toughie. Or maybe that's why she became tough. Who knows? In any case, this wasn't easy for the children. I often think that living in a bad marriage is worse than divorce.'

'You could be right,' Cordelia said as she remembered bitter arguments between her parents during her early childhood. 'I think my parents fought a lot before my dad left. But I was only three, so the memories are faint.'

'There could still be some kind of residual trauma,' Sally remarked.

'Could be. But it's not a big deal any more.'

'Because of the bad marriage,' Sally continued, 'Phil and her brother spent their childhood summers and other holidays here in Sandy Cove without their father. Brian McKenna worked in Dublin and came down for the odd weekend, but most of the time they were here on their own with their mother. But she made sure the kids were happy, and where could a child be happier than here?'

'Heaven for kids, especially in the summer, I'd say,' Cordelia remarked.

'Your table is ready, lads,' Nuala called from the door that led to the glassed-in part of the pub where round tables were laid for dinner. 'You can eat outside, too, if you like, but that wind is a bit chilly tonight.'

'We'll stay inside, thanks,' Sally called back and got up from the barstool.

They walked through the now crowded pub and into the relative calm of the restaurant part, where only a few tables were occupied by people enjoying the excellent seafood on offer.

Nuala led the way to a table by the window with views of the harbour and the ocean beyond, where the craggy outlines of the Skellig Islands contrasted against the pink-tinged evening sky. 'Wait till the sun sets behind the islands,' she said. 'It's spectacular. And tonight there's a full moon so that will be another sight for sore eyes. We don't need fireworks here,' she said to Cordelia. 'Mother Nature provides the best show in town. I never get tired of it,' Sally said with a happy sigh. 'Those are the things I missed the most when I was away. The sunsets and the stars at night.'

Nuala handed them the menus. 'It's only seven thirty. Plenty of time to eat and drink before sunset. Sean Óg will come over with the blackboard with tonight's specials. But I can tell you straight away that if you want crab, you'd better order right now. They're going fast and some people are ordering by phone before they even arrive.'

'We'll definitely have the crab,' Sally said. 'OK with you, Cordelia?'

'Oh yes,' Cordelia replied, her stomach rumbling.

'We serve them with new potatoes but you can have chips if you prefer.'

'The new potatoes for me,' Sally said. 'And extra salad and bread on the side. Then we won't need a starter. A bottle of that lovely Sauvignon would be great, too.' She darted a look at Cordelia. 'I hope you'll join me.'

'Of course,' Cordelia said. 'I'm sure you know wines better than me.'

'Better than a woman called Mirafiore?' Sally said with a laugh.

'Oh, that.' Cordelia shrugged. 'I don't think I'm related to the wine people in Italy. Or if I am, it's a long way away. It's just a name in the US.'

'I suppose it is.' Sally handed the menus to Nuala. 'There you go.'

Nuala took the menus and tucked them under her arm. 'Chips or new spuds for you, Cordelia?'

'New spuds,' Cordelia replied without hesitation.

'Good choice,' Sally said with an approving nod. 'Maybe we could have the wine while we wait? And the bread, please, Nuala.'

'Coming up,' Nuala chanted. 'Enjoy the evening, lads. See you later.'

The wine was brought to the table by a tall man with a round pleasant face who was introduced by Sally as publican and restaurateur extraordinaire, and one hell of a chef.

Sean Óg took Cordelia's hand in his big warm one and shook it. '*Fáilte go dtí ár sráidbhaile, mo chroí*,' he said.

'Oh, eh… thanks,' Cordelia replied, shooting an inquiring look at Sally.

'He said, "Welcome to our village, my dear."'

Sean Óg nodded. 'That's right. You'll have to learn a bit of the old language if you're going to stay.'

Sally snorted. 'Go away out of that, Sean Óg. Stop having us on. There's not much Irish spoken on a daily basis around here, even if some people pretend it's an Irish zone. They'll all have to go back to school if that's to be kept up.'

Sean Óg laughed. 'There are no flies on you, Sally O'Rourke. I was just having a little fun.'

Cordelia joined in the laughter. Sean Óg seemed so full of fun and there was an irresistible bonhomie about him. His sing-song Kerry accent was a joy to listen to and she found herself basking in the warmth of his presence. 'That's OK,' she said. 'I'm only happy I don't have to go to Irish classes. I'm sure I'll pick up a bit here and there though, if I keep listening.'

'That's the spirit,' Sean Óg said approvingly and took a corkscrew from his pocket and expertly opened the wine, pouring a little into each of their glasses. 'Well, cheers and bon appetit and all that. Got to go and see to the food. Nice to meet you, Cordelia. See you around, girls.'

'He's very nice,' Cordelia said when he had gone.

'He's a pet and Nuala is a lucky girl,' Sally agreed. She picked up her glass and took a sip, her eyes on Cordelia. 'So what about you and your plans? You're going to stay?'

'For the time being at least,' Cordelia replied, echoing the thoughts she'd had since leaving The Two Marys'. Declan asking her about Christmas had made her decide to prolong her visit. She would stay until the holidays and by that time she would have a firm plan about what she would do next, depending on what she found out about her mother. 'I've applied for Irish citizenship.'

'Oh, that's fabulous,' Sally said, beaming. 'We'll have a party when that comes through. Won't be long, as your mother was born in Ireland.'

'Yes, she was.' Cordelia drank some wine and helped herself to a slice of bread. 'My mother and Phil were first cousins. But...' She paused.

'But?' Sally asked.

Cordelia swallowed her mouthful. 'I got some strange news today. I received my mother's birth certificate for my citizenship application. I thought it was going to be straightforward, but it wasn't. My grandmother seemed to have called herself by her maiden name, Brennan, not Fitzgerald, and it says "father unknown" where her husband's name should have been.'

'What?' Sally exclaimed. 'Really? How strange.'

'Did Phil ever talk about my mother? Or about my grandfather?'

Sally put her elbows on the table and leaned forward, looking thoughtful. 'Sometimes. We were talking about you when I visited her in hospital. Just a few weeks before she... left us. She said she was so happy you had found each other and how important you had become to her during the past year. She told me she didn't know much about what had happened to make Frances – your mother – go off to America. But she said it had been a year or two after Frances' mother had died. And there had been some kind of falling out about something, but she didn't know the details. Your mother didn't stay in touch with her cousins and was forgotten and only mentioned as "that cousin who went to America" and was never heard of again. That's all Phil knew. But… "father unknown"? That is a mystery to me. I'm sure Phil had no idea.'

Cordelia sighed and drained her glass. 'No. And it came as a huge shock to me. Phil told me she didn't know much about my grandparents, but she was sure my grandfather was known as Jimmy Fitz, and apparently, he was fond of drinking and gambling. But…'

Sally looked thoughtful. 'Why isn't he mentioned on the birth certificate as the father? And why did your grandmother call herself Brennan and not Fitzgerald?'

'Maybe she didn't want to change her name?' Cordelia suggested. 'I know that she was quite progressive and a real feminist.'

'Like my mother,' Sally said. 'She never took my dad's name so I ended up being an O'Rourke and she was always known as Mary Watson. Quite shocking in those days. Could have been the same scenario there.'

'Could be. I have to find out more. I need to know who my grandfather was, if he wasn't this Jimmy Fitz. I just can't leave this alone. It's as if a piece of me is missing and I need to find it.'

'Absolutely,' Sally said with feeling. 'You need to find out what happened. It's about your family and your identity. You must try.'

'I know. But will it be possible to find anything? It was all so long ago.'

'Well, Ireland is a small country. And Dublin was even smaller then than it is now. I'm sure we could do a bit of research.' Sally was interrupted by a young waitress arriving at their table with two plates of dressed crab in their shells, buttered new potatoes, lettuce and coleslaw and a pot of garlic mayonnaise. 'Let's enjoy this feast, though,' Sally continued. 'And I'll have a little think while we eat.' She topped up their glasses and picked up her knife and fork. 'It's too nice an evening to be sad. Just look at that sky.'

Cordelia looked at the sky turning a riot of pink and orange, the sun slowly sinking behind the islands and the wild waves of the ocean crashing against the rocks sending sprays of water high in the air. What a wild, wonderful place that could never be tamed by man or technology. You had to take whatever nature sent and accept it, cherishing good days and taking shelter during bad days. It seemed to Cordelia that a place with this beautiful clear sky at night was so much nicer than Miami where the stars were rarely visible. But the smell of the food lured her away from her musings and the wonderful view. She smiled at Sally and picked up her fork. 'This looks fabulous.'

'Heaven,' Sally said through a mouthful of crab.

And it was. Cordelia attacked the food with gusto, savouring the taste of fresh crab laced with lemon and chives, the nutty flavour of the new potatoes and the crisp lettuce and crunchy coleslaw. It was a meal fit for a king and they didn't talk until the last potato was gone and the crab shells empty. Then they sat back, wiped their mouths and finished the last of the wine, smiling at each other.

'Oh my God,' Cordelia groaned. 'That was delicious. But I'm stuffed.'

'I know.' Sally laughed and leaned back. 'I won't be able to move for a while.'

'Me neither,' Cordelia agreed.

Sally sighed and discreetly unbuttoned the top button of her trousers. 'Puah. That helps a bit. So how could we get going on this research into your family—'

'I said to Declan that I might need some help without giving him the details,' Cordelia interrupted. 'Do you think he might be able to find something for me?'

Sally nodded. 'Oh yes. Good idea. Declan O'Mahony used to be a hot-shot reporter and could find out anything about anybody. If you give him what you know, I'm sure he could do some digging for you. Can't think of anyone better.'

'Oh, good.' Cordelia paused. 'I'll get back to him on this. He said he'd be glad to help. It feels a bit odd to share family secrets with someone I've only just met. But I like him.'

Sally nodded approvingly 'Of course you do. He's a very attractive, interesting, fun man. And you're pretty and smart and good company. I'm sure he likes you a lot already.'

Cordelia smiled. 'I hope he does. He's taking me on an outing tomorrow. To Skellig Michael. I can't wait to see it.'

'That's terrific. You'll love it. See? I knew he liked you. He wouldn't go to the trouble if he didn't.' Sally patted Cordelia's hand. 'And he's a terrific sleuth, so you should definitely ask him to help you with your family research. I'm sure he'll find what you're looking for in no time.'

Cordelia smiled and nodded, feeling suddenly optimistic. The shock of what she had read on the birth certificate slowly faded and she knew she had to do everything she could to find out the truth, even if it was bad. But did she want Declan to dig into her family history?

Chapter Fourteen

The next day was breezy but warmer than the day before and Cordelia did her chores with happy anticipation of the day ahead. Nothing could ruin her bright mood, not even a grumpy Roisin, who kept shouting orders from the office, where she sat at the desk doing the accounts and bookings. She was still pale with faint red marks on her face and arms despite the lotion Cordelia had made up for her, but she seemed to have regained her energy, including her mood, which Cordelia knew by now was just the way she was.

They had heard that the probate would come through soon, and they needed to do an inventory of the contents of the house for those records. It was a huge task and Cordelia had volunteered to help out. It was a perfect opportunity to search through the house for clues about the family history that might provide a link to her mother's past.

But right now, her outing with Declan was on the top of the agenda. Cordelia looked through her meagre wardrobe that morning trying to decide what to wear. *Casual*, she thought, *with a dash of sexy, like maybe that silk camisole with lace around the edge…* She had washed her hair early that morning and now it was a mass of shiny curls around her face. She already had a slight tan which enhanced her blue eyes and she needed only a touch of mascara to look her very best in a natural, wholesome way, which belied what she was thinking every time Declan came into her mind. She smiled to herself as she fried blueberry pancakes and nearly burnt them as she forgot to flip them over. But she dribbled a generous amount of maple syrup over them and added a dollop of whipped cream and the guests were happy.

Cordelia rushed through the washing up after breakfast while Kathleen made the beds, checking her watch. Declan would be here soon, and that thought made her forget everything that was going on around her. She jumped and nearly dropped the frying pan she was drying when Roisin called her from the office.

'Yes?' Cordelia replied, walking to the open door.

'If you're not busy today, could you work on the website? We need to update the availability page for the rest of the year, now that we've prolonged the season. I have written it all down on a piece of paper. All you have to do is put it into the schedule.'

Cordelia put the frying pan on the kitchen table and went back to the office. 'OK. But can it wait until later? I... I'm going out with – someone.'

Roisin looked surprised. 'Oh? Who?'

'Uh, Declan O'Mahony. He's going to show me around the peninsula and we're going to see the Skelligs.'

Roisin stared at her. 'Declan?' she said in a near whisper.

Cordelia nodded. 'Yes. I need to learn about the history and culture of this part of Ireland and he's showing me the best places to go.'

'Oh really?' Roisin looked at Cordelia with suspicion. 'So that's why you're all spiffed up this morning.'

Cordelia laughed. 'Thank you for noticing. I'm sure I don't look that great, but—'

'You look stunning, darlin',' Roisin interrupted. She laughed and shook her head. 'Sorry, I'm just a little envious. You're standing there looking so fresh and healthy and glowing and here I am all pale and spotty still. You make me feel old.'

'But you're looking so much better,' Cordelia protested. 'You'll soon be back to normal. Keep putting on the lotion. That should help the redness fade and get your skin back to normal.'

'Yes, the lotion is helping and my skin feels softer. It was so kind of you to go to all that trouble. That's why it's impossible to hate you for looking so good. You'll have a good time with Declan, he's fabulous company. But do be careful. He might take you out under false pretences—' Roisin stopped. 'Sorry. Forget it.'

'Forget what?' Cordelia asked, confused by the look in Roisin's eyes.

'Oh, just an idea. I might be wronging him, but he could just see you as an interesting subject for a story. He is a reporter, after all.'

'He said he's put all that behind him,' Cordelia argued. 'He said he now wants peace and calm and to write about politics and things like that. No more digging into other people's secrets.'

Roisin looked doubtful. 'Yeah, maybe that's true, but you never know with journalists. Always hungry for a mystery to solve and a story to make headlines.'

'Mine would hardly make headlines,' Cordelia protested.

'It could if he made up a few things.' Roisin shrugged. 'Oh forget it. I'm being paranoid. I'm sure he's learned his lesson by now.'

'What lesson?' Cordelia asked.

'Nothing to do with you,' Roisin said, looking slightly uncomfortable 'Declan and I are friends, but we got our wires crossed a bit last year. That's all I'm going to say and it's in the past by now. So please, do go out with him and enjoy yourself. You're free as a bird and can do what you like. None of my business at all.' She drew breath and turned back to the computer. 'You can do the website stuff when you come back.'

'OK. I will,' Cordelia said, hovering in the door. 'If that's all, I'll…'

'Great. Have good time,' Roisin said with a weak smile. 'I'll be done here soon and then I'm going for a walk on the beach. Fresh air and sunshine will be good for me.'

'I'm sure it will. See you later,' Cordelia said and left to get changed for her date, her mind turning to her outfit for the day. White jeans, a dark blue linen shirt and that cream lacy camisole underneath, peeking out of the neckline as if by accident… Her skin tingled as she put it on, feeling the soft silk slide down her body. A subtle hint of something less wholesome, exactly how she felt deep inside. She grabbed her windproof jacket and a sweater, sprayed on a light mist of Coco Mademoiselle by Chanel and took a final look in the mirror before she went outside as she heard wheels on the gravel in front of the house.

A red Audi had just pulled up outside and Declan got out as she came through the front door. He was dressed in jeans, a white T-shirt and a black bomber jacket and he had pushed his aviator sunglasses into his short hair. He put them on as she approached. 'You look all fresh and lovely,' he said and kissed her cheek. 'And you smell wonderful.'

'And look at you,' Cordelia teased. 'That jacket and the sunglasses. Wow. Very James Dean.'

He grinned. 'That was the idea, darlin'.' He opened the passenger door with great flourish. 'Have a seat in my old jalopy, madame.'

'Old jalopy?' Cordelia said incredulously, sitting down on the cream leather seat after having put her jacket and sweater on the back seat. 'This is a nearly new Audi if I'm not mistaken. Couldn't be less jalopy-ish if it tried.'

'Two years old,' Declan corrected. 'But I keep her in good nick. Bought her after an especially good year which was the end of the glory days for me. But let's not go there right now. Or ever.'

'OK. I won't ask any questions.'

'I'll hold you to that.' Declan got into the passenger seat and started the engine, smiling at Cordelia. 'Off we go. Are you ready for a bit of an adventure?'

'Never been more ready,' Cordelia replied, the sparkle in his eyes giving her a thrill. This wasn't a real date, just an outing, she told herself. But whatever it was, she knew she was ready for whatever the day would bring.

They stopped for coffee at a roadside café that was perched on a cliff and had spectacular views of the coastline and the sunlit ocean. Seagulls glided above, peering in at the guests, squawking loudly. They picked a table near the large picture window that was out of the glare of the sun but still offered a view of the sea. Declan ordered coffee for them both. 'They serve a really good carrot cake if you like that,' he added.

'I'll just have coffee, please,' Cordelia said, feeling too much on edge to eat anything. But she still stole a piece of Declan's cake when it arrived which made him laugh.

'I can see you're one of those picky eaters. You say no, but then steal a bit from whoever you're with.'

Cordelia laughed. 'Yeah, that happens a lot. It's because I have a small appetite and a full helping of anything is too much for me.'

'Have another bite,' he said and held up a forkful of cake.

'OK.' She opened her mouth and let him feed her while he held her gaze, and then smiled slowly before taking a bite himself. Then he dabbed her mouth with his napkin. 'You have a little bit of icing just here.'

She pushed away his hand. 'No I don't.'

He laughed and finished his cake. 'You're not easy to cod, are you?'

'Cod?'

'Fool. Irish expression.'

'Oh. One of those. I'll put that into my memory bank.'

'It'll be full by the time you learn all our little quips and sayings.'

'Is there a dictionary?'

He smiled. 'No. But there should be one. Maybe we should write one together?'

'In a year or two when I have added all those Irish words to my vocabulary. Can't wait to see the Skelligs. But—' She looked out the window. 'We're not anywhere near where the boats dock. Isn't this the way to Waterville? Why are we going this way?'

'Because we're not going to the Skelligs. The boat was fully booked. They only allow twelve people at a time to go out there. It's a heritage site and the flora and fauna are also very delicate. So another time, I think.'

'Oh, that's a pity,' Cordelia said.

'Sorry to disappoint you. But look on the bright side. You won't have to climb up six hundred very steep steps with a bunch of kids waving lightsabres to relive their favourite *Star Wars* moments. And…' He paused for effect. 'I have an excellent plan B. I think you'll love it.'

'Oh? What's that?' Cordelia asked.

'It's a trip around Bull Island, which is a little further south. We'll get on the boat at Caherdaniel, and then head out to this massive marine mountain. It's part of the chain of rocks off Dursey Island at the edge of the <u>Beara</u> Peninsula. The islands are called the Bull, the Cow and the Calf. The Bull is the biggest island and it has an arch running through the rock. In Irish mythology, it was supposed to be the home of Lord Duinn, the lord of the dead. Souls passed through the arch after death on the way to the otherworld. A little dark, but quite fascinating. You might see dolphins and seals and maybe even a whale or two.' He leaned back, beaming at her. 'How about that?'

'That sounds amazing,' Cordelia replied, impressed. 'Can't wait to see that.'

'Great. We'll be going in a rib, so might get a bit wild.'

'Rib?'

'A rubber dinghy thing. Like the ones that go out to rescue people. I hope you're not prone to seasickness.'

'Not as far as I know. But I've only ever been in a rowboat so I can't promise.'

'We'll hope for the best. You can always puke over the side, should you feel queasy.'

Cordelia laughed. 'How romantic.'

'Well, it might break the spell, of course,' Declan said, waggling his eyebrows. He got up. 'We have a bit to go yet. Caherdaniel is about half an hour from here. We can have lunch on the boat if we get sandwiches in the shop near the caravan park. He held out his hand. 'Come on. Let's go on an adventure.'

It proved to be the best adventure Cordelia had ever experienced. The skipper of the rib, who was called Conor O'Shea, was waiting at the quayside when they arrived. He shook their hands and gave them each a collar with straps that tied around their waists, which was a life vest, he explained, and it would expand and inflate on contact with the water should there be an accident or they fell overboard. 'Much more comfortable than the old bulky vests,' he said. 'And safer, too, because it's easier to move around boats with those. So when you're ready we'll take off. There's a bit of a swell but it's not too bad, so you won't get too sick.'

'Just a little bit sick, then,' Declan murmured in Cordelia's ear as he helped her on board.

She giggled despite feeling nervous, hoping fervently she wouldn't get seasick. She settled on the seat, Declan beside her and looked around for other passengers.

'No other passengers,' Conor announced behind them and started the engine. A young boy on the quay cast off the ropes and the rib started to move through the crystal-clear water.

They were soon on the open sea, moving south along the coastline towards a dark mass ahead, which was the end of the Beara Peninsula.

'The Bull is part of Dursey island like I told you,' Declan shouted over the noise of the engine, pointing in the direction of the islands sticking out of the sea. Cordelia nodded, held on to the edge of the rib and looked ahead, watching the huge rock get closer.

The boat suddenly swerved and slowed down. 'Here they are,' Conor shouted and pointed to the side, where shiny blue-grey backs stuck out of the water. 'Dolphins.'

Awestruck, Cordelia watched as the glossy backs tumbled in the water, as the dolphins surrounded the boat. It was as if they were playing a game and the boat was part of the group, a friend to play with. 'It's called a pod,' Declan said in her ear. 'A pod of dolphins. Isn't it amazing?'

Cordelia nodded, unable to speak. She watched in awe as one of the dolphins rose from the water and jumped beside the boat and felt a jolt of pure joy, like an electric shock to her heart. Then another dolphin jumped, and another and she gasped each time, not wanting this amazing show to stop.

Declan put his arm around her. 'They're showing off for you,' he muttered in her ear.

'Oh God, I love them,' she said, breathless. 'They're beautiful.'

They continued the journey toward the rock, the dolphins still trailing behind and then dropping off to follow a shoal of fish, Conor explained.

They arrived at the rock that rose above them like a mass of dark stone, the sides made up of steep rugged cliffs with a lighthouse on top and daylight shining through the arch. Conor said it would be safe to pass through and steered the rib towards it.

'Is the lighthouse still working?' Cordelia asked.

'It is indeed,' Conor replied. 'That beam sweeps across the ocean and the sky every night. Built in 1889.'

Then they were inside the arch and travelling through what felt like a space journey or something spiritual, Cordelia thought, as they left the islands behind them and were suddenly out on the immense Atlantic Ocean. There was only sea and sky here, and seabirds above them gliding around.

'Look!' Conor suddenly shouted and pointed ahead, where an immense dark shape rose out of the blue water. 'A killer whale.' He handed Cordelia a pair of binoculars and she gasped as a huge black-and-white head emerged, a plume of water shooting out of the back of it. Then it disappeared and didn't come up again, but they could see the enormous dark shape sinking deeper into the water and then it was gone.

Cordelia stared out over the sea, stunned by what she had seen, unable to utter a word. She looked at Declan, wanting to thank him. Their eyes met and she could tell he knew how much she had loved the experience of this trip. The rib slowly turned and they travelled back, the shifting light of the sun through the clouds painting the water all kinds of shades from indigo to glittering silver. When they arrived back at the quayside in Caherdaniel, Cordelia felt she was leaving a world of pure magic and delight behind. They handed the life vests back to Conor and thanked him, then walked to the car, Cordelia still in a daze after all she had experienced.

They sat in the car drinking water and enjoying the sandwiches they had forgotten to eat, both lost in their own thoughts, looking out at sea through the windscreen.

'Strange how that kind of trip can make you feel you've been on another planet,' Declan said, wiping his mouth with a paper napkin.

'Oh yes,' Cordelia agreed. 'It was incredible.' She finished her sandwich, drank some water then turned to Declan. 'I… I didn't know what to say. But I want to thank you for this amazing trip. It was truly magical and I won't forget it. Ever.'

'I knew you'd like it,' he said, leaning towards her. 'Not a history lesson, more like a marine wildlife field trip.'

'It was amazing, whatever you call it.'

'You have stars in your eyes,' he remarked, laughing.

'Do I?' she sat back, feeling flustered. 'It's because it was all so beautiful.' She looked at him, wondering if he was going to kiss her, but he sat back while he kept looking at her. Did he feel what she was feeling? Could he read her thoughts and discover the stars in her eyes were not only about the outing?

He touched her cheek. 'You have a lot to get used to right now. A new country, a new family and the mystery about your mother and her parents. It's not wise for you to rush into anything with me right now.'

Sobered by his serious tone, Cordelia straightened up. 'I suppose you're right,' she said, slowly coming to her senses. How did he know what she had been thinking? That she wanted to dive in, to kiss him, to forget everything else that was going on. She looked into his earnest grey eyes and saw a hint of fear there, fear of going too fast and messing up what had started with so much promise. 'I want to get to know you,' she said. 'I want to find out what you like to eat, if you prefer beer to wine, what books you read, what makes you laugh and what makes you cry, what music you like and all about your life before we met.' She drew breath. 'Everything.'

'Me too,' he said, smiling, and started the car. 'But let's not rush it. Let's continue the voyage of discovering Ireland. We'll go on a little trip along the coast to Kenmare and then take the mountain road through Moll's Gap and have dinner in Killarney. And we'll talk. We have all day, don't we?'

Cordelia thought fleetingly of having promised Roisin to update the website, but pushed it away. She could do that later tonight, there was no rush. 'Yes, we do,' she said and leaned her head back against the headrest, closing her eyes, enjoying the smooth motion of the car. She was feeling relaxed and happy, even though he had pushed her away when she wanted to take things to another level. But even that felt good and he was right. There was no rush. And in any case she had something more important than romance on her agenda. She needed to keep searching and now she felt comfortable about asking Declan to help. She didn't know Dublin at all and she knew that had to be the next place to go looking. But where would she start in a city she had never even visited? Declan had grown up in Dublin and knew the city inside out. *Yes*, she thought, *I will ask him to help me.* Would he understand how much it meant to her?

Chapter Fifteen

The drive up the mountains and through the mountain pass called Moll's Gap was spectacular. Declan pulled up at the top and they got out to admire the view of the Gap of Dunloe on one side and McGillicuddy's reefs with Carrantoohill, the highest peak, rising up in the distance. 'Ireland's highest mountain,' Declan said. 'And a tough climb, but worth the pain. Maybe I'll take you up there when you've had a bit of practice.'

'That'd be fabulous,' Cordelia sighed, looking out over the mountain range, shivering in the chilly wind. 'Why is this called Moll's Gap?'

'It's after a woman called Moll Kissane who was famous for her poitin – or home-made brandy to you.'

'Like hooch?' Cordelia asked.

'Something like that. The Kissane family still run the sheep farm near here. I bet they're very proud of old Moll.'

'She must have been a strong woman.'

'They all were in those days. Had to be to survive. Making poitin must have been a nice little earner for them.'

'I could do with something like that right now,' Cordelia said, hugging herself.

He put his arm around her and held her tight for a second before he let her go. 'You're freezing. Let's go down to Killarney and have dinner.'

They drove down the steep, narrow road full of hairpin bends. Cordelia glanced over the edge of the cliffside and shivered, wondering if they'd survive if the car pitched over the side. She whimpered as a car approached, grasping the handle of the door and shutting her eyes as Declan swerved. But the cars miraculously managed to pass each other without incident.

'You can open your eyes now,' Declan announced as they arrived at the crossroads. 'We're down safe and sound.'

Cordelia breathed out. 'Thank God for that.'

'Scary road. But I've driven there a few times. Worth it for the views.'

'And for the fright.' Cordelia sighed and drank the rest of the water from the bottle. 'It was pretty scary up there.'

'You should try it in the fog.'

'No thanks.'

He grinned and shook his head. 'You little chicken.'

'I'm sensible, that's all.'

He nodded, pretending to look serious. 'Ah. The sensible type. That's quite a challenge. I'm more the devil-may-care kind of guy.'

'I can tell.' Cordelia put away her bottle. 'And right now, I'm the hungry type.'

'Dinner coming up.' He turned onto the main road and then continued through the enchanting landscape with rolling green hills, the majestic mountains in the distance and the brief glimpse of lakes and rivers through the lush foliage of the trees that lined the road. The sun was setting in the west casting a golden light on the countryside. They drove into Killarney while the sky turned a darker blue and the evening star glinted above the rooftops.

'It's nearly eight o'clock,' Declan said as he parked the car in a small parking lot behind the main street. 'But I think we can get a table at the Steakhouse, if you like that sort of thing. Steak and chips and salad. Simple but excellent with the best Irish beef.'

'Fabulous,' Cordelia replied, her stomach rumbling, which made them both laugh.

The restaurant wasn't full and they were soon sitting at a table near the back, tucking in to steaks while Declan answered some of Cordelia's questions about himself. He told her about his time as a political reporter and how he had revealed a big corruption scandal, which had resulted in him being hounded by politicians and eventually fired from the newspaper. His TV show had also been cancelled and he had left Dublin to try and recover and to start his career again. 'Whistle-blowers are never popular,' he said. 'Peace and quiet and a place where nobody bothers you is what I was looking for, and found right here in Kerry.'

Cordelia listened while she ate most of Declan's chips.

He laughed as he watched her and declared he had ordered a double helping because he suspected she might want some despite having declined them earlier. 'I see I was right,' he said, laughing as she picked up a chip and ate it.

'I know,' she said, 'I *think* I don't want any when I order, but then they looked and smelled so delicious I couldn't help having a nibble.' She looked at him across the table. 'Do you find it irritating?'

He leaned over and kissed her cheek. 'No, I find it sweet.' He sat back. 'So… I've told you some of my story, how about yours?'

'My story?'

'Yes. Well, I know why you're here and all that. But not much about how you grew up or if you knew anything about your Irish family before you met Phil.'

Cordelia wiped her fingers on her napkin. 'I didn't know much about Mom's family in Ireland. She didn't talk much about them and she said she had left so long ago and they were all dead so there wasn't much to tell. But now that I have to prove—' She stopped.

'To prove what?' Declan said, looking intrigued. 'That you are who you are? Because of the will?'

'No.' Cordelia hesitated. 'Yes, well, it's all a bit of a mess. You see, I…' She swallowed, not knowing how to continue. How would he react if she told him she had contacted Phil and lied to her about being her cousin – not lied exactly, but pretended something she had no idea was true or not.

'Yes?'

'I don't know how to explain,' she said in a near whisper. 'You might think…'

'Tell me,' he said, pushing his plate away. 'Don't hold back. I won't judge you. I have an inkling you're going to say you made it all up.' He laughed. 'Is that it?'

'Not quite.' Cordelia took a swig of water from her glass to ease her dry mouth. 'It's a little complicated. Strangely enough, what started as a lie is turning out to be true. I mean, my mother is probably who I pretended she was.'

Declan frowned, what was left of his steak forgotten. 'How do you mean?'

Cordelia put her hand on her forehead. 'Oh, it's so hard to explain.'

'But you have to. Start at the beginning and don't leave anything out.'

'OK.' Cordelia knew he was right. She had to tell him everything. She took a deep breath and told him the whole story right from the start, ending with the mystery of her mother's birth certificate. When she had finished, Cordelia drew breath and looked at Declan, her eyes bleak. 'It feels like I don't know any more than I did before.'

'And you lied to Phil?'

'Not really, but I didn't tell her I had doubts we were related,' Cordelia mumbled, not daring to look at him for fear of what she'd see in his eyes. Dislike? Maybe even disgust? 'I couldn't help myself. It was as if someone else was telling me not to. Someone deep inside. Oh, God, now you must think I'm some kind of gold digger.'

'No, I don't. I'm sure it wasn't about money.'

'No, it wasn't. It was about having someone to care about me, having a family. But that doesn't make it OK, though. I know that,' Cordelia said, looking at him at last, ready to take the criticism she was sure would follow.

'It's OK,' she heard him say to her surprise. 'We've all been swept up in the odd lie from time to time.'

She darted a look at him. 'You have? Just the odd lie, though?'

He suddenly laughed. 'I know how you can get carried away and lie, not thinking it does any harm. It's just like adjusting the truth a little in your favour. A bit like wishful thinking out loud. You want it to be true so you make it up, nearly believing it yourself. And then...' He stopped. 'Then it's too late to change it.'

'Yes, that's exactly how it was,' Cordelia said, relieved to hear he had been there, too. She looked at him as something dawned on her. 'Has this something to do with Roisin?'

He sighed and nodded. 'Yeah. But I don't want to go there right now, except to say I didn't exactly behave like the perfect gentleman.' He shifted on his chair and looked at his plate, then back at Cordelia. 'So I'm no angel and neither are you. You lied to get what you never had – a family – and I'm going to help you. Your story has awakened my reporter brain. I want to get to the bottom of this.'

'You do? That's wonderful. I was going to ask you to help but I didn't know quite where you'd start looking.'

'That's not a problem. I'm going to Dublin tomorrow for work. While I'm there I'll look into births and marriages and stuff like that. And I'll look for the man you thought was your grandfather. What was his name again?'

'Jim Fitzgerald. Jimmy Fitz, they called him. Apparently he and my grandmother lived in a part of Dublin called Ranelagh.'

'I know where it is. I'll start looking there. Parish records should be available. And who knows? He might still be alive.'

'If he is, he's very old,' Cordelia protested. 'I'm sure he's dead.'

'When would he be born? In the late nineteen twenties?'

'Something like that. But I bet you won't be able to find him.'

Declan raised an eyebrow. 'I've had tougher assignments, you know. I'd bet all I have in the bank I'll find him, alive or dead.'

'How much do you have in the bank?'

'After all the repairs on my house? Uh, a couple of thousand. But OK, I'll throw in the house too.' He squeezed her hand. 'Come on, Cordelia, have a little faith.'

She smiled at him with a huge sense of gratitude and hope. 'I believe you. I'm sure you'll succeed. You don't know how good it feels to have you to help me.'

'That's the spirit.' He checked his watch. 'It's getting late. We'd better get back.'

They paid the bill and left, walking down the dark street toward the car. 'Look,' Declan said, pointing to the sky. 'The stars are out. They will guide us home.'

Cordelia looked up at the stars and the wide, glittering band of the Milky Way far up in the endless dark sky and felt suddenly very small. 'The universe,' she mumbled and pulled her jacket tighter around her. 'It's so immense.'

'To infinity and beyond,' Declan said, putting his arm around her. 'I always thought Buzz Lightyear was so clever saying that.'

'I thought he was silly. I always shouted, "There is nothing beyond infinity,"' Cordelia countered. 'But what did I know?'

'What does any of us know?' He guided her into the car. 'Come on. It's late and it's been a long day.

'The best day,' Cordelia said and kissed him on the cheek.

They didn't arrive back until eleven o'clock, after a drive in the moonlight with the stars dotting the sky like glittering gems set in dark blue velvet. Declan finally pulled up outside Willow House and turned off the engine. 'Here we are. I brought Cinderella back before midnight.'

Cordelia stretched and shot him a sleepy smile. 'Thank you.'

'For what?'

'For this day, the boat trip, the dolphins, the whale and the ocean. And for dinner and for listening to my story and offering to help.'

'You're welcome. Happy to help, and you were wonderful company.'

'So were you.' Cordelia yawned and opened the door. 'I'd better get some sleep.'

'Yes, me too.' He got out of the car and went to her side to help her. As she got out, he wrapped his arms around her. 'How about a goodnight kiss?'

'Oh yes.' She stood on tiptoe and touched her lips to his in a light kiss. But he had other ideas and pulled her tighter, kissing her deeply. She couldn't help herself and responded, parting her lips and pressing her body against him.

The light over the front door suddenly came on, bathing the front garden in a bright neon glow. They sprang apart, panting and laughing while the door opened to reveal Roisin standing there, staring at them.

'Hi,' she said. 'Sorry. I thought I heard someone, so I turned on the light. For security, you know.'

'Of course,' Declan said. 'Security. Can't be too careful in this dangerous part of the country. Could have been Mad Brendan's donkey out for a stroll.'

'Very funny,' Roisin snapped.

'But I forget my manners,' Declan said unperturbed. 'Hello, Roisin. How are you this fine evening?'

'I'm grand, thanks. Are you coming in, Cordelia?'

'Yes, I am.' Cordelia walked across the gravel to the front steps. 'Bye, Declan,' she said over her shoulder. 'Thanks again.'

'The pleasure was all mine, darlin',' Declan replied. 'Goodnight and sleep tight. Both of you.' He got into the car, slammed the door shut and started the engine.

Roisin looked at the car disappearing into the darkness. 'I suppose he was charm personified all day.'

'We had a good time,' Cordelia replied, taken aback by the sarcasm in Roisin's voice. She pulled the door open. 'I'm going to bed. I'm sorry I didn't get back in time to update the website. I'll get up early tomorrow morning to do it before breakfast.'

'Terrific.' Roisin followed Cordelia inside and closed the door before making her way up the stairs, leaving Cordelia standing in the dark hall, wondering what was biting Roisin. She'd been very snappy with Declan and curt to Cordelia. Was she sad that her friendship – or whatever it had been with Declan – seemed to be over? Or maybe she was just being protective, in which case it felt good that a family member was worried about her like this.

Cordelia walked down the long corridor, deciding to leave it alone. She had bigger problems to sort out that didn't look as if they would ever be resolved. Who was her mother's real father? What had happened between her and Jimmy Fitz to make Frances leave for America and never to come back?

Chapter Sixteen

Declan left for Dublin the following day. He sent a brief text message to Cordelia saying he'd always remember their day together. That felt like some kind of goodbye to Cordelia, as if their day together had been lovely but that was all it was going to be: a nice memory. He didn't say when he'd be back, but she was sure he'd be in touch to let her know if he found out something that might cast a light on her mother's parentage. Even if he didn't want to embark on some kind of relationship, he would keep his promise to help her. At least that was something she could be sure of.

With the day she had spent with Declan and the memory of his kiss burning in her heart, Cordelia occupied herself with the day-to-day running of the guesthouse, updating the website and taking care of bookings. Roisin announced that she wanted to help with the inventory, so she and Cordelia went through the rooms, starting with the study, which had once been a small library. The walls were lined with shelves crammed with old leather-bound books, which had taken a while to go through as they kept finding gems: early editions of classics by Dickens and Jane Austen and even George Bernard Shaw. Those books were put aside until they could decide what to do with them.

'Incredible,' Roisin declared. 'I had no idea they were here. I never really looked at any of these dusty old books. I used to read Enid Blyton and later Agatha Christie that I found in Phil and Uncle Joe's bookshelf upstairs.'

But Cordelia was more fascinated by the names written in some of the books by family members who had owned them. She found a few that had belonged to Brian and Olive McKenna, some with Phil's and Patrick's names and even a copy of *Gone with the Wind* with 'Clodagh Brennan' written on the title page, which made her gasp. She showed it to Roisin. 'Look, my grandmother.'

Roisin looked at the name and nodded. 'Must be. You should keep that one and any others you can find with her name in it.'

But there had been no more and they finished the inventory of the study and decided to move on to the dining room next, when Maeve could join them. Cordelia put the book away in her room, often opening it and running her finger over the name written in neat handwriting. She was now desperate to find out what had happened to her grandmother and why her husband had not recognised her mother as his child. It seemed more and more urgent and she hoped she'd hear from Declan soon. She found great solace in the work she had to do and managed to push her thoughts of him away during most of those busy days.

It was the end of August and the busiest time of the season, so there wasn't much opportunity to brood. The guesthouse was fully booked every day and cooking breakfast, tidying up and greeting new guests was all she had time for. Maeve and Roisin were supposed to run the guesthouse on their own, but Cordelia was often called on to help out when things got hectic. Roisin was a strict taskmaster but she put in as much work as anyone else which made it all fair and square, as Kathleen put it.

The inventory had to be done in bits and pieces but after the dining room – with its huge amount of china and glassware – was finished, the bulk of it was done and only the living room remained, which would be more fun than hard work, Roisin declared. Despite all this, Cordelia managed to get down to the beach for a swim or a walk most days, usually in the early afternoon when things were reasonably quiet and guests were out sightseeing, swimming or walking. She even managed to get away to meet Sally one evening at her house for 'a chat, beer, sausages and mash', as Sally put it.

Sally's charming centuries-old cottage was just off the main street, on a slight incline, surrounded by a beautiful garden crammed with hydrangeas and other flowering shrubs. A meandering path led to the red front door, where a sign said 'Journey's End'. The door was half open, and Cordelia peered in, not sure she could just walk in. She rang the doorbell and the chimes echoed through the house without a reply. 'Out here,' a voice shouted from the side of the house and Cordelia walked around the corner to discover a patio with wooden chairs and a round table where Sally was lighting a barbecue.

She turned around. 'Hi. Just getting this going. Thought we'd barbecue some sausages and stuff. Sausage and mash seemed a little boring on a night like tonight. I asked Nuala to come around but she won't be here until later.' Sally gestured at the garden table and the rows of bottles. 'Grab yourself a beer and we'll sit down and have a chat while we wait.'

Cordelia took a bottle of Harp and sat down at the table, admiring the sweeping views of the cliffs and the ocean. Up here, she could see the whole village all the way to where the roof of Willow House was sticking up above the trees. Maeve's cottage could be seen in the distance and she noticed a plume of smoke from the chimney. 'Maeve's just lit the fire,' she said.

Sally followed her gaze. 'Yes. And I can see Paschal walking up from the beach with little Aisling in his arms. Or at least I think that's them. Father and child. So lovely.' She sighed and sat down at the table, sipping beer from her bottle. 'Seems like a hundred years since my own little girl was that age. And my husband...' She smiled. 'In those days I thought nothing would ever change and that I'd always be married to the man I loved.'

'You still love him, don't you?' Cordelia said softly.

Sally nodded. 'Yes. Can't stop myself, even if he didn't behave so well in the end. He didn't cheat on me, but he left me high and dry with nothing to live on, except the child support. I suddenly had very little money, which was hard to get used to. But at least I had the apartment, which he was decent enough to put in my name. Lovely four-room place on the Left Bank overlooking the Seine. We lived there, Jasmine and I, until she was eighteen and left to go to university in Toulouse and live with her father.' Sally shrugged.

'What did you do when your husband left?' Cordelia asked. 'For a living, I mean.'

'I got a job with an haute couture house, first as an assistant and then later organising their fashion shows. I also worked a little in marketing and advised on some of the designs. I loved my job and my life. It was fun and interesting and I met a lot of people. And of course, I had a boyfriend or two, glamorous men who were fun to be with. Paris twenty years ago was wonderful. But then later, it became less so with all the violence and terrorism. Like all big cities these days. My mother had retired and lived in this house with a bunch of women her age. They were very happy here. I visited often and then moved here when Mum died last year. She left me this house. I had sold the apartment which made me a lot of money and I used it to buy the shop. So here I am back where I began.'

'And the glamorous men?' Cordelia couldn't help asking.

Sally let out a laugh. 'Oh, them. They were just arm candy, really. Nothing serious but sweet while it lasted. I waved goodbye to François and Jean and Philippe and all the hunks of my past and came home.' Sally smiled like a contented cat. 'But of course I think about them from time to time and enjoy the memories.'

She sighed happily and glanced at the barbecue. 'Nearly ready. Oh, and by the way,' she continued, 'I must thank you for that Magic Shop tip. Telling me about that little shop in New Jersey and how they go around markets and craft fairs and get things to sell on in their own shop really inspired me. I went around to the markets and little stores around Kerry last Monday when the shop was closed. I've picked up some amazing bits and pieces and they are selling like crazy. More and more people are coming in to look from all kinds of far-away places, all the way from Cork and even Limerick. I've set up a Facebook page and I drop my card all over the place wherever I've been. My shop is hopping with customers right now. I feel that the decision to buy the shop was the perfect choice for me after all the turmoil.'

'And now you're happy?'

Sally nodded and put her bottle on the table. 'Happy? Content, I'd call it. A feeling of having landed at last. There's no such thing as lasting happiness, really. Only happy moments, and I have lots of those. And men? Who needs them? They're a load of trouble and very demanding as they grow older.' Sally studied Cordelia with a serious look in her eyes. 'I know you're falling in love right now, and that's such an incredible feeling.'

'What do you mean?' Cordelia asked, shocked at this comment. Was it so obvious?

Sally laughed. 'Oh, please. Don't deny it. It shows in your eyes when you mention his name.'

'Oh.' Cordelia felt her face flush.

'And Declan is probably just as smitten with you,' Sally continued. 'And I don't blame him. You're gorgeous and sweet and smart. But do remember one thing: you should never lean on a man, or depend on him. Stand on your own two feet and stick to your guns, never agree to anything you don't feel is right for *you*. Women have a habit of adjusting their lives to suit the men they're in love with and that will always end in tears.'

'I never thought of that,' Cordelia said with a shiver. 'But I'm sure you're right.'

Sally laughed. 'OK, I'll stop now. I can see I'm scaring you.'

Cordelia looked back at Sally while she digested what she had just said. 'No, you're not. And you're right. It's easy to fall into that traditional trap. Women are still thinking that way and letting men decide for them. I think that's what might have happened with my parents. My mother was strong and independent and I'm sure my father wanted her to comply with his will and his decisions. But she didn't, so he left. I remember her being sad and often crying in bed when she thought I was asleep. But that stopped after a while and then we were this happy little family. Mom went out on dates sometimes and I have a faint memory of her having a relationship with a man called Ralph for a while. But that ended and then there were no more men, except for friends and acquaintances.' She sighed and took a swig from her bottle. 'Ah, Mom, she was so special. So strong and gentle at the same time.'

'Like Phil,' Sally said. 'Hey, have you found out anything? About your Irish family?'

'Not yet. But Declan's gone to Dublin and he's looking up some stuff for me.'

'You should go there. To Dublin. Look around yourself. See if you can find anyone who knew them in the area where they lived.'

'Oh?' Cordelia stared at Sally. 'Go to Dublin?' Her heart started to beat faster at the thought. Of course she had to go and see what she could find out herself. This was her quest, her pursuit to find that missing piece of her identity. She couldn't leave it entirely to someone else. 'I should go. I can ask for a few days off after the weekend.'

Sally let out a derisory snort. 'Gee, you'd think they were employing you, instead of you being a part-owner. Just say you're going and that's it. Don't be a doormat. I like those girls, but they're a little too precious sometimes, especially Roisin. Phil spoilt them rotten. Maybe she knew that and gave you a part of the estate because of it? She might have thought you'd teach them the sun doesn't actually shine out of their behinds.' She suddenly looked contrite. 'I don't mean to make them sound mean or anything, they're lovely women and very fair, but there is that unshakeable McKenna confidence about them.'

Cordelia couldn't help but giggle, even though she was a little shocked at Sally's words. But there was a grain of truth in it. Maeve and Roisin were lovely and had been very friendly and helpful, accepting her as part of the extended family despite the question mark about her mother. But there was that touch of assumed royalty about them and that slight feeling of Cordelia not quite making the cut in their eyes. Maybe she was right, she thought, watching as Sally put hamburgers on the barbecue. It was time to put her foot down and not be the nice doormat she had become...

'I'm going to Dublin on Monday,' Cordelia announced as she and Roisin were sitting in the office doing the accounts on Saturday evening.

Roisin looked up from the receipts and stared at Cordelia. 'Dublin? Why?'

'I want to go and look around and see if I can find something out about my grandparents. Walk around Ranelagh.'

'What could you possibly find out? They lived there over fifty years ago. Clodagh Brennan died in the seventies, and...' She stopped. 'Is Jimmy Fitz still around?' She shook her head. 'No idea, but he must be dead. There'd be nobody around who'd remember them.'

'I just want to go there,' Cordelia insisted. 'Walk the streets and look at the houses in the part of Dublin where my mother grew up. Maybe go and see her school and...'

Roisin sighed. 'I see. But that'll be a bit of a pain for us. This is the busiest time of the season, coming to the end of August and all. And we haven't finished the inventory. The living room still has to be done, and there are a lot of things to go through.'

'I know. But you'll just have to manage. We can leave the living room until I come back.' Cordelia straightened her back and gave Roisin a steely look. 'I've been working hard since I came here – you were sick and Maeve had her hands full with little Aisling, so I did what I could. But now you're better and can get back to doing what you did before. And Maeve can, too. Paschal's on leave so he can help out with Aisling. Your husband and the boys will be back at the end of the week, and when they do, why not get them to help, too?'

Roisin looked slightly shell-shocked. 'Oh, well… yeah.'

Cordelia jumped up from her chair. 'Great. I'm going to make a cup of tea. You want one?'

'Yes, please,' Roisin said, still looking stunned.

'OK. I'll bring it in and then we can finish the accounts. Tomorrow will be busy as we're full tonight. Loads of pancakes to make. They're getting very popular.'

'Who's going to make them when you're gone?' Roisin asked.

'Maybe you can? I'll give you the recipe. It's easy, really, but hard work when there are a lot to make. You'll have to use two frying pans, and then there'll be the full Irish breakfasts. But you'll manage, just like everything else you do so well around here.'

'I'm good at the paperwork. But housework and pancakes…'

'Ah come on, Roisin. A smart woman like you will whizz through it in no time,' Cordelia breezed on, secretly enjoying Roisin's discomfort. She shot Roisin a cheery smile and went to make the tea.

Her heart sang as she thought of her trip to Dublin. Sally had promised to drive her to the train in Killarney and she had booked into a B&B in Ranelagh, which she knew she could reach by the tram called Luas. She hadn't told Declan she was coming yet, but she'd call him later that night to tell him. Things were looking up. She still didn't know what her future held, but during the next few days, she might get started on the trail of her mother's past.

Declan saved her the trouble of calling him when he called himself as Cordelia walked on the beach to watch the sun set behind the Skelligs. It was a calm, cool evening with the promise of a chilly night. The sea lay like a mirror and the sun had already started to sink behind the islands. Cordelia sat down on a piece of driftwood and looked out over the bay, lost in the lovely view. She gave a start as her phone rang in the pocket of her jacket and she hauled it out and looked at the caller ID. Declan.

'Hi!' she chortled. 'I was just going to call you. Guess what?'

'No, you guess,' he interrupted, breathless with excitement. 'You'll never believe it.'

'Believe what?'

'That I've found him.'

'Who?'

'Jimmy Fitz.'

Chapter Seventeen

Dublin was busy, noisy and crowded. Not like New York, but the noise and hustle and bustle of Heuston station was a still little unnerving after the peace and quiet of Sandy Cove. Cordelia stood on the platform for a while to get her bearings while all around her people were hurrying towards the exit. Then she walked on, through the turnstile, into the big hall and out through the entrance doors, where she could see the trams arriving at the platform. In true New York fashion, she grabbed her small suitcase and ran, pushing into the packed carriage just as the doors closed. Panting, she smiled at a man who offered her his seat. 'Thank you,' she said, smiling gratefully, trying her best to manoeuvre the suitcase so it wouldn't block anyone.

He returned her smile, then nodded. 'You're welcome, darlin'. Going far?'

'To Ranelagh,' she said, wondering if she should really be talking to a stranger like this. But he was quite old with grey hair and a kind glint in his pale blue eyes.

'Then you have to change at Abbey Street,' he said. 'Get off at Wynn's Hotel and then it's just up the next street. That line will take you straight to Ranelagh.'

'Great. Thanks. Is this tram always so crowded?'

'Usually, yes,' he replied. 'But not this bad. The Dublin Horse Show is on this week, so lots of people come up from the country. I bet the train was pretty packed too.'

'Yes. But I managed to get a seat by the window. Are you going to the horse show?' she asked.

He laughed. 'Nah, I'm not one of them people from the horsey set. Not interested in show jumping and dressage and whatever else those fancy lads get up to. I have a bit of a flutter at the Curragh during the Irish derby from time to time though. That's our most famous racecourse,' he explained. 'We have the best racehorses in the world, you know,' he said proudly.

'So I've heard.'

'Of course you have. You from America?' he continued.

'Yes. New Jersey.'

'Ah. I have a cousin in Boston. Like most Irish people. But here's my stop,' he said as the tram slowed down and came to a halt. 'Have a grand day, my dear. And good luck.' He waved at her, got off and disappeared into the crowd.

While she looked out at the streets of Dublin, and the mishmash of old and new buildings, Cordelia turned her attention to the day ahead and that meeting. The meeting with Jimmy Fitz. How incredible that Declan, after just a few days, had managed to track down the old man. But he had been lucky, he said. He had started at the wrong end, really, and gone through the nursing homes in Dublin, instead of looking up parish records or any of the Census reports that existed since the nineteen twenties.

'That would have been a huge chore, but maybe the only way,' he said to Cordelia. 'I thought I'd have a go at nursing homes just in case and struck gold after the third one. Please don't ask how I managed to get them to reveal the names of the patients,' he added with a laugh. 'Not very ethical, I'm afraid.'

'As long as it doesn't get you into trouble,' Cordelia remarked.

'I covered my tracks quite well,' he replied.

He had wanted to meet her at the train, but she said no, she preferred to make her own way to the B&B in Ranelagh. She wanted to see Dublin and get the feel for the city on her own. This was her journey, not Declan's, even if he was the one who paved the way.

She got off the tram outside Wynn's Hotel, which looked old and Victorian, and hurried up the next street where she got on a less crowded tram that took her across the River Liffey, past Trinity College and up Dawson Street, lined with Victorian houses, shops and restaurants. At the top of the street, they went past the Mansion House, a large white wedding cake of a building, where the Lord Mayor of Dublin resided, according to her guidebook. Then onto Stephen's Green with its leafy park where people strolled around or sat on benches.

Cordelia looked around as they went down Harcourt Street with its tall Georgian buildings which would have been the townhouses of rich families centuries ago but had later been turned into offices. It was nice that the buildings had been restored instead of knocked down, she mused, admiring the façades, the pretty front doors and sash windows. There were little shops and cafés in the downstairs areas of the houses and people milled around, looking at menus or sitting down for a tea or coffee before heading home. Dublin seemed such a nice town to live and work in, with a less hectic pace than New York and a friendlier feel as people around her chatted to each other and the woman beside her smiled and asked if she knew where to get off. Cordelia told her where the B&B was and the woman told her to get off at a stop called Cowper.

They travelled through the quiet streets lined with two-storey houses inside pretty front gardens and came to Cordelia's stop in no time. To her surprise, she spotted Declan leaning against the railing, smiling at her.

'Hi,' she said, lifting her suitcase off the tram. 'How on earth did you know when I'd arrive?'

He tapped his head. 'In here lurks a detective's brain. You told me which train you'd take from Killarney and then I calculated how long it would take from Heuston to here. Your B&B is just around the corner. Good choice, by the way.' He kissed her cheek and took her case and started to walk swiftly down the street.

Cordelia half-ran behind him. 'Sally gave me the tip. It's a family-run place. She stays there when she's in Dublin.'

'You'd better be on your best behaviour then,' he teased.

'Aren't I always?' she replied primly.

'Of course you are.' He looked more serious. 'And you're here to find something very important – or someone, really.'

'Yes,' Cordelia said, butterflies dancing in her stomach. 'When do you think I can see him?'

Declan stopped and checked his watch. 'It's twenty past five. They said after tea, so that would suit. Or we can go in the morning, if you prefer to wait and catch your breath.'

'No!' Cordelia exclaimed. 'I don't want to wait. I want… I *need* to see him today. Otherwise I won't be able to sleep,' she pleaded. 'Can we go there now?'

'Yes, if we get our skates on. Let's just leave your bag at the B&B and then we'll go to the nursing home. It's about ten minutes' walk from here.'

'Great.'

They reached the B&B which was situated in a white two-storey house with a nice front garden. Cordelia rang the bell and when a woman came to the door, she explained breathlessly that she was going out on an errand but would be back later and could she leave her bag here and check in later? The woman took her bag and said she'd put it in Cordelia's room, which was number two, the second door on the left on the upstairs landing. 'I'm going to collect one of the kids from Irish dancing anyway,' she continued. 'So I won't be back until half past six. But no need to check in at all. Just make yourself at home and we'll see you in the morning for breakfast.' She handed Cordelia a set of keys. 'This is the one for the front door and this one's for the room. Have a lovely evening,' she said and shot Declan a shy smile.

They thanked her and continued down the street, Cordelia quickening her step, anxious to get to their destination as soon as possible. She looked around at the large red-brick Victorian houses with their bay windows and well-tended front gardens where cars were driving in, mothers unloading shopping and children with schoolbags. She watched them walking up the front steps, opening the door and going inside, chatting with each other, and imagined them all sitting around some kitchen table together for the evening meal.

Men and women in business suits walked from the tram, carrying briefcases and hugging their children as they arrived at the door. Families, Cordelia thought, all doing mundane things, being together and not alone like she had been. Would she ever have a family of her own? She glanced at Declan walking ahead and wondered if he had ever wanted a family. He had told her about his three failed marriages and many relationships, and she wondered if theirs would end the same way one day. Even though they hadn't known each other long and had only had that one date, she still felt such a strong pull towards him whenever they met. It was as if they were meant to be together and nothing could break them apart. But maybe that was just wishful thinking?

Cordelia pushed the thoughts away as they arrived at a large yellow one-storey building surrounded by trees and shrubs. A sign said, BRAMLEIGH LODGE NURSING HOME.

'Here we are,' Declan said. 'Nice place. Not your ordinary old folks' home – this is for old folks with a lot of cash.'

Cordelia looked at the house. 'Is it? So Jimmy Fitz is rich?'

'He was before he started paying the fees to stay here. He made a lot of money in his heyday. Owned a chain of cinemas among other things. And those dance halls that were so popular in the nineteen fifties. He's ninety-seven now and a bit shook. The nurse in charge said his nephew is managing his estate.'

'Oh,' Cordelia said, her heart beating like a hammer at the thought of meeting this man who had been married to her grandmother and might have been her own mother's stepfather. As it had said 'father unknown' on the birth certificate, Cordelia had to assume that Jimmy Fitz was not her grandfather – but who was?

Declan squeezed her hand. 'Here we go,' he said and pulled her along up the gravel path to the entrance door. 'Time to hear the truth at last.'

'OK,' Cordelia said as she walked on shaking legs, her mouth dry. 'Does he know we're coming?'

'The nurse told him someone was coming to visit. He loves visitors, apparently. Doesn't get that many.'

Cordelia suddenly stopped dead. 'Flowers,' she said, panic rising in her chest. 'I should have brought flowers or chocolates or something.'

'No need, I'm sure. He'll probably be delighted to have visitors. Or visitor, really. I think I'll let you talk to him on your own.'

'Oh, er…' Cordelia said, not sure she really wanted to be on her own with him.

'Let's see how we go.' Declan ushered her up the stairs and pushed the heavy oak door open.

They walked into a large, bright hall where there was a reception desk and a group of chairs around a table in the middle of the shining linoleum-covered floor. The place smelled faintly of furniture polish and soap, and classical music could be heard in the distance. '"Nocturnes" by Chopin,' Cordelia said absent-mindedly. She looked around. 'Where can we find him?'

A nun appeared through a door near the reception desk. 'Who are you looking for?' she asked in a pleasant voice.

'Jim Fitzgerald,' Declan replied. 'I called earlier.' He pushed Cordelia forward. 'This is his… niece who has come all the way from America to see him.'

The nun nodded. 'I see. I'll take you to him. He's waiting for you in his room.' She turned to Cordelia. 'I have to warn you that his short-term memory isn't so good. So try to be patient if he asks you the same questions over and over again. He's very frail, so you need to be gentle and not upset him in any way.'

Cordelia nodded. 'Of course.'

She nodded. 'Good. Come this way.' She proceeded to walk through the door and down a corridor, her rubber soles nearly silent on the linoleum. Cordelia tiptoed after her, glancing behind her to see if Declan was still there. He was and gave her a reassuring smile.

The nun came to a stop in front of a door and knocked gently, opening it and peering in. 'Jimmy?' she called. 'There's someone here to see you.' They could hear a muffled reply and the nun waved them inside. 'He seems to be quite alert,' she whispered. 'Have a nice visit.' She smiled and walked away, closing the door behind her.

The room was bright and airy with a French window overlooking the park. There was a bed and a night table by the opposite wall and a group of chairs by the window. A hunched figure sat in one of the chairs, facing the view. Cordelia walked forward and peered at the old man. He wore a grey cardigan and a blue blanket over his knees, his sparse white hair was neatly brushed across his pink scalp and he had a moustache above his thin mouth. His face was face covered in a myriad of wrinkles and he peered at Cordelia through rheumy blue eyes with a confused expression. 'Who are you?'

'Hello,' Cordelia said and took his bony hand. 'I'm…' She stopped and looked at Declan for help. But Declan shrugged and made a gesture with his hand.

Cordelia sat down on the edge of a chair opposite the old man. 'I'm here from America,' she started, not knowing what else to say.

The old man gave a start. 'America? I don't know anyone there. Do I?' He looked at her as if trying to remember something. 'Except,' he continued, 'a girl called Frances who went there long ago. Are you Frances?'

'No,' Cordelia said. 'I'm Cordelia, her daughter.'

'Daughter?' Jimmy said. 'I don't have a daughter. *She* wasn't mine, you know.'

'Yes, I know,' Cordelia whispered, barely able to speak. Here was the confirmation of her suspicions. She had felt in her bones that this must be the explanation of what it said on the birth certificate. 'Father unknown' echoed through her mind as she stared at the old man. 'But whose child was she if she wasn't yours?' she finally managed to ask.

'What?' Jimmy asked. 'Speak up, girl. What time is it? Can we have tea?'

'I'll get you both some tea,' Declan offered. He nodded at Cordelia and left.

'Who was that?' Jimmy asked. 'My bloody nephew? No good, that boy. Always slacking off. Do you know him?'

'No,' Cordelia said, desperately trying to think of how to get him back on track. 'I just came here from America. I'd like to ask you some things about my mother and my grandmother.'

'Who?' Jimmy coughed and took a handkerchief from his pocket and wiped his eyes. 'Your mother, you said? Who is she?'

'Frances,' Cordelia said. 'Frances Brennan. Like your wife, who was Clodagh Brennan, wasn't she?'

Jimmy nodded. 'She was. Fine woman. Died young, poor thing.' He leaned forward. 'Wouldn't take my name, the stubborn girl. Even though I *saved* her,' he hissed.

'Saved her from what?' Cordelia asked, recoiling slightly. She felt he was derailing from the point she was trying to make.

'From the shame,' Jimmy replied. 'The shame of being an unmarried mother.'

'Oh.'

'Yeah.' He sat back and nodded. 'She was already pregnant when we met, you see.'

Cordelia stared at him. So Clodagh had already been pregnant with Frances when she met Jimmy Fitz. Had he married her knowing this? She suddenly knew she had to hear the story from the start. 'How did you meet Clodagh?' she asked.

Suddenly, it was if saying the name had triggered something in the old man's brain and he looked straight at Cordelia, his eyes clear. 'Clodagh,' he said. 'My darling wife. How did I meet her? Oh well,' he began, looking wistfully at Cordelia. 'That's something I will never forget. I was on holiday in Clifden. That's a village in County Galway. Pretty seaside place. I was in this café one beautiful morning in June when I struck up a conversation with this pretty girl at a table next to mine. We chatted about the weather and such and found we were both from the same part of Dublin. She was a teacher in a Gaelscoil in Rathmines.'

'Gaelscoil?' Cordelia asked. 'Does that mean an Irish-speaking school?'

Jimmy nodded. 'That's the lad. Anyway... Where was I?'

Cordelia smiled. 'In Clifden with Clodagh Brennan.'

'Oh yes. That's right.' His eyes softened. 'She was a lovely girl, you know. Dark hair and the brightest blue eyes I had ever seen. And a smile to charm the birds out of the trees.' He sighed. 'I fell for all of that, and her laugh and her lovely voice and her soft skin. And the way we talked and joked… I felt I could have sat there all day talking to her.' He shook his head. 'Love like I've never felt before, you know? That feeling of… of just clicking and getting on and seeing the world through the same eyes. You know what I mean, girl?'

'I think so,' Cordelia said, Declan popping into her mind. She had felt the same way about him the moment they met.

Jimmy rubbed his eyes. 'Yes. That's the way it was. But then, a few days later, when we sat on the beach, she told me about the baby. And that it was the result of a brief affair with a married man. She was staying with relatives and would have to have the baby adopted when it was born. But she said she was planning to keep it. She supposed I wouldn't want to know her after that. It was a great shame in those days, and she wasn't sure what she was going to do. Going to England for an abortion wasn't an option for her. She was fiercely Catholic and felt she had committed a great sin. That guilt would stay with her for the rest of her life.'

'How did you feel about it?'

Jimmy thought for a moment. 'I was shocked at first. Felt like leaving her there on the beach with her great shame. It wasn't my problem. But then… I stayed and we talked and… I couldn't help myself. We had known each other three days, but I loved her already. I said I'd marry her as soon as we could organise it. She… she started to cry. And then she said she couldn't accept. But then later, when I insisted, we talked some more and she finally agreed to marry me. She said she wouldn't expect me to recognise the child and put my name on the birth certificate as the father. That would be a lie, she said. So I didn't.' He paused. 'Not very gentlemanly, was it?'

'But honest,' Cordelia said.

He nodded. 'I suppose. I hope it hasn't caused you any problems.'

'Not for me, but maybe for Frances. My mother.'

'Frances is your mother?' He leaned forward and peered at her. 'You don't look much like her. Except for the colour of your eyes. Exactly the same as Frances – and Clodagh.' He sat back and wiped his eyes with the back of his hand. 'We were happy, you know. One happy little family in that house in Ranelagh. Thirty-two Cherry Lane. Because of the cherry trees.'

'Sounds lovely.'

'It was.' He gazed at her with a far-away look in his pale eyes. 'Until she died and I had to look after Frances. She was fifteen and had turned into a pretty girl. Loved her music. I paid for her to go to the Music Academy. And then she wanted to study in America. So we applied for a passport. That was the first time she had seen her birth certificate. And then she found out. About me not being her father. It was a great shock to her. She was angry with me and with her dead mother. She demanded to know who her father was, but I refused to tell her. I couldn't bring myself to say that name and to reveal that her late mother, who she had adored had had an affair with... with—' He stopped abruptly, his face suddenly red. 'It would have been too much for the poor girl. But she kept asking and I kept refusing and then she went to America and I never heard from her again.' He drew breath. 'But here you are, my dear.'

'Yes,' Cordelia whispered, not knowing who he thought she was. His mind seemed to wander all the time, which was probably normal for someone that age. She put her hand on his bony knee. 'Do you feel all right? Shall I call a nurse?' She was dying to find out more, to ask him to tell her who Clodagh's lover had been, but he seemed suddenly so frail, as if telling her his story had exhausted him. It seemed unfair to push him further.

'Yes,' he mumbled. 'Please get Sister Attracta. She's nice. She'll help me get into bed.'

Cordelia got up. 'I'll call her. It was nice meeting you, Jimmy.'

'Lovely to see you again, Frances, darlin'. Will you come and see me again?'

'I… Yes, I will,' Cordelia promised, suddenly dying to get out of there, out into the fresh air and away from the smell of the nursing home. There was one piece missing in the story, but she had a feeling old Jimmy wouldn't be able to tell her who the father of Clodagh's baby had been. He seemed too exhausted to talk further. It was frustrating but she could visit him another day when he was feeling better. 'Goodbye for now,' she said.

He nodded. 'Bye, dear girl.' She was about to walk away, when he grabbed her hand. 'Just one thing,' he wheezed.

Cordelia stopped. 'Yes?'

'That man… your father. You deserve to know the truth at last, Frances.'

Cordelia's heart flipped. 'Who was he?'

Jimmy made a gesture with his hand for her to come closer. 'Nobody knows except me, you see.'

Cordelia leaned down so her ear was close to his mouth. 'Tell me,' she whispered.

And then he softly said a name. A name she had heard before, a name she hadn't expected.

Cordelia gasped, pulled back and stared at him. It couldn't be true. Her grandfather was— No, it couldn't be. Not possible. Cordelia suddenly felt sick. Without a word, she walked out of the room, her knees like jelly, that name echoing through her mind.

Chapter Eighteen

Declan met her halfway down the corridor. He took a look at her face and ran to catch her as she nearly fell. 'What happened?' he asked. 'You're as white as a sheet.'

'Jimmy,' she stammered, hanging on his arm. 'Get that nurse – nun, or whatever she is.'

'Is he dead?'

Cordelia shook her head. 'No. But he needs help to go to bed.'

'Oh. OK. We'll ask at reception.' He looked at her. 'But why are you in such a state?'

Cordelia felt unable to speak. 'Take me out of here,' she croaked. 'I need air. I need to sit down, I need—'

'OK. There's a bench in the garden. I'll take you there.' He half-carried her down the corridor, across the entrance hall and out through the door, down the steps and across the gravel. They came to a quiet corner of the garden and Declan led her to a bench in front of a flower bed and helped her sit down. 'There.'

'Thank you,' she whispered and closed her eyes for a moment, taking deep gulps of the rose-scented air. Felling slightly better, she opened her eyes. 'Could you get me some water?'

'I will. I'll go back to the reception area. There's a dispenser with bottles of water there. And I'll get that nun to take care of old Jimmy. Are you OK?'

She nodded. 'I'm fine. I need to be on my own for a bit.'

'Of course. I'll get you the water.'

'Thanks.' Her mind still reeling with shock, she watched him walk away. Then she was alone and had a chance to take stock of what she had just heard. She knew Jimmy wasn't her grandfather, had known it in her heart for some time. She had thought Jimmy wouldn't know either, and that Clodagh had never revealed the name of her child's father to anyone. But obviously she had told Jimmy. Cordelia had no doubt that what he had told her was the truth, the truth that she had been looking for, the missing piece of the jigsaw of her mother's past. And her own. But… Oh God, how was she going to handle this? Who should she tell? Or should she keep it to herself? But how could she?

When Declan came back with a bottle of water she had calmed down, and could focus on drinking it and eating a slice of cake he had bought in the cafeteria. She realised she hadn't eaten since lunchtime when she had bought a sandwich on the train. She wolfed down the cake and smiled at Declan, feeling instantly better. 'Thanks. I needed that.'

'Thought so.' He kept looking at her with concern. 'Are you OK? You seem to have heard something shocking.'

She nodded and drank some water. 'Yes.' She met his gaze and wondered if she should tell him. Was this something she should keep quiet about? She did trust Declan, who had supported her through all of this, but what she had just found out might be too sensitive to share with someone outside the family. Then she suddenly felt she had to tell someone; this was too heavy to carry alone. 'It was about my grandfather,' she started. 'My real grandfather, I mean. Jimmy told me who he was. I thought he didn't know, but Clodagh – my grandmother – must have told him.' She drew in a ragged breath. 'Oh God, I can't believe I heard it. Can't believe that…'

Declan put his arm around her. 'You don't have to tell me if you don't want to.'

She pulled away and stared at him. 'But I do. I have to tell someone, or I'll explode. I don't know what to do about this either.'

He took her hand. 'OK. Tell me when you're ready. No rush.'

Cordelia put her hands on her hot cheeks and closed her eyes. 'This must be a nightmare.' She opened her eyes and looked at him again. 'My grandfather was… Brian McKenna. Roisin and Maeve's grandfather. Which means my grandmother had an affair with her own sister's husband.'

Declan gulped. 'Holy mother. Really?'

'Yes, really.'

Declan looked at her for a long time before he spoke. 'Bloody hell, what a mess. OK, so then, that means Phil and your mother were…'

'Sisters. Or half-sisters.' Cordelia shook her head in disbelief. 'Nobody could have known. Or maybe Olive, the sister, did? Was that why they fell out? And did Mom know but never told me or anyone?' She sighed deeply. 'Nobody knows what really happened. They're all dead. Phil can't have known or she would have said something. All I know is that her father was "a bit of a lad" as Sally put it. A philanderer, in other words. Cheated on his wife right, left and centre. Poor Olive, that can't have been easy. But why didn't she leave him?'

'In nineteen fifties Ireland?' Declan said. 'That couldn't happen. Divorce was illegal and the stigma would have been enormous, especially for the children.'

'So my grandmother had an affair with her brother-in-law, got pregnant and went to Clifden in the west of Ireland to have the baby,' Cordelia said as if to herself, 'and then she fell in love with Jimmy Fitz… My mother only found out Jimmy wasn't her biological father when she applied for a passport to go to America. Did she learn only then who he actually was? Or did she never know? Is that why she called herself by her mother's maiden name?' Cordelia put her hands over her face. 'So many questions that will never be answered. Oh, I wish I never started this search. I should have left it alone. I wanted to find out the truth. And then the McKennas started worrying that I wasn't really part of the family and Maeve and Roisin's mother said we had to do a DNA test. So I thought I'd see if I could get proof some other way.' Cordelia drew breath.

Declan let out a snort. 'Well, the DNA test will prove you're related to them all right. I bet all three of you have very similar genes. You should do it.'

'I don't want to.' Cordelia looked at Declan for help. 'But what should I do? Tell Maeve and Roisin about this? It's their grandfather, after all.'

Declan shrugged. 'I don't know. You have no proof, only Jimmy's word. Would it affect the will?'

'No.'

'Maybe let sleeping dogs lie, then.'

'I'm not sure. It's hard to carry this on my own. And in any case, it means we're first cousins in a way.'

'In every way.' He shook his head. 'What a dilemma. But you don't have to tell them anything yet. Let's go and have dinner, a glass of wine and then you'll go back to the B&B and try to sleep. Everything will look better in the morning.'

'How could it?' Cordelia asked bitterly. 'Nothing can change the facts.'

'No, of course not. But it's what you'll do about it that matters. Tomorrow you will think more clearly.'

Cordelia nodded. But she had already come to a decision.

They had dinner in a gastropub in Blackrock, a suburb by the sea. It was a beautiful late summer evening with light breezes and a calm sea. The tide was out and people were walking on the beach all the way to the water's edge. The sea stretched to the horizon where a long line of cargo ships rode at anchor waiting for the tide to turn. Howth Head, the headland across Dublin Bay, could be seen clearly and the lighthouse on top of the cliff reminded Cordelia of the one in Sandy Cove. The sun dipped behind the mountains to the west, casting a golden glow on the sea and the coastline.

Cordelia found it hard to concentrate on her surroundings while she slowly ate fish and chips and sipped a glass of Pinot Grigio Declan had insisted she needed. He drank only water as he was driving but seemed to enjoy the meal while he tried to distract Cordelia with anecdotes from his past as a journalist. She nodded and smiled, her mind far away but appreciating his kindness and his attempt at cheering her up. She looked fondly at him and felt lucky that he was with her.

He looked up and smiled as their eyes met. 'A penny for your thoughts.'

Cordelia smiled. 'Oh, I was just thinking. Mulling things over, you know. I find it hard to talk about this right now.' She looked out the window, suddenly noticing the nice view. 'This is a pretty part of Dublin. It seems such a great place to live. Why did you move?'

He laughed. 'You've only seen the good parts. There is an ugly underbelly to this town. The traffic is terrible and housing is impossibly expensive. My mother has a one-bedroom flat in Dundrum and I can stay there while she's away. I sold my flat and bought my entire house in Sandy Cove for nearly the same amount. Besides, why live in a city if you don't have to?'

'I guess you're right. And now that I've lived in Sandy Cove for nearly a month, I never want to leave. But of course I haven't seen it in the winter.'

'It's not that bad. Lots of storms and heavy rain but it's often nice and mild. It can rain for days on end but you get used to it. The trick is to have something to do. I have my writing job and the radio slot once a week. And Killarney and Cork are near should I yearn for a bit of entertainment.'

'I loved hearing you on the radio.'

'You might be the only listener.' He took her hand. 'But let's talk about us. You and me. You're so quiet tonight and things are so confused for you right now. But I can't help wondering if some of that has anything to do with me. Has it?'

'It's not you, it's just that everything is getting on top of me. The house, Roisin and Maeve, the will, my mother and now my grandfather. I think I need a little space now, to come to terms with everything and plan my life. So,' she continued with a little sigh. 'I feel we have to take a break for a while.' She looked at him, surprised by the words that had come out of her mouth. When they first met, the attraction between them was undeniable, and she had longed to fall into Declan's arms. But with all that had happened lately, she suddenly felt she couldn't deal with a romantic relationship at the same time as she was trying to cope with the latest revelations. 'It's not anything to do with you, Declan, It's just that I…'

He let go of her hand and laughed. 'That old "It's not you, it's me," you mean?' He shook his head. 'I've heard that a few times, too.'

'No,' she protested. 'That's not what I was saying. Please try to understand.'

He sighed. 'Yeah. I do understand, of course. But I don't like it much. I've been living like a monk the past year, working hard and trying to make some sense out of my life. Last year, with Roisin, that was a bit of madness.'

Cordelia stared at Declan. 'So what happened exactly? I know it was something really bad, but no one has explained it to me in detail.'

Declan looked away for a moment while a shadow seemed to cross his face. Then he looked back at her. 'You deserve an explanation as you have been so honest with me. So…' He paused. 'I suppose we were both desperate for someone to confide in when Roisin came to Sandy Cove and I suppose I was more desperate than her. I thought she was ending things with her husband, but she wasn't, and I nearly lost her friendship by being stupid and selfish.'

'In what way?' Cordelia asked.

'We were at a social event together and there was a photo in one of the national newspapers of us. Roisin got a little tipsy and I offered her a bed in my room at the hotel. Nothing happened, of course, but the press blew it out of all proportions, me being a high-profile reporter in the not-so-distant past. Then the tabloids got ahold of it and it went kind of viral.'

'Oh God,' Cordelia exclaimed. 'How horrible.'

'Yes, it was. And what made it more horrible was that I did nothing to stop it.'

'Oh,' Cordelia said, trying to take it all in. 'But hey, maybe what you did turned out to be good in the end. You pushed them together instead of breaking them apart.'

Declan let out a laugh. 'Yeah, if you want to look at it in a Pollyanna kind of way. But sure, it's true of course. Could have been worse.' He shrugged.

'Thanks for telling me,' Cordelia whispered, his sad expression bringing her close to tears.

He looked into her eyes. 'And now you're appalled and never want to see me again.'

'No,' she protested. 'Not at all. But I do still need some space. A little time to sort all this out and to decide what I'm going to do after all these strange events have been put into proportion. So many questions need to be answered still. Will I stay here or go back to New York? Betsy left the door open and said there would always be a job for me with her. And my mother is buried in Morristown. Staying here would mean cutting all my ties with my country. I'm not sure I can do that. It's a big decision. But first of all I must decide what to do about what I have found out. Sort things out with Maeve and Roisin. And most of all, sort out my feelings about you.' Cordelia looked at Declan, willing him to understand.

Declan put his hand over hers. 'I know. And I do see that you need to deal with all this, and that's OK. You've been through a lot.'

'Yes, I have.' Cordelia blinked away tears that threatened to well up. 'There's been too much death and sadness lately.'

He touched her cheek. 'Yes. Too much for a lovely young woman. You're tired. Let's get out of here and get you back to the B&B. You need a good night's sleep.'

'I think I do.' Cordelia suddenly felt a wave of fatigue wash over her.

'I was going to Galway tomorrow to interview someone for an article before I meet my mother when she comes back to Dublin from Scotland, but I can stay, if you…'

'No. It's OK. You've done so much to help me and I'm very grateful for that. And you need to go to Galway and then see your mom. In any case, I want to be on my own for a bit. And I want to walk around Ranelagh and look at the house where my mother grew up. Then I'll take the train home.'

'And then—?'

'You mean, will I tell Maeve and Roisin?' Cordelia thought for a moment. 'I think I must.'

'They might not believe you.'

'In that case, I will do something that proves it's true.'

He looked intrigued. 'What?'

Cordelia smiled. 'I'm not going to tell you. Not yet.'

Chapter Nineteen

Sally met Cordelia at the train station in Killarney.

'So how was your trip?' she asked once they were on their way.

'Weird,' Cordelia replied. 'Overwhelming. I'm still trying to digest everything.'

'I'm sure.' Sally turned to take the road past Muckross and continued towards Sneem. 'You can tell me about it later. I have something to tell you. And a suggestion.'

'Oh?' Cordelia asked, intrigued. 'What about?'

'You'll find Willow House a bit chaotic. Cian and the boys have arrived back from their camping trip. Roisin is trying to organise them and welcome guests at the same time. I think the boys are a bit miffed at having to sleep in the same room. So we thought that you might move in with me for a bit. Would that be OK? That way Cian and Roisin can sleep in Phil's room and the boys will then have the two attic rooms. Roisin said they'd mentioned this to you a while ago.'

'Oh yes, they did. But I didn't pay much attention with all that was going on. But it's a great idea,' Cordelia said with a relieved sigh. It would be nice to be away from Maeve and Roisin and it would give her a chance to take stock of everything away from the family. 'Thank you so much, Sally. I'd love to stay with you.'

'Good. We'll go there first so you can collect your things and then head over to my place.'

'Great. Your place is so close that I can easily walk over to the house in the mornings to help out with breakfast and do the inventory with Maeve and Roisin.'

'Exactly. That's all settled, then.'

'In the best possible way.'

They had a pleasant drive along the coast and didn't talk much other than comments about the weather and the busy holiday traffic, Sally complaining loudly about the state of the roads.

Cordelia's thoughts turned to her morning in Dublin, when she had walked around Ranelagh and stood outside the house where her mother had grown up. It was a red-brick Victorian house like all the others in that street with bay windows and a front garden with rose bushes and a large oak from which hung an old swing. Cordelia wondered if her mother had sat on that swing as a child, but maybe not as it would have been sixty years ago – any swing would have rotted by now. She looked up at the top windows and wondered which room had been her mother's and tried to imagine what the house had looked like in the nineteen fifties. Then she had walked on around the corner and found a primary school where Frances would have gone before she went to secondary school at Loreto College in St Stephen's Green. She promised herself to go and look at it before she took the Luas to Heuston station to go back to Sandy Cove. But there had been no time as she risked missing her train, so she made a mental note to go and see it next time she was in Dublin.

It had been nice to walk in her mother's shoes for a while through the leafy streets where she had grown up. It would have been even nicer if they could have done it together, Cordelia thought with a dart of sadness, trying not to feel resentful that she hadn't been told anything about her mother's childhood or how she had found out that Jimmy wasn't her father. But she'd been reticent, a very private person and also someone who always said she preferred to look forward and not carry grudges. Cordelia had thought she was talking about her failed marriage and her errant husband, but maybe she had also meant what had happened in Ireland? Cordelia sighed. There were some similarities to her own fatherless childhood that they could have shared. But now it was too late. She would never find out.

Sally glanced at Cordelia. 'That was a deep sigh. Feeling sad and lonely?'

Cordelia smiled. 'A little. I walked around the streets where my mother grew up and looked at the house. It was nice even if it made me feel sad.'

'Of course it did.' Sally slowed down and turned into the lane. 'But here we are, nearly at Willow House. I'll help you pack your stuff while you talk to Roisin. Maeve's gone to Cork to meet a client and Paschal's minding Aisling. Everybody's busy.'

Cordelia was grateful that Roisin was occupied settling the boys in. Two guests had appeared and Cordelia helped them check in while Sally went to her room to start packing whatever Cordelia would need for the next few days. She'd get the rest later when she had decided if she wanted to stay. But the house was big and Sally had said she'd be delighted with the company.

Roisin looked up from the computer when Cordelia came into the office. 'Hi. How was Dublin?'

'Great,' Cordelia replied. 'It's a nice town. I met up with Declan and he showed me around. We had dinner in a nice place in Blackrock.'

'And you were able to do a little research, too?' Roisin's question hung on the air as Cordelia met her gaze.

'Eh, yes. I saw the house where my mother grew up. And I met someone who knew her.'

Roisin's eyes widened. 'You did? What did they say?'

'It's a long story. Maybe later?'

'Definitely,' Roisin said with a laugh and switched off the computer. 'I have to sort out the boys and move Cian and me into your bedroom. Thanks for moving out, by the way. It doesn't seem fair but right now it's a life saver. The boys have another two weeks until they go back to school and then we get access to the house we've bought when the sale closes in September. So things will settle down then and you can move back in here.'

'No problem,' Cordelia said, smiling. 'I knew you couldn't squash three teenagers into one room. And you and Cian would have to share a bathroom with them. A total nightmare, I can imagine.'

'Oh yes,' Roisin said with a sigh. She focused on Cordelia. 'So you met Declan in Dublin? And had dinner with him and all?'

'Yes.'

'So you're… together then? Dating?'

'Not really.' Cordelia hesitated. 'We're just friends for the moment. I'm not in the mood for romance right now, to be honest. Nothing to do with Declan. He's been terrific.'

'That's very wise,' Roisin said approvingly. 'Rushing into things with a man is never a good idea. But who am I to talk? I fell in love and into bed with Cian straight away.'

Cordelia laughed. 'Ah but you were so young. And it all worked out and you're still happy together.'

Roisin smiled. 'Yes, we are. Happier than ever as we grow older and wiser. But still… It doesn't hurt to be careful. Especially with…' She stopped. 'I'm sorry if I've been a little snappy about Declan.'

Cordelia put her hand on Roisin's arm. 'He told me what happened. I understand why you were a little tense and that you were worried about me. No need to go over it again.'

'No need at all. What a relief.' Roisin squeezed Cordelia's hand and got up from the desk. 'Case closed, I think. I have to go and sort out the lads upstairs. The guests have all arrived so there's nothing to worry about. Have a nice evening with Sally and then I'll see you in the morning.'

'I'll be here at seven thirty to start breakfast. And then we can get started on the living room for the inventory.'

'Great. See you then.' Roisin smiled and walked out and Cordelia went to her bedroom where Sally had put her laptop in its bag and gathered together some of the things she thought Cordelia would want to bring. 'I started packing your clothes that were hanging in the wardrobe. Roisin will want some space for her own and Cian's.' She gestured at the open wardrobe. 'I can see some of Phil's amazing Paris collection in there. Takes me back to the glory days. How nice that she kept it all.'

'Yeah, but it's a little sad to see the clothes she wore. But we're going to share it between us when the probate comes through.'

Sally nodded. 'That's nice.' She pointed across the room. 'Hey, I took everything in the top drawer of the chest of drawers and put it in that carrier bag. That was all yours, wasn't it?'

'Yes. Thanks. Just my toiletries and underwear and my swimsuit left.'

'Great. I'll take what I've packed to my car and wait for you there.'

'Thanks. I won't be long,' Cordelia said and went to the bathroom. She gathered her toiletries and make-up bag and then packed the last of her clothes into her suitcase. She took a last look around the room wondering if she'd ever sleep here again. She hoped she would, as she now felt more connected to Willow House and the McKennas than ever. She was one of them and McKenna blood flowed through her veins. But telling them about what she had found out would be a huge bombshell and she wasn't sure she could bring herself to do it.

Later that night, after a delicious poulet *basquaise* – or chicken casserole in a tomato-based sauce – Cordelia and Sally sat on the terrace watching the sunset and talking.

'Fantastic dinner,' Cordelia said.

'I love cooking and now I have you to cook for. I went to cordon bleu cookery classes in Paris and learned all about French cuisine. So you'll be eating your way through my repertoire while you're here.' Sally held her glass of red aloft. 'Cheers, by the way. And welcome to my humble abode.'

'Not so humble,' Cordelia protested and glanced in through the patio doors at the large, bright living room with its comfortable sofas, colourful rugs on the polished oak planks and the array of watercolours on the walls. 'It's fabulous house. And the bedrooms are so cute. I love my little bathroom and the power shower. I think I'll use it twice a day.'

'You'll be the cleanest girl in Ireland,' Sally joked. 'This house was designed for four elderly women with the best equipment for the slightly disabled. I think it was a brilliant idea for the old girls to live here together with a housekeeper instead of a dreary nursing home. I intend to do the same if I'm lucky enough to live as long as they did.' She sipped her wine.

Cordelia drained her glass and put it on the table. 'So… about what I found out…'

'Yes?'

Cordelia took a deep breath. 'It's hard to talk about it, but if I don't say it out loud, I'll never believe it's true.'

'I'm all ears. And my lips are sealed.'

'I know.' Cordelia told Sally everything that had happened in Dublin, including the revelation about who her grandfather was, which she still found hard to believe.

'What?' Sally gasped. 'Oh my God! That's unbelievable.'

'I know.'

'Could it be true? Or was he a dithery old man who would make things up?'

Cordelia shook her head. 'No. He was a little forgetful at times but he was clear as crystal when he told me the story. It's true all right. I feel it in my bones and in my heart. It explains everything about the family row and why Frances just took off like that. Doesn't it?'

Sally nodded. 'Yes. It does. But holy mother, what a scandal that must have been. Who knew about it then, I wonder?'

'I reckon it was why the sisters fell out. But did my mother know who her biological father was? I'm not sure. Jimmy said he never told her who it was, but that she was upset when she found out he wasn't her father and hadn't been told. She left to go to America to attend a music school in New York that he had paid for. And then she cut all her ties and never went back or contacted anyone again.' Cordelia drew breath. 'That's why she didn't want to talk about her family or tell me anything about them. So I never knew who they were until I met Phil.'

'At least it turns out you really are related. With knobs on,' Sally remarked. 'How incredible.'

'That's what Declan said.'

Sally's eyes widened. 'You told him?'

Cordelia nodded. 'Yes, of course. He was there when I came out of Jimmy's room, looking like a ghost. And in any case…'

'You're getting to be very close to him?'

'Yes.' Cordelia turned her head and looked out across the bay and the headland bathed in a rosy glow by the last rays of the setting sun. 'It's funny, but I feel as if I've known him for a long time – or that he has been here, waiting for me.' She sighed and turned back to Sally. 'Crazy, huh?'

'He's been married three times and been fired from national TV, not to mention that little flirt with Roisin last year,' Sally filled in. 'But at the same time he seems a little lost and lonely. A nice man who's had a lot of bad luck, and made the wrong decisions, I think.'

Cordelia nodded. 'I get that feeling about him, too, sometimes. He probably has a lot of baggage, but who doesn't?'

'His might be a little heavier than most,' Sally remarked dryly. 'But hey, who am I to judge with my track record? I fall for the wrong man all the time. They have always looked so right but turned out to be the worst.'

'There you go,' Cordelia said, smiling. 'He couldn't look more wrong, so he must be my Mr Right.' She sighed. 'I know what you're saying, joking aside. But Phil always said you should think with your heart, not always with your head. I'm not sure she was right. While I was searching for my grandfather, Declan was there for me. He looked after me and supported me. And I fell in love with him, that's true. But then I started thinking with my head and took a step back and told him we should take a break. I think he hated the idea and he hasn't been in touch since we said goodbye in Dublin. So maybe it – whatever it is – will never happen. If it does, it will be up to him. And then I'm sure we'll be happy together.' She sighed heavily. 'But it might not happen at all, even if I'd want it to. He seems perfect for me. So he has a bit of a back story? Who cares what happened before we met?'

'Nobody,' Sally said with feeling. 'And here we are, you and me, becoming friends. Isn't that grand?' Cordelia smiled, touched by the words and the emotion in Sally's voice. She held up her glass. 'Cheers to that.'

Sally lifted her glass and smiled. 'And cheers to Phil who brought us together. I can feel her putting her arms around us. Can't you?'

'Oh yes, I can.'

They clinked glasses and drank, both turning to the view of the sunset, both feeling that there was someone looking at them from above, smiling. When they had finished their meal, Sally asked if Cordelia had managed to pack everything she needed from Willow House.

'I haven't checked, but I'm sure it's all there,' Cordelia replied.

'There was a box in the top drawer. I think it had photos in it. I put it in the case with your laptop.'

'A box with photos? No, that's not mine. I'll go and have a look.'

'I'll make some tea while you look,' Sally suggested.

'Great.' Cordelia went to her bedroom and picked up the bag with her laptop and personal papers. She found a flat box crammed into the front pocket and pulled it out. It was an old box, stained by damp and frayed at the edges. She had seen it in the top drawer in the bedroom in Willow House but had thought it belonged to Roisin and Maeve. But now she saw the words 'Mum's photos' in Phil's spidery handwriting that had faded with time on the box. Family photos, maybe? Cordelia picked it up and brought it to the living room and put it on the coffee table in front of one of the large sofas by the fireplace at the same time as Sally arrived with a tray loaded with two steaming mugs and a plate of tiny muffins.

She looked at the box as she put the tray beside it. 'That's the one. Not yours, then?'

'No, it must be Phil's,' Cordelia replied, sitting down in the sofa. 'I think there are photos here that belonged to her mother. I'll give the box back to Roisin, but I want to see what's in it first.'

'Open it,' Sally ordered.

Cordelia didn't hesitate and opened the box, discovering a stack of black-and-white photos, some of them yellow with age. She picked up the top one and discovered a little girl in a white dress and veil with a woman and a man standing behind her, all smiling broadly. She peered at the girl with the pretty face, large dark eyes and curly hair. 'It's Phil,' she exclaimed. 'Her first communion. And that must be her parents.' Cordelia studied the couple. The man was tall with a shock of dark hair. He was very handsome and his smile told her he knew it. The woman was attractive with classic features but there was a sad look in her eyes, despite her smile. 'My grandfather,' Cordelia mumbled.

Sally took the photo and looked at it. 'He's like a film star. But his wife looks miserable. What year would that have been?'

Cordelia turned the photo. 'It says 1955 on the back.'

'Must have been around the time of the affair.'

'Yes,' Cordelia agreed. 'My mom was born in 1956.'

Sally frowned. 'What a smug gobshite he was, standing there at his daughter's first communion with all that going on behind the scenery.'

'She must have known,' Cordelia said, picking up the next photo – the same woman in a pretty dress holding a baby in a christening gown. 'Look, Phil when she was a baby.'

Sally looked at it. 'She was so cute. And here the mother looks very happy. Just look at that smile.'

'Sad to think of what happened afterwards.'

'Well, they had a son a few years later. Maeve and Roisin's dad.'

'That's right.' Cordelia focused on Sally. 'You're about five years younger than Mom. Did you know the family when you were growing up here?'

'No,' Sally replied. 'We didn't live here then. My mother was from Sandy Cove but my father was from Cork and he worked there. He was a doctor and had a very busy practice. We used to come here for our summer holidays, but I don't remember much about the McKennas, other than that they lived in the big house. It wasn't until I went to Paris that I got to know Phil through the Irish club there.' She paused and drank some tea.

Cordelia and Sally flicked through the photos of other first communions, christenings, weddings, assorted family parties and holidays at Willow House all through the nineteen twenties and thirties, trying to find any of her grandmother, but there didn't appear to be any, until she came to the bottom of the pile and found a photo of two women. One of them was definitely Olive and the other a much younger and prettier version of her. Cordelia turned and looked at the back. 'Olive and Clodagh at the Kildare hunt ball 1944,' she read aloud. 'Wow,' she whispered, 'look at them in their ball gowns.'

'What?' Sally tore herself away from the photos of Willow House in the early nineteen thirties and looked over Cordelia's shoulder at the two women in the photo. 'Gorgeous dresses. Clodagh must have been a lot younger than Olive. Like ten years or so. She looks about seventeen there. Stunning young woman. Just look at those eyes and the dimples. No wonder old Brian was smitten.'

'But he must have been married to Olive already by then.' Cordelia looked closer at the older sister. 'Yes. She's wearing a wedding ring and a diamond engagement ring.'

'Yes,' Sally agreed. 'She could have even been pregnant.'

'Phil was born in 1945, I think,' Cordelia said after a moment's reflection. 'Hopefully she had a few happy years before...'

'I'm sure she did. Until he got bored and started flirting with the younger sister.' Sally put the photos back in the box. 'What are you going to do about all this?'

'I'm giving the box back to Roisin. It belongs in Willow House.' Cordelia picked up the photo of Olive and Clodagh. 'But I'm keeping this one.'

'I didn't mean the photos, I meant the news that Brian McKenna was your grandfather. Are you going to tell them?'

Cordelia sighed and reached for the mug of now tepid tea. 'I don't know. I think they'll be very upset, and so will their dad.'

'Your uncle,' Sally said, looking thoughtful.

'I guess he is,' Cordelia said with a shiver. 'He must never know. It'd be too hurtful for all of them and they'll never believe me anyway. I hardly believe it myself. But I have decided one thing,' Cordelia continued. 'I'm going to agree to that DNA test. In fact, I'm going to insist.'

Chapter Twenty

Cordelia didn't have an opportunity to mention the DNA test during the following week. They were all so busy with a fully booked guesthouse and all kinds of administrative details to sort out when the probate came through, including the inventory of the contents of the house. Roisin was busy organising the boys and the final details of the new house they were buying, and Maeve had to combine work with family life while Cordelia did her best to keep the guesthouse running smoothly.

But the big question that burned in her mind was the revelation of the identity of her grandfather. She couldn't get it out of her mind. While they were doing the inventory of the living room, going through old papers and photos in the drawers, she'd kept looking for traces of the relationship between her grandmother and her brother-in-law. But she found nothing at all, only photos of family events, weddings and christenings and birthday parties of people she didn't know. Even Maeve remarked on the number of relatives who had been passing through, often celebrating their big events in Willow House in the nineteen thirties and forties.

'Gosh,' she said, adding yet another family photo to a pile on the coffee table. 'This house seems to have been used by even the remotest relative as a place to celebrate special events.'

Roisin held up a photo of a fat man bursting out of a tuxedo dancing with a tall woman in a backless evening dress. 'Look at this lad, whoever he is, doing the Charleston or whatever they did in those days. Who is he, anyway?'

Maeve peered at the photo. 'Haven't a clue. But look at the dining room. They must have pushed the table to the wall and rolled up the carpet to dance. I can see the sideboard stacked with champagne bottles and some glammed-up people in the background.'

'That's a gorgeous dress,' Cordelia said. 'I wonder who she is.'

'No idea. "Charlie's fiftieth, 1932",' Roisin read from the back of the photo. 'It's a fun photo. We should put in a frame and hang it on the wall in the dining room.'

'Great idea,' Maeve said. 'What do you think, Cordelia?'

'Love it,' Cordelia said, looking at a photo of a family group. 'And look, here's another one from 1919. The clothes and hats are amazing.'

'We'll get that one framed as well,' Roisin said. 'And the one of the house when it had just been built. It's so lovely to have memories of this house in years gone by.'

'Oh yes,' Cordelia mumbled, shifting through the pile of photos. Looking at the family groups with the secret knowledge that these were her family, too, gave her a frisson of pleasure, a feeling of belonging, of her own history now connected to the house. She looked at her cousins, wondering if or when she would break the news. She should also tell them about the box of photos she had found. She felt an urge to do so, but the feeling passed as they moved on to the rest of the contents, furniture, lamps, silver bowls and ashtrays, none of it of any real value but intrinsically connected to Willow House and its history.

'We should decide what to do with it all,' Roisin said with a sigh. 'And divide it into three parts or something. What did the solicitor say about it, Maeve?'

Maeve shrugged. 'He just said that we should see who wanted what. As long as there is no dispute, there is no legal problem, he said. Or we could just leave it all here.'

'In that case, I vote for it all to stay here,' Cordelia said. 'I mean, what would I do with any of it?'

'Or either of us,' Roisin agreed. 'It all has to stay here. Willow House should remain the way it's always been.'

'Absolutely,' Maeve declared. She got up from the sofa. 'If that's all, I'll go back home. Can someone get those photos framed and any other ones that look nice?'

'I'll do it,' Roisin said. 'I'm going into Killarney with the boys tomorrow to buy some sports gear for school anyway.'

Cordelia was going to say she had a photo that should be hung with the others, but decided to leave it for now. If she started explaining why she had them it would lead to other questions. Later, she thought. And, when they had tidied everything away, she went back to Sally's house with a feeling of having come a tiny step closer to some kind of conclusion. She would have to tell them. The only question was when.

Later that week, Cordelia opened an Irish bank account and, as her passport arrived, was able to apply for Irish residency and get herself a personal public service number which would register her with the

Irish Revenue and make sure she got all the welfare benefits that were due to any Irish citizen. It was a proud moment when she held her Irish passport in her hands, but she was relieved she could retain her American citizenship, feeling she hadn't burned all her bridges at once. She suddenly felt a little bit Irish. It made her feel she belonged in an odd way. The money coming in from her inheritance was a welcome addition to her strained finances and she knew she would have an income from Phil's royalties for the next few years at least.

'We should celebrate,' Maeve said one evening as she popped in to help out with the laundry. 'We'll have a drink in the living room later,' she said as they were folding sheets in the kitchen. 'No guests tonight and the new ones won't arrive until mid-morning tomorrow. So we can have a nice evening all to ourselves. And we have a lot to talk about.'

'OK. Sounds great.' Cordelia gathered up the stack of sheets. 'I'll put these in the hot cupboard or whatever you call it.'

Maeve laughed. 'Hot press. Linen cupboard with the water heater under it. I don't think any other country in the world has that contraption.'

'Except England,' Roisin said as she came in from the office. 'Did I hear the word drink?'

'Yes. We're going to raid the wine cellar,' Maeve replied. 'And there's a runny Brie in the larder for some reason. But you share the wine with Cordelia. I'm off the booze at the moment.'

'Oh?' Roisin said with a surprised look. 'Why? Please don't say you've come down with chicken pox as well.'

'No. It's something else. Is that piece of Gubbeen cheese yours?'

'It's Cian's. But he took the lads to the cinema in Killarney, thank God, so he won't miss it. They'll be going to a pizzeria after the film, so I have oodles of free time, bless him.'

'And Paschal's putting Aisling to bed,' Maeve interjected. 'So I can put my feet up for a bit.'

'Me too,' Cordelia chimed in. 'Sally's having dinner with Nuala, so I'm at a loose end. In any case, I need to tell you something.'

'Oh?' Maeve looked at Cordelia. 'Sounds ominous. Let's get organised then. If you put away the sheets in the hot press, I'll get the wine and Roisin will do the cheese and crackers.'

'Great.' Cordelia went upstairs to put away the sheets with a tight knot in her stomach. She had a feeling this was a watershed moment and, judging by the look in Maeve's eyes, Cordelia wouldn't be the only one to break some startling news.

They all settled on the big yellow velvet sofas by the fireplace in the living room in front of the antique coffee table, where Maeve had placed a tray with wine, elderflower cordial, glasses and a jug of water. Roisin followed behind with a cheese board and a basket with crackers and crispbread. The cream muslin curtains billowed in the breeze from the open sash windows and birdsong could be heard from the garden.

Maeve sighed and leaned her head back against the cushions. 'Oh, how peaceful. We haven't been together like this since… since, I can't even remember.'

'Last week,' Cordelia remarked. 'When we sorted through the contents of this room.'

'That was just work,' Roisin argued. 'I think the last time we had a real talk was last month. At the lunch in Muckross after that visit to the solicitor,' she added, pouring herself a glass of wine from the dusty bottle she had found in the wine cellar. 'Help yourself, Cordelia. We can share the bottle. Did you get anything to eat earlier?'

Cordelia nodded as she helped herself to wine. 'Yes. I had a burger and chips at The Two Marys'. Sally wasn't cooking tonight so I got a break from the haute cuisine.'

Maeve laughed. 'Sally must be happy to have someone to cook for.'

'More than happy,' Cordelia agreed with a grin. 'And she serves up the most amazing dinners every evening. But sometimes I long for a little bit of junk. I mean boeuf bourguignon or bouillabaisse á la whatever is fabulous most days, but it can be quite rich.'

'I'm sure it is,' Maeve agreed. She put a piece of Gubbeen on a cracker. 'So here we are,' she started. 'All bursting to tell our news. Who'll go first?'

'Me,' Cordelia said, taking a large swig of wine, hoping it would give her courage. 'I… God, I don't know how to say it…'

'Go on,' Roisin urged, 'we're friends, aren't we?'

'I want to do the DNA test,' Cordelia interrupted. 'I have been thinking about it and realised it's a good idea.'

Roisin stared at her. 'Why now all of a sudden? I know Mum has been bugging us to do it but we never thought it was necessary. You provided all the papers we needed and—'

'If Cordelia wants to do it, we should,' Maeve cut in. 'It'll get Mum off our backs too. Then we can all carry on and decide what to do about the house.'

'The house?' Cordelia asked. 'This house? But we own it together, don't we?'

Roisin and Maeve exchanged a look. 'Yes, of course,' Roisin said after a moment's silence. 'But we've been talking, Maeve and I, about the future of Willow House.'

'The future?' Cordelia said, confused. 'You mean the guesthouse?'

'Yes,' Roisin replied. 'We've been looking at the accounts and the repayment of the loan Phil took to do the rebuilding work and we've seen that if we run it for six months, taking in guests at the weekends even during the winter months, we can break even and close down the guesthouse in the spring. And then…'

'Then what? Who's going to live here then?'

'We haven't thought that through yet,' Roisin replied.

'But I have,' Maeve announced. 'This is what I wanted to talk to you both about.' She paused and blushed. 'You see… I'm… I'm pregnant.'

'What?' Roisin exclaimed, staring at Maeve. 'You are? How did that happen?'

Maeve rolled her eyes. 'Duh, how do you think?'

Roisin waved her hand in the air. 'Yeah, yeah, I know. But I thought… Given your age and what the doctor said and all…'

'He was wrong,' Maeve said, beaming. 'OK, so I'm forty-three and never thought I'd even have one baby, but it appears that wasn't true. Then I had Aisling and the doctor said there would be no more, but my hormones had other ideas. So here I am with sore boobs, puking every morning. The baby is due in early March next year. Isn't it brilliant?'

Cordelia couldn't help smiling. 'Congratulations. That's terrific. Paschal must be so happy.'

Maeve nodded. 'He's ecstatic. He thinks it's a boy this time.'

'Aisling will only be a year and a half,' Roisin remarked. 'This will keep you busy, my friend. And where the heck are you going to put that baby? Your cottage is already small. Are you going to build an extension?'

'No. The site the house is on wouldn't allow it. But I have a suggestion. Paschal and I have been talking about it, actually.'

'Without consulting me?' Roisin grumbled.

'Well, yes,' Maeve admitted, looking a little guilty. 'I wasn't sure about the pregnancy until yesterday. There's some more news. We did our first ultrasound scan and… they think it might be twins.'

'Oh God,' Roisin muttered. 'Three children under two. That'll be a killer. How do you feel?'

'Great,' Maeve said brightly. 'Apart from the morning sickness and all that. But this will mean we have to move house. And our lives and work have to be rejigged a lot.'

'Of course,' Cordelia said, looking at Maeve in awe. Twins. And then the very lively little girl. Her career in interior design had been put on hold but her husband was so busy with his research and the university lectures and might not be able to help much. 'I can't even begin to imagine what you're going to do.'

'Well,' Maeve started. 'We have a suggestion, Paschal and I. We obviously don't fit in the cottage any more, so that will be sold.'

'But where are you planning to live?' Roisin asked.

'Here,' Maeve said. 'In Willow House.'

Roisin and Cordelia stared at Maeve. 'Here?' Roisin said.

'In Willow House?' Cordelia asked.

Maeve laughed and took another cracker. 'Yes. Here. We want to buy the two of you out and be the sole owners. We can afford it now that we have Phil's money to help us and we can take a mortgage for the rest. We'll find out the market value and then…'

'And then you'll buy us out. Just like that,' Roisin snapped, looking angry. 'Forget it, Maeve. I don't want to be bought out. This is as much my house as yours. I'm a McKenna, don't forget. And this house is our heritage. It's in our blood. Not in Cordelia's, of course. You can buy *her* out. She's not a McKenna, after all.'

Cordelia sat up, glaring at Roisin, anger boiling in her chest at Roisin's words and her dismissive tone. 'What would you say, Roisin, if I told you I'm a McKenna, too?' she heard herself ask, regretting it the instant she had said it. But it was impossible to take it back. She returned Roisin's bewildered gaze with a look of defiance. Roisin had been nice on the surface but her secret suspicions and misgivings had been obvious at times when her guard was down. And just now she'd felt like she was being pushed away.

'How do you mean?' Maeve asked. 'That's not possible.'

'I'm afraid it is,' Cordelia replied, knowing she had to tell them everything now that she had started.

Roisin frowned. 'What are you going on about? You're not a McKenna, you're a Brennan,' she added as if an afterthought.

'You think?' Cordelia asked. 'Well, I have news for you. When I went to Dublin, it was not just for a bit of sightseeing or to go on a date with Declan. I went to find out who my grandfather was. We knew it wasn't Jimmy Fitz. Who was that man who made my grandmother pregnant and then left her in the lurch? A married man, of course. But here's a twist: guess who he was married to?'

'Who?' Roisin asked.

'Her own sister,' Cordelia said grimly.

Maeve gasped. 'Not—?'

Cordelia nodded, feeling an odd dart of satisfaction at the shocking news she was about to deliver. 'Oh yes. Olive, your grandmother.'

Maeve shook her head in disbelief. 'Holy mother,' she said, her voice hoarse. 'Can it be true?'

'So your grandfather, that man who left Clodagh in the lurch was… our grandfather?' Roisin said in a near whisper, her face ashen.

'Yes,' Cordelia replied. 'The very man.'

'How did you find out?' Maeve asked.

'Jimmy told me. He's ninety-seven and in a nursing home, but his mind is crystal clear. He told me about Clodagh's brief affair with her brother-in-law.'

'This is shocking,' Maeve mumbled. 'Even now it seems such a vile thing to do. I wonder why? I mean, Clodagh was a schoolteacher and very respectable, I would have thought.'

Cordelia shrugged. 'Who knows? He was very handsome and charming. He might have hit on her at a vulnerable moment. She was young and pretty and maybe impressionable. There are a hundred ways it could have happened. They might have been alone in some house or something. Or,' she added to soften the blow, 'they might have been in love.'

'We'll never know,' Roisin said with a sigh. 'Is Jimmy the only one who knew about this?'

'I have a feeling he is. Or the only person alive that we can ask.' Cordelia poured wine into her glass, her hand shaking slightly, feeling a stab of guilt. They were obviously upset and bewildered and she was beginning to have regrets. 'I shouldn't have told you,' she started. 'But when Roisin started to talk about me not being a McKenna, as if that made me less than you…'

'Sorry,' Roisin mumbled and took a big swig of wine. 'I didn't mean…'

'That's OK. I understand,' Cordelia said. 'I know this must be a terrible shock.'

Maeve nodded. 'It's difficult to accept that our grandfather behaved in this way.'

'And my grandmother,' Cordelia interjected.

'I have to say that this Jimmy Fitz must have been a real trouper,' Roisin remarked. 'Marrying a woman who was pregnant with another man's child was so brave. He must have loved her very much.'

'He adored her,' Cordelia said. 'That came across very strongly while we talked.'

'That's the best part of the whole story,' Maeve said, her eyes sad. 'But oh God, what a holy mess it must have been. Jimmy saved Clodagh from having to give up her baby. That's what women had to do in those days.'

'If she had, we wouldn't be sitting here now,' Roisin said with a smile. 'Frances would have been adopted and we would never even have heard of her. Isn't that incredible?'

Cordelia returned her smile. 'I hadn't thought of it that way.'

'And you're part of the family even more,' Roisin continued. 'And Willow House. I'm really sorry I made you feel – excluded, Cordelia. I didn't mean it that way.'

'I shouldn't have told you like that,' Cordelia replied, feeling remorseful. 'I thought you wouldn't believe me. I've worked so hard to help run the guesthouse because that's what Phil wanted us to do. And then I started to feel I belonged here in an odd way. Then what I learned in Dublin made me realise that it was part of my heritage, too. That's why I want to do the DNA test. It'll prove Jimmy told me the truth.'

Maeve touched Cordelia's arm. 'If you want, we'll do it. But I believe you anyway.'

Cordelia stared at Maeve. 'You do?'

'Yes.' Maeve nodded. 'It all fits. Our grandfather died before we were born. I think he died in 1972 or something. But our granny was still alive and lived in this house until she died in 1986. I was ten and it was my first summer in Willow House with Phil and Uncle Joe. Remember, Roisin?'

Roisin looked thoughtfully at Cordelia. 'Yes, I do. And I remember Granny from when we were younger. She was always so happy and smiley. I heard later that she was called "the merry widow" in the village. It was as if she changed after her husband's death, they said. And… she never talked about her sister. Phil said later, after Granny died, that she always wondered why the sisters had fallen out but Granny wouldn't tell her. She just closed up like a clam when she was asked and then they stopped asking. Daddy said much the same thing.' Roisin nodded. 'Yeah, it all fits, doesn't it? In a terrible, sad way. It makes me feel very strange.'

'Me too.' Maeve piled some cheese on a cracker. 'It makes me hungry, as well.'

'That's just you being pregnant,' Roisin remarked.

'Very true.' Maeve sighed and stuffed the cracker into her mouth. 'Sorry but being pregnant seems to distract me from everything else. When I'm not puking, I'm starving. Food calms me down.'

'Same here. Stress makes me hungry even if I'm not pregnant.' Roisin picked up her phone. 'I'm going to order pizza from Nuala's new take-out service. Anyone else?'

'Oh, yes,' Maeve groaned. 'Get me a margherita, will you?'

'Of course.' Roisin looked at Cordelia, who shook her head. Roisin dialled the number and quickly ordered two pizzas. She slipped the phone back into her pocket and looked at Maeve and Cordelia. 'What do we do now, then? Who do we tell?'

'Nobody,' Maeve said sternly. 'What would be the point? We'll do the DNA thing and send it off. It'll show we're related with more DNA than you could shake a stick at. That should make Mum happy. Then we'll just carry on and make plans.'

Roisin frowned. 'Yes. We have to decide about the house. Maybe...' She glanced at Cordelia. 'Maybe we should just let Maeve have the house but still own part of it? Be sleeping partners? It means a lot to me to own it. I spent all my teenage summers here and I so love it. I can't bear to part with it. What about you, Cordelia?'

'I'm not sure how I feel. It's nice to own a part of this gorgeous house. But...' Cordelia thought for a while, an idea popping into her head that made her gasp. 'Oh...' she mumbled. 'That would be...' She looked at Maeve. 'I just had this thought... But maybe it won't work for you.'

Maeve looked intrigued. 'Come on. Tell me.'

'Well, how about we swap?' Cordelia suggested. 'Houses, I mean. You get my part of Willow House and I get your cottage. It would be ideal for me. I love that little house and it would be my very first real home and I'd live close to you and I can stay here in Sandy Cove and—' Cordelia drew breath, smiling. 'That just came out on a gush. No idea where it came from. It's just that I feel so at home here in Sandy Cove. And with you. I've never known that feeling of having a family and you gave that to me. I know the cottage might not be worth as much as my part of Willow House, but that doesn't matter to me. I'd be so happy if I could have my own place close to you. It would mean so much.'

'Oh.' Maeve's eyes were full of emotion as she looked at Cordelia. 'I always had that feeling of us being related, but I had no idea it was that close.'

'And we like you whatever the family circumstances,' Roisin filled in. 'I have to admit I was wondering at times if you were for real. Your story was somehow too neat and convenient. But the way you came over and rolled up your sleeves and got stuck in was truly impressive. You've been a star, Cordelia, and I'm sorry if I've been a bit prickly at times.'

'That's understandable,' Cordelia replied. 'I might have had misgivings myself if I were you. I was so worried telling you about who my real grandfather was. I even thought I should keep it to myself.'

'I'm glad you didn't,' Roisin said with feeling.

'Me too,' Maeve agreed, reaching for another cracker. 'Where is that pizza?' She laughed. 'Sorry, but I just have to eat soon.' She turned to Cordelia. 'But about the cottage…'

'Forget it,' Cordelia said. 'It's too crazy. I'll think of something else.'

Maeve flew up from the sofa. 'No! I won't forget it. It's perfect! I'm sure Paschal will love it too. What about you, Roisin?'

Roisin laughed. 'Yeah. I think it's brilliant. The perfect solution for you, Cordelia. And for us. We'll all be together but not in each other's hair. We should work on that. No real rush, but it should all be done before Maeve has the baby – or babies if it's twins. If we all stick together, we'll make it work.'

Maeve sat down again. 'Yes, we will.' She brightened as the doorbell rang.

Roisin got up. 'I'll get it. Then we should eat in the kitchen. I'd hate to get tomato stains on the sofa.'

'My sofa, you mean,' Maeve corrected, looking prim.

'Oh yes, your ladyship,' Roisin retorted. She winked at Cordelia. 'Watch her becoming the lady of the manor. We'll have to curtsey next.'

Cordelia laughed and turned to Maeve when Roisin had left. 'Are you sure this works for you? Me buying the cottage, I mean.'

Maeve grinned. 'Oh yes, I love the idea. It'll be so nice to have you next door. Maybe you could babysit sometime?'

'I don't know anything about babies, but I'm willing to learn,' Cordelia replied, smiling at her new-found cousin. What a relief that she had shared the terrible secret with the sisters and a bigger relief that they had been able to deal with it so sensibly and without too much trauma.

A family, she thought. *That's a greater gift than all the money in the world. And that was what Phil wanted to give me. And the only way she could do that was to include me in the will. What a clever, wonderful woman she was.*

Chapter Twenty-One

Declan picked Cordelia up from Sally's house the next evening. He had called the night before just as Cordelia was beginning to think he'd never want to see her again. Now that the mystery of her grandfather's identity had been resolved and all the missing pieces had fallen into place, she had the time to think about her feelings for Declan. There had been no word from him since they had said goodbye in Dublin and she had come to the sad conclusion that she had driven him away for good. But then he called, and even if he sounded a little curt, the fact that he wanted to see her gave her hope. He said he'd cook her dinner at his house, because he had something to tell her. Then he had said a quick goodbye and hung up, leaving her puzzled, not knowing if he wanted to meet her to announce he was leaving Sandy Cove for some reason, or that he wanted them to get more serious.

Her stomach full of butterflies, Cordelia prepared for the evening. The weather had turned wet and windy after several weeks of warm summer weather. But that was Kerry, Sally said, adding that Ireland didn't really have seasons. 'But we have weather. It can be balmy as a summer's day in December and cold and stormy in July,' she explained. 'That's the charm of living here. You never know what the weather gods are going to hit you with next.' Cordelia had nodded, the weather being the least of her concerns, and gone to her room to get ready.

Having worried about what to wear and going through her meagre wardrobe, Cordelia had given up and just put on her usual jeans and a white shirt under a navy Irish knit sweater. She brushed her hair and applied mascara, not needing any other make-up as she had acquired quite a tan that made her eyes even bluer. No matter what he was going to tell her, the thought of seeing him again gave her a buzz she couldn't hide. Her eyes sparkled with happy anticipation and a smile hovered on her lips as she looked at herself in the mirror. She walked into the living room on her way to the door.

'Look at you,' Sally said from the depths of the sofa by the fireplace. 'You're blooming.'

'It's nerves,' Cordelia confessed. 'I have no idea what he's going to tell me. Maybe he'll never want to see me again?'

'I doubt that very much. If he breaks up with you, he's a fool. I'm sure you'll come back with even more stars in your eyes.'

'Thank you,' Cordelia said, throwing her a kiss. 'You're a darling for cheering me up. Don't wait up.'

Sally laughed. 'Have a lovely evening whatever time you get back. But I don't have to tell you that.' She sat up and put another log on the fire. 'I'm going to laze around and make myself something nice and then go to bed early. I have a busy day tomorrow. The shop, then I'm closing early to go to Cork. There's a craft fair there, where I hope to pick up some things to sell. My last collections were snapped up very fast. All thanks to you. I'm looking into extending the shop now and adding a new section with things for the home. If

I can raise enough money for it.' She smiled and shooed at Cordelia. 'But go on. I hear a car outside. Must be your Prince Charming.'

Cordelia glanced out the window. 'Yes, it's him. He's on his way to the door.' She picked up her bag and grabbed her jacket. 'Goodnight, Sally. See you tomorrow evening.'

She opened the door and walked straight into Declan. She looked at him for a moment without speaking. He met her gaze and smiled and she felt her insides melt. That smile and the look in his eyes told her he wasn't about to push her away. 'Hi,' she said shyly. 'Nice to see you again.'

'Nice?' he growled and pulled her close. 'It's more than nice, girl.'

'I know,' she whispered.

'Ohh, how I've missed you,' he said and kissed her on both cheeks. 'But let's go. Or do I have to go in and be polite?'

Cordelia laughed. 'No. Sally's half asleep in the sofa.'

'Good.' They walked back to the car and set off into the wet, windy night, Declan glancing at Cordelia now and then. 'I have everything ready. Food, fire, wine. The only thing missing is you.'

'I'm here,' Cordelia said and touched his hand.

He smiled. 'Then everything will be perfect.'

Declan's house was just outside the village on the road to Ballinskellig. On a steep incline, the one-storey building overlooked Sandy Cove Bay and the islands beyond. It also had sweeping views of the coastline all the way to Waterville. The house had once been a farmhouse with a thatched roof and a tiny front garden, which Declan had turned into a terrace with a walkway that went around the corner to the back of the house, sheltered from the winds by a low stone wall.

Cordelia looked at the roof. 'I see you had it redone.'

Declan turned off the engine. 'Yes. I put a slate roof instead of the old thatch. More durable, I thought.'

'They say a thatch roof lasts about twenty-five years,' Cordelia said, thinking of the cottage that would soon be hers.

'It might but with the winds here, I feel more secure with the slates.' Declan got out of the car and went around to open the passenger door. 'But let's go inside. It's going to rain all night. I lit a fire and everything is ready for dinner.'

They walked up the steps that had been cut into the cliff and arrived at the front door. Cordelia looked at the view and the dark clouds gathered at the horizon. 'Wow. It looks so dramatic from here.'

'I love it. Wild and beautiful and unpredictable.' Declan pushed open the door. 'Welcome to my humble abode, your ladyship.'

Cordelia laughed and stepped inside, arriving straight into a huge living room. She looked around in awe. The interior of the house, which must have consisted of several small rooms, had been knocked into one big space, the rough walls painted white and covered with all kinds of paintings and posters in bold colours. The large window took in the view in such a way that she felt she was at one with the ocean and the sky – except in here, the warmth from the blazing fire made the room welcoming and protected from the elements. Two small green sofas flanked the fireplace and there was a window seat under the largest window. The rest of the furniture consisted of a desk at the back wall, a dining table and chairs by the smaller window, and a huge rug with a Celtic design in red and blue covered the wooden floorboards. The windows were bare of curtains but as the house was not overlooked, it didn't seem necessary to cover them. This way the old window frames, painted a light grey, formed part of the view and enhanced the room.

Declan smiled as their eyes met. 'Do you like it?'

'I love it,' Cordelia said, rendered breathless by the beautiful room and the feeling of intimacy between them. She looked around. 'But where's the kitchen? And the bedrooms?'

'Through there.' He pointed at a door in the far wall. 'A corridor. Kitchen to the right, bedrooms to the left and the master at the end. It's an extension but so cleverly done you'd think it's always been part of the house. Not done in my time, but by the previous owners. I did the interior of the kitchen, though,' he said proudly.

Cordelia walked to the door and opened it, finding a bright modern kitchen with all the latest appliances including a wall oven and induction hob with a stainless-steel hood over it. Modern and stark, it suited the house and its spartan feel. Two of the bedrooms were large and airy and sparsely furnished, sharing a bathroom. The master, on the other hand, was opulent, with a four-poster bed piled with cushions, an Oriental carpet on the floor and windows that overlooked the back garden swathed with deep red velvet curtains held back with thick silk ropes. 'Oh,' Cordelia mumbled as she looked into the room. 'Not quite what I expected.'

Declan put his arms around her from behind. 'It's my secret hideaway,' he whispered into her neck.

'It looks like some kind of sheik's boudoir,' she said with a giggle. 'Is this where you seduce women?'

'Haven't seduced anyone here yet.' He let go of her and went to sit on the bed. 'This is my secret space, the place where I rest, read, dream and sleep. It's been where I have thought of you the most, ever since we met. Nobody but you has ever seen it.'

'I'm honoured to be the first,' Cordelia said with pretend flippancy. She was touched by what he'd said, and the look in his eyes made her feel something more.

He held out her hand. 'Come here.'

Cordelia sat beside him. She touched his cheek, wondering what he was going to tell her. Was he leaving and wanted to let her down gently with sweet words? 'I meant to say this before but never got the chance,' she said, wanting to prolong the moment before he gave her the bad news. 'I want to thank you for your help. Without you I would never have found Jimmy. What he told me was the final piece of the jigsaw and it gave me the closure I needed.'

'I'm glad I could help.' He took her hand. 'I knew how shocked you were when you saw your mother's birth certificate. The despair in your eyes when you told me made me want to do something, anything to help you. I could feel your pain and how lost you were. I didn't know if I'd find anything, but I was determined to try my best. It was sheer luck to hit the jackpot straight away.'

The empathy in his voice made Cordelia's eyes sting. She blinked away the tears and smiled at him. 'I could never thank you enough.'

'The look in your eyes right now is the only thanks I need.'

'You're too good to be true,' Cordelia said with a sigh.

He laughed and kissed her and she did the only thing she'd wanted to do since she met him. She kissed him back, trying to push away her fears that this might be the last time they were together.

If that was the case, she was ready to do anything just so she would have something to remember when he was gone.

He sat back, smiling, and they looked at each other, while the vibes between them grew even stronger than before. She touched his face, then kissed him lightly on the mouth, closing her eyes as he pulled her close and returned her kiss. Then they drew apart and smiled at each other, both knowing what would happen next. Cordelia started to unbutton her shirt before he pulled it off her in one smooth movement, laying her on the bed and looking into her eyes. 'This is the moment,' he said without taking her eyes off her.

'The moment of no return,' she whispered and gave herself up to his mouth and hands and body. They took off their remaining clothes and slid naked up the bed and under the covers in one movement. Cordelia looked at him and knew that this was a man who had fallen in and out of love more times than she could imagine. But despite all that, she felt as if she was making love for the first time and that she would never feel like this with anyone else. And neither would he, even if they never met again.

Afterwards, as they lay in each other's arms smiling, Declan traced his finger along her cheek and down her throat. 'I can feel you in my heart and soul,' he said, kissing her. 'My wild beautiful girl from the other side of the ocean. You won't believe this, but with you, I felt new-born somehow. All the old stuff washed away.'

'I know.' She took his hand and kissed it. 'Me too. You make my heart sing.' Then she laughed. 'I feel as if I'm stuck in some Hollywood movie, saying corny stuff like that. But I mean it, I really do. Whatever happens next, nothing can ruin this moment.'

'Nothing,' he agreed. 'I'll never forget it.' He drew her close. 'You're the best thing that ever happened to me. I feel complete when I'm with you.'

'Even when I steal your French fries?'

'Especially then.'

She sighed and snuggled closer to him. 'You make me feel safe and – cherished.'

'I do cherish you more than I can say. But I'm no good at romance. I find it hard to express what I really feel.'

Cordelia smiled. 'You're doing a great job so far.'

'Glad you think so.' He buried his nose in her hair. 'I love the way you smell and the way you…' He stopped. 'What was that noise?'

She giggled. 'My stomach rumbling. I'm starving.'

He looked suddenly stricken. 'I forgot about dinner. I was supposed to ply you with food and wine and then…'

'And then lure me to your boudoir?'

'Something like that. But I didn't have to lure you. What a relief. I'm not that good at luring.' He laughed.

'I'm glad it happened like that…' *Even if we never see each other again*, she thought, feeling a chill go through her.

'Me too.' He kissed her and sat up. 'But I'd better do something about dinner… How do you like your lamb cutlets?'

'Medium rare,' she replied.

'Coming up.' He put on his trousers and shirt and walked to the door. Then he stopped and looked at her.

'I'll have a shower while you cook.'

After her shower in the state-of-the-art bathroom, Cordelia dried herself with the soft, thick towel, marvelling at the luxury and comfort of his master suite, feeling relaxed and happy. They hadn't had a chance to talk much, but that would come while they had dinner and now that the sexual tension had been defused, it would be easier to talk about everything, including whatever he was so obviously dying to tell her. It couldn't be so important it would change anything between them, she thought. Or could it?

He went straight to the point when he had served them lamb cutlets, salad and a baked potato and poured wine into glass goblets. 'So,' he said, grabbing his knife and fork.

Cordelia nodded and cut a piece of lamb. 'I'm listening. And eating,' she added, putting the piece of meat into her mouth. 'But tell me what's on your mind,' she said, feeling that his news couldn't be as bad as she had feared.

He nodded. 'OK. It's about my mother.'

'Your mother?' Cordelia said, her heart sinking as she saw how worried he was. 'Is she seriously ill?'

'Not really. But her health is deteriorating.'

'I'm so sorry to hear that. Is she in hospital?'

'No, but when she came back last week, she was in very bad shape. Her asthma was worse and she was exhausted after her trip and all that walking in Scotland. Her doctor wasn't happy and said she needed rest, preferably in a place where the air is clean. Somewhere by the sea. So she's letting her apartment and coming to stay with me in a couple of weeks. She'll be here for quite long time, maybe until the spring. The winters are milder here and this house is dry and warm. She can walk on the beach and maybe get into some of the activities that are run by the local retirement group here.' He smiled wryly. 'Knowing her, she'll be running the group in no time.

She is eighty-two but very young in her mind and body, apart from the asthma. But she needs to slow down. You'll like her very much, I think. But…' He frowned. 'This means I'll have to go away again at the beginning of September for a bit to help her organise things in Dublin. And then, when she comes here…'

'You'll be all alone in your sheik's boudoir,' Cordelia teased. 'With Mommy next door asking if you have clean underwear and if you've done your homework… And no girls in your room, please.'

He looked slightly annoyed. 'Yeah, right. Very funny. But it'll mean a big change for me. And you, if…'

Cordelia stared at him. 'If what? Was this the news I've been so worried about? I thought you were going to tell me you never wanted to see me again, or that you were leaving.'

He looked surprised. 'Why would you think I'd say that? What about you? I have no idea what you're planning, come to think of it. I am sitting here, not knowing if you're going back to America or not. You haven't said anything about what you're going to do now that your search for your grandfather is over.'

'That's because I wasn't sure myself. But now… Well, recent events have decided things for me.'

'What events?'

Cordelia laughed, drained her glass and held it out to him for more wine. 'The most amazing events. I had a long talk with Maeve and Roisin last night. We did the DNA test, by the way. That all happened after I told them what I had found out about my grandfather – and theirs.'

'That must have shaken them up.'

'Of course. They were shocked to say the least. We also talked about Willow House and the possibility of them buying me out. There are reasons why this should happen, but we decided that I should have Maeve and Paschal's cottage in exchange for my share as they want to move into the big house in the spring and the house will be a family house again.' Cordelia drew breath.

Declan stared at her. 'Maeve and Paschal's cottage? Next door to Willow House?'

'Yes. It will be Cordelia's cottage now,' she remarked, feeling a dart of excitement. 'My very own house for the first time in my life.'

'So you'll be living there? Permanently?

'Gosh. Is anything ever permanent?' Cordelia mused. 'But yeah, this is what I want right now. My own house, my own space. And it's a good investment. If I ever want to move, I can let it or sell it. But that's for the future. Right now I know I want to live here. And I know I want to be near you.'

'Oh,' he said, looking relieved. He took her hand. 'That's wonderful to hear. I thought… I was worried you were planning to leave. I thought this was going to be yet another broken relationship, and that I'd never see you again.'

'Oh, no,' Cordelia exclaimed. 'I had no idea that was on your mind. I know I've been preoccupied with the search for my roots, and I honestly didn't know what I was going to do when that was over. But now with what's happening between us and the cottage and everything, it's as if everything is falling into place and I've found my groove, if you know what I mean.' Cordelia put down her knife and fork, meeting his troubled eyes, trying her best to reassure him.

'You could stay with me whenever you need to. I'm not planning to leave Sandy Cove or Ireland any time soon.'

'Oh.' He let out a long sigh and looked at her thoughtfully. 'I don't know where we're going, except I want us to be together.'

Cordelia smiled. 'Me too.'

They retired to the sofa where they enjoyed a chocolate cake he confessed he had bought at The Two Marys', and talked until night fell and the fire died. Then they went to bed and made love again. And then they slept, their arms around each other while the rain beat against the window and the gale-force winds howled in the chimney, knowing they had found the best thing in life.

The next morning, Cordelia woke up early. Declan was sleeping peacefully beside her and she slipped out of bed, trying her best not to wake him. She glanced at her watch on the bedside table. Seven thirty. The sun was poking a finger of light through a slit in the curtain. The wind seemed to have dropped and she could hear birdsong from the garden. She put on Declan's shirt that was draped on a chair and tiptoed into the kitchen where she made herself a large mug of tea and toasted some brown bread she found in the bread bin.

She walked into the living room with her breakfast and settled on the windowsill, looking out at the beach where the waves were crashing in and the seagulls sailed above in the bright blue sky. It was one of those spanking bright days when the world seemed to have been washed clean by the wind and rain. She longed to go out there, run across the sand and dive into the waves, feeling the cool salty water against the skin.

Memories of the night before popped into her head, making her smile. She brought the sleeve of the shirt to her nose and breathed in Declan's smell of soap and aftershave and a slight whiff of smoke from the fire he had lit last night. *And a fire in my heart*, she thought. *A fire that will never go out.* And then her two cousins who now felt nearly like sisters. Such amazing women, who had without question accepted her as one of them. They had even gone against their own mother when she wanted proof of Cordelia's identity. Well, now she'd have it, Cordelia thought with a wry smile. They had done the DNA test late that evening after the pizzas had been delivered and eaten, spitting into the test tube and sealing the envelope. Maeve was going to send it off by post on Monday and they would have the result three weeks later. They had agreed not to tell anyone, not even Maeve and Roisin's father, about the identity of Cordelia's grandfather. 'Let the dead rest in peace,' Roisin had said. Cordelia had confessed that she had told both Sally and Declan, but neither of them would ever breathe a word about it to anyone. 'I know Sally won't,' Maeve had said. 'But what about Declan?'

'He won't,' Cordelia promised. 'He even said it was something that should never be told.'

'Then he will never say a word,' Roisin agreed, giving Cordelia a knowing look. 'Because he would lose so much if he did.' They had carried on making plans and talked about the future which looked so bright and promising.

Now, Cordelia drank her tea and stayed at the window, making her own plans and furnishing her new cottage in her imagination.

She gave a start as she suddenly noticed Declan, dressed in jeans but no shirt, standing beside her. 'So that's where my shirt went to,' he said, dropping a kiss on her head.

She laughed and touched his bare chest. 'You'd better find another one. I like this one and I'm going to keep it.'

He sat down beside her. 'You may. You have stolen more than my shirt. Much more.' He took the mug from her and put it on the floor and wrapped his arms around her. 'I think this is the happiest moment for a long, long time. Finding you here, wearing my shirt and knowing you're not going away, that we will live here, in Sandy Cove in your house or mine and nobody can take that away from us. Can they?'

Cordelia leaned her head on his shoulder. 'No.'

'There's no better place for a fresh start than Sandy Cove, is there?'

'No better place in the whole world,' she said, knowing it was true.

Epilogue

Cordelia moved into her new home two weeks before Christmas. It had taken several months to finalise the house deal, as everyone wanted it to be as fair and as legally correct as possible. They had had two different estate agents to look at the two properties in order to work out the market value of both and then an independent assessor had also sent them their report. Once they had agreed, Maeve and Roisin had bought Cordelia's share of Willow House and the amount had come to quite a bit over the price of the cottage, so Cordelia had enough money to buy it and also redo the interior to suit her needs and her own taste. Maeve had left her the red velvet sofa and the big double bed, but the rest of the furniture went to Willow House where it fitted perfectly. Cordelia bought a thick wool carpet in reds and blues for the living room and pale blue curtains for both bedrooms. She had great fun in the antique shops in Cork, where with Declan's help she found lovely old side tables, lamps and two seascapes for the walls along with assorted posters and photos, some of which included the framed photo of the two sisters, and one of Phil and Frances together. The result was a gorgeous mix of styles and colours which made the cottage homely and inviting.

Roisin and Cian had, by that time, settled into their new house overlooking the main beach, only a few minutes' walk from Willow House. Maeve moved into Willow House in 'the nick of time', she said, as it had been confirmed she was definitely expecting twins. The bedrooms upstairs provided ample accommodation for Maeve and Paschal and little Aisling and the babies would spend their first year in the nursery next door to their parents' bedroom. They would need someone to help mind the children and Kathleen had already offered her services, having plenty of experience as the sister to three younger siblings. The sitting room downstairs would be the perfect office for Maeve, and Phil's bedroom would be kept as a guest room.

'It's all fallen into place beautifully,' Cordelia said to Sally as she popped into the shop one chilly afternoon to look at the Christmas decorations Sally had bought on her recent trip to Normandy.

'Oh, yes,' Sally agreed as she unpacked the parcels. 'Everything seems to be oddly perfect at the moment. Especially you buying into my business and us extending into the building next door in the spring.'

'That's the best part,' Cordelia said, taking off her gloves. 'I'm so glad I took the plunge. Show me what you got.'

'Help me unpack, and you'll see. It's all so gorgeous and different.'

They unpacked everything and laid it out on the counter. Cordelia stared at the beautiful Christmas baubles, the little angels carved out of wood and the silk flowers in deep reds and purples, and the rest of the Christmas decorations. There was also an array of hand-made silver jewellery: earrings, necklaces and bracelets adorned with semi-precious stones that glowed in the lamplight. 'It's all so beautiful. Was it expensive?'

'No,' Sally replied. 'All artisan work from various village markets. I enjoyed driving around but it was very tiring. Especially the drive from the ferry port in Rosslare to here. But it was worth it, don't you think?'

'Oh yes,' Cordelia agreed. 'And I got some fabulous hand-printed wrapping paper in Killarney. So we can do gift-wrapping.'

'Brilliant.' Sally put the items on a shelf and folded the paper and cardboard for the recycling bin. 'You'd think it's too close to Christmas to sell decorations and presents, but a lot of people do that kind of shopping at the last minute. I think the jewellery will sell very well. So many men looking for the perfect present for their wives or girlfriends.'

'I think you're right. We can price everything before we open tomorrow and then we'll display some of it in the window.'

'Speaking of men and girlfriends,' Sally said. 'How are you getting on with Declan's mum? She's not being the typical Irish mammy is she?'

'God, no.' Cordelia laughed at the thought. 'She's great. In fact we often chat so much Declan can't get a word in.'

It was true, Cordelia thought. She and Derval had clicked immediately and soon became firm friends. There was no standing on ceremony or being polite to the elderly, as Derval was that kind of ageless woman who was simply herself. She had driven a rented van loaded with her belongings herself from Dublin and done a lot of the unloading and unpacking, shooing Declan and Cordelia away, saying she wasn't a hundred years old yet. With her tall athletic frame, short grey hair and strong features only marked by a few lines around her eyes and mouth, she didn't look her age at all. But that evening, while they were having supper, Derval had nearly fallen asleep over her plate of Irish stew and Cordelia had helped her to bed while Declan did the washing up.

She smiled as she remembered how Derval had been full of beans the next morning, making plans, asking about the village and its people. It hadn't taken her more than a few weeks before she was running the active retirement group and started a walking club for older people who met on the beach for a brisk walk twice a week. She also played bridge in the village hall and forced everyone on the Tidy Towns committee to make them clean up the village and tidy up the grass verges and flowerbeds. 'We'll have hanging baskets all over the place in the spring,' a woman remarked to Cordelia in the grocery shop. 'And we'll be the tidiest village in Ireland,' she added. 'All thanks to Derval O'Mahony. You'd think she had lived here all her life instead of only a few weeks.'

'She's already running everything around here,' Sally said, pulling Cordelia out of her thoughts. 'But if you've been such a high-profile journalist and the most vocal feminist in the country, I suppose it's hard to tone down and just be an old lady. But I love her and so does everyone else. She's a true life force. I hope I'll be like that if I'm lucky enough to live that long.'

'I'm sure you'll be even better,' Cordelia replied, thinking of how Derval wasn't always so gung-ho and strong. She was tired in the evenings and often had her dinner in bed, and when she had her asthma attacks, she had to rest for a long time afterwards. But her health was improving, she slept better and the attacks seemed to come further apart. Declan looked after his mother with great affection and tenderness which made Cordelia love him even more.

'Christmas dinner,' Sally said while she put the jewellery away in little velvet pouches. 'Maeve and Paschal are having a big do and they invited me. So kind of them. And the whole family is coming. Maeve and Roisin's parents are flying in from Spain and Roisin, Cian and the boys will be there, of course. And you and Declan and Derval. How is Maeve going to cope with everyone? She's as big as a house already.'

'Paschal and I are cooking dinner, Roisin will do the table and the boys have promised to help serve and wash up,' Cordelia replied. 'We've offered them a very generous reward, of course, or they would never have agreed. It took quite a bit of negotiation before we came to a good price. But they're Roisin's children so that kind of thing is as natural as breathing to them.'

'And we're dressing up,' Sally said. 'Black tie, no less. What are you wearing?'

'It's a surprise,' Cordelia replied with a secretive smirk. 'But it won't be boring, I promise.'

Sally laughed. 'I can't wait. It'll be the best party for years.'

'The best and the happiest,' Cordelia agreed, feeling a dart of excitement. It would be the best, even if the two women she had loved most wouldn't be there. But they'd be there in spirit, she thought, trying to picture them in the next life, their arms around each other like the sisters they had been but never knew.

It was a starlit evening with the crescent of a new moon rising above the roof of Willow House. There had been a cold snap the day before and the branches of the trees were coated with ice, and the frozen grass glimmered in the light from the windows. Maeve had hung a Christmas wreath adorned with red bows on the front door and lit candles in the hall. The house smelled of wood burning in the fireplace in the drawing room and roast turkey from the kitchen.

The three cousins – all dressed up in various items from Phil's vintage fashion collection – gathered in the hall to greet the guests. They stood in front of the mirror looking at their reflection, smiling at each other. Roisin, wearing a black skirt and a dark blue ruffled blouse, did a twirl, while Cordelia wondered if that dark-haired woman in the red Dior sheath was really her, and Maeve pulled an embroidered shawl across her baby bump.

'Gee, look at the two of you,' she said. 'Such glamour pusses while I look like a fancy tea cosy.'

'You look beautiful, Maeve,' Roisin said. 'That shawl is stunning on you. And Cordelia, you look like one of those nineteen sixties models from Phil's fashion magazines. I can't wait for Declan to see you.'

There was a clatter of heels on the stairs as Anne-Marie McKenna came tripping down in a lurex skirt and top, her blonde hair piled up in a chignon. 'There you are,' she chortled and air-kissed them all. 'You look fabulous.'

Cordelia smiled politely, thinking about all the family secrets she could never share. As Anne-Marie chatted with her daughters, Cordelia gazed at herself in the mirror. She looked confident and happy, like someone who had finally arrived at her destination after a long, eventful and sometimes heart-breaking journey. It seemed incredible that in just five months, she had acquired a new country, a family, financial independence, and met the man she knew she would love for the rest of her life.

When the doorbell rang, she walked to the door and opened it, smiling at Declan, handsome in black tie, and pulled him inside, into the light and warmth of the bright future they would have together.

A Letter from Susanne

Many thanks for reading *Dreams of Willow House*. I hope you enjoyed it as much as I loved writing it. I am busy writing more stories set in this wonderful part of Ireland! If you want to keep reading them and stay up-to-date with all my new releases, just sign up at the following link. Your email address will never be shared and you can unsubscribe at any time.

www.bookouture.com/susanne-oleary

I would be hugely grateful if you could write a review. I'd love to hear your thoughts about the story, and it will also help new readers discover my books.

I love hearing from my readers – you can get in touch on my Facebook page, through Twitter, Goodreads or my website.

Many thanks,
Susanne

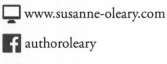

www.susanne-oleary.com

authoroleary

@susl

Acknowledgements

My very first thanks must go to my wonderful editor Jennifer Hunt, who with a firm but gentle hand steers me in the right direction. Also many thanks to Debbie Clement, who designed the wonderful covers for this series, Kim Nash and Noelle Holten, marketing managers extraordinaire and all at Bookouture, who continue to be the best publishers to work with ever! Many more people to thank, family and friends who support me and cheer me on. Hugs and kisses to you all who are with me on this amazing journey!